From the Banks of the Tamar
Stories of Country Characters from the 1950s

With My
Warmest Best Wishes

Ted Sherrell

Also by Ted Sherrell:

Kingdom of Cain
The Lonely and the Lost
Milltown
A Bitter Wind from off the Moor
Nor the Years Condemn
Point of Order, Mr Chairman
And the Days Grow Short
Fire and the Phoenix
The Cutting of Mary Park. . . and Other Devonshire Tales
Looking Towards the Tamar – More Tales of Devonshire Life
Back to the Tamar – Country Tales from Early Post-War Days

From the Banks of the Tamar

Stories of Country Characters from the 1950s

Ted Sherrell

UNITED WRITERS
Cornwall

UNITED WRITERS PUBLICATIONS LTD
Ailsa, Castle Gate, Penzance, Cornwall.

British Library Cataloguing in Publication Data:
A catalogue record for this book is
available from the British Library.

ISBN 9781852001773

First printed in 2015
Reprinted in 2015

This edition published in 2016

Printed in Great Britain by
United Writers Publications Ltd
Cornwall.

To my lovely Ann
– the centre of my world and my best friend,
and
to our wonderful family
– all treasured.

Contents

I

The Show

'Tiddler' Tom Dawkins was almost certainly the best gardener in the parish – and certainly valued by his employers Joe and Beryl Foster, growers and farmers of Brookdale Farm. He was also a war hero twice mentioned in dispatches during the North African campaign, a valiant member of Montgomery's famed Eighth Army. Clearly his diminutive stature (which gave rise to his long held nickname), being only five feet two inches tall and weighing a mere eight stone, did not impact in the slightest degree upon his courage; and clearly it would have no relevance regarding expertise.

Mind you, he was not the sole member of his family with such ability; for if he was the most accomplished gardener in the community, then his brother was surely the second best, nicknamed 'Deadeye' because of his prowess as a marksman during his service in the Home Guard (being ten years senior to Tiddler, he had been too old to be conscripted during the war), Jack Dawkins was a master in the art of growing fruit, flowers and vegetables – especially the last – and was much appreciated by Harry and Sarah Martin of Downside, a farm virtually evenly divided between the growing of horticultural crops and the maintenance of cows, bullocks, sheep and poultry.

If Deadeye was second only to his brother, then he was a close second. In fact, in the growing of vegetables he was, at his best, possibly the better of the two, but when it came to

9

fruit and flowers, Tiddler certainly had the edge, and a noticeable one.

Such prowess was marked, clearly, every July when 'The Show' was staged in the capacious village hall. This annual event had been staged for the best part of a century, interrupted only by the two world wars, and was adjudged the finest and most prestigious in all of West Devon and the Tamar Valley. Indeed, whoever won most points across the myriad range of classes, was adjudged the best, most able practitioner of the horticultural art within a radius of a dozen miles and more. Ever since the show had been re-started in 1946, Tiddler had been the champion (as he had been for a few years before the war), with older brother, Deadeye, as runner-up – a state of affairs which irked the latter considerably.

To be fair to Deadeye, he had no problem with 'young' Tiddler being a bit of a local hero in terms of the war; indeed, he was quite proud of the fact. His attitude, though, to being perpetually in his brother's shadow regarding the show, was radically different; he resented it, and being a touch jealous, sadly, this resentment led, over the years, to a gulf between the two. Not that they had ever actually quarrelled over this – in fact, over anything; it was just that increasingly they had ever less to do with each other. It got to the stage that if one came into the bar of the Tamar View Inn of an evening and saw the other there, then he would retreat instantly. Tiddler Tom was saddened very much by his older brother's behaviour but, as he reasoned he had done nothing to cause such pettiness and spite, felt it was down to Deadeye to make overtures of peace, not him.

What made the situation even sillier in the younger brother's mind – and to many other folk aware of Deadeye's fraternal antagonism – was the simple fact that there was so very little between the two of them in terms of skill and expertise. Show results, year on year, proved that the brothers were in a league of their own. The vast majority of classes they entered, they dominated, with first and second positions coming their way. And Deadeye would accrue a decent number of first prizes – especially in the veg section – but overall, for every top spot achieved by Deadeye, his brother would score a brace. That which Deadeye produced, and exhibited, would be, at worst, high quality – at best, close to perfection; his brother, though, was able usually to lift his standards even higher. Even he could not usurp the vagaries and contrariness of nature and achieve total perfection, but so often – so very often – he would produce a plate of soft fruit, a collection of vegetables, a vase of traditional blooms which would grace any produce show in the country.

Not content just to shrug his shoulders and accept that Tiddler Tom had a touch which he did not – and thus save himself stress, as well as taking a sword to the envy and resentment which had destroyed his relationship with his younger brother – Deadeye tried different ways of growing his wide range of produce in his capacious, immaculately kept, garden and allotment, listened to tips from other, generally older, veterans of shows (though invariably from the lips of men who had enjoyed far less success than himself), and determined that somehow, someday he would be the best in the Peninsula, and claim the sizeable, most ornate cup which had sat on Tiddler's mantelpiece, continuously, for so very many years. It could take the greater part of his lifetime, though (if it ever happened at all) – of that he was well aware. Yet, totally unexpectedly, from a visit he did not wish to make, came the possibility of salvation – a door was opened to him which could provide the opportunity, at last, for him to gain the ascendancy in his perpetual struggle against his brother; he could yet be the 'Show King' – which would be apt, in a way, for it was at Christmas of the year in which Elizabeth II had been crowned Queen.

It came about through his sister-in-law. His spouse, Harriet, had a sister – several years her senior – who worked as a housekeeper in the fine home of a minor aristocrat near Exeter. Celia had gone into service as a young girl in the 1920s and due to diligence, aptitude and ambition, had risen quickly. By the age of 25 she had become assistant housekeeper in the sturdy, sizeable but very ugly house of the local squire, who still owned a considerable acreage of land both sides of the Tamar – much of it worked by tenant farmers.

Marrying just before the war, she gave up her position to care for her two sons who had come along in quick succession in 1940 and 41; sadly, in 1945 she was in sole command of their upbringing, when her husband, Eric, was killed at Arnhem.

Quickly realising that a war widow's pension would not be remotely sufficient to keep them all, she returned to service. She had been able to secure a position as assistant housekeeper at the end of the war at the Exeter mansion, and after just four years had become housekeeper when the incumbent of the role retired. Thus Celia, for a number of years, had a good, interesting and relatively safe job, plus excellent accommodation for herself and her growing sons, a small apartment in a wing of the house set aside for their use.

Then, in the autumn of that coronation year, Celia's situation had changed again – she remarried. The head gardener at the house, one Maurice Miller – of similar age to herself – had become a widower some three years previously. Celia had been good friends with his wife, Mary, and had been almost as shocked as her husband when she had been struck down by a severe stroke, something most unexpected in a woman under 50 years of age. Within days she had passed away, and the housekeeper saw it her duty to ensure the widower was, in the early stages of his solitariness, well looked after. Both of them being of similar nature – gentle, kindly and even tempered – they got on very well, an accord which, within a year or so, had turned to love. Thus, when Maurice proposed marriage, Celia had no hesitation in accepting him.

They had married very quickly in the church of the village near the estate with very few guests attending, and Celia had gone to live with her new husband in the large lodge some quarter mile from the big house. She was, though, on very good terms with younger sister, Harriet, and invited her and Deadeye up to spend Christmas with them so that they could both meet Maurice.

Harriet Dawkins was delighted with the invitation, but her husband was infinitely less keen. Not that he had anything against Celia – on the contrary, he had always liked her; and he had no problem meeting her husband – his profession suggested that they

would assuredly have something in common. The head gardener
would probably not share Deadeye's other passion – a lifelong
devotion to the triumphs and, all too often, disasters of Plymouth
Argyle – but a man dedicated to creating masterpieces in the
horticultural world (as a head gardener, he must surely be good at
his trade) would be decent company. The problem was that
Deadeye had always spent Christmas by his own fireside and had
no desire to change. Christmas Eve in the Tamar View Inn,
Christmas Day in his own home; his legs under his own table, his
stomach filled with good food, much of it provided by Farmer
Martin, always generous with poultry, vegetables and the odd
flagon at Yuletide.

The other two long term employees at Downside, Alfie
Tremain and Herbie Parsons, also received the victuals, but they
would both spend time on the farm during Christmas and Boxing
Days, milking, feeding stock and so forth, invariably assisted by
the farmer himself. Very occasionally, Deadeye had done a stint,
but only if through illness, or possibly family reasons, one of the
others were not available; but such times were most rare.

Not that Deadeye lacked the skills of animal husbandry but his
working interests, and certainly his major talents, lay in the
tending of the soil; in the bulb and strawberry fields, amongst
sprouts, carrots, potatoes and the like, was where his value lay,
and Harry Martin was much aware of it. Thus his feet rarely
touched Downside's rolling acres over the Yuletide, except on
Boxing Days when Argyle were away; then he and a couple of
friends from the village would descend with ferret and nets to
spend a large part of the day attempting to encourage rabbits from
their holes to augment their still quite meagre meat supplies (that
of the Martins also, who would, in accordance with custom, be
presented with a brace). This was something Deadeye was also
good at, he having the rare knack of being able to assess into
which hole the placing of the ferret would prove the most
effective in terms of bringing hapless rabbits into the daylight. He
pointed out to Harriet that, seeing as his beloved team were
travelling on Boxing Day, he had promised to go rabbiting with a
couple of his regular mates and, seeing as he was the one with the

ferret (two, in fact), he had an obligation to do just that. If he did not, then their usually much enjoyed day could not take place.

This moved Harriet not one iota, she pointing out that, as responsible men, he could certainly entrust them with the ferrets for the day, enabling them to rabbit to their heart's content. In desperation he thought about approaching Farmer Martin and volunteering to go out to the farm to help out on either Christmas Day or Boxing Day – or both – but knew that whilst such an offer would be received with courteous thanks, it would not be accepted. The farmer knew that when it came to cows and sheep, Alfie and Herbie were more than able and also – possibly more importantly – both were more than happy to work on Yuletide, pleased to earn the overtime, especially Herbie who had three young children to keep.

So it was that Harriet and Deadeye Dawkins caught a train from the village station on the afternoon of Christmas Eve, arriving at St. David's Station, Exeter, just before dark. They were met by Celia and her new husband – a tall, thin fellow whose somewhat studious face was wreathed in smiles, his lips giving forth copious words of welcome to his recently acquired sister and brother in-laws.

Introductions and welcomes complete, they were ferried back to the Miller's snug, comfortable lodge some three miles from the city, in Maurice's rather elderly Austin saloon. Whilst Deadeye was still pining somewhat for home and the Tamar View Inn, he had to concede that Maurice seemed very pleasant and welcoming, whilst the lodge was most comfortable and cosy. Celia, of course, was charming and warm as she had always been, though he had never spent much time in her company even though he had been married to her sister for almost twenty-five years.

Within an hour of arriving, though, Deadeye found himself convinced that this visit to the residence of the head gardener of an old and significant country estate, could prove both enjoyable and of very long lasting benefit to himself. For following the consumption of a brace of cups of tea and a large slice of scrumptious Christmas cake, his host invited him to his office-

14

cum-study, leaving the two sisters to 'women's talk' as Maurice put it – and to prepare an evening meal, inviting aromas of which were already permeating the air.

"Come in here, Deadeye," invited his brother-in-law, leading him out into the small hallway and opening a door next to the sitting room. He put on the light, closed the door behind him, turned to his guest and enquired, "Are you a whisky man, Deadeye?"

"I am – when somebody else is offering it, Maurice," said he with a grin. "Best thing to come out of Scotland."

Whilst the gardener poured, into small tumblers, two large portions of single malt from a bottle standing on a shelf above a bureau against the far wall, Deadeye cast his eyes around the office. He was stunned into silence, for the sizeable room was festooned with rosettes and prize certificates about its walls, whilst trophies, large and small, occupied shelves and desktops – a shrine to success, accomplishment and excellence. He took the proffered glass with muttered thanks, his mind, his entire being transfixed by the treasure house of triumph about him. He drank deeply of the liquor, continuing to gaze around, then emptied the glass – far quicker than he normally would have done.

"Drop more, Deadeye?"

The softly spoken words from his host brought him out of his reverie; he looked down at the empty tumbler, then up at Maurice.

"Good heavens, boy – I'm sorry; truly I am. I didn't realise I had drunk it all. I don't usually drink Scotch this quickly. . ." – words which were totally true. "It's just that I'm – I'm – I'm, well, stunned by all this. I've never seen anything like it in my life. . ." He realised he'd not answered his host's question. "Yes, Maurice, I will have a touch more if I may. Cracking good whisky, this – first class."

The statement was true, but it was the sheer wonder of all around him which had caused him to gulp down the liquor in such haste. Receiving another generous portion, he gave his thanks, wished his host, "Good health, boy," took another gulp, then began pursuit of that which firstly had astonished him but now was puzzling him.

15

"These cups, Maurice – the rosettes, certificates – mostly for first prize, I see; what are they for?"

The head gardener looked at him with an expression of puzzlement upon his face – and took a few seconds to answer.

"Well – I'm a gardener, Deadeye; they're for shows – shows where we've exhibited various produce grown here on the estate; fruit, flowers, vegetables – a wide range of all three. It's something I've always enjoyed doing, showing – and the chaps who work with me do as well, all three of them. Fortunately Sir Henry is all in favour – especially as we tend to do very well. I doubt he'd be so keen if we were not so successful, but as it is, it shows the estate in a good light – and Sir Henry likewise. He's very fair, though, as he doesn't stint on money when it comes to the gardens and the shows, and any cups or whatever we win, he leaves it to me to display as I see fit; he doesn't expect them to be kept in the big house. Well, the only place I can put them is in this office – so, as you see, here they are displayed for those folk who actually come in here; not that many, really, to be honest, but so much of the satisfaction is simply knowing that we've won them. Nothing, and I mean nothing, can beat that feeling, Deadeye."

His guest nodded. "Oh, yes – you're right there, boy. I only show locally, of course – the show at home, always in July it is; fruit, flowers, veg – I show the lot. Good show, Maurice – probably the best in the Tamar Valley; could well be the best in West Devon as well, for that matter. I – I don't do too badly," he added, somewhat modestly.

He looked around him again, aware that the array of awards which filled – almost cluttered – the office, had most probably been won at events bigger and more prestigious than that of his own admirable parish. Despite such awareness, however, he was still not prepared for the answer to the question which hastened from his lips.

"Where do you show, then, Maurice – with the remarkable number of cups, rosettes and so on you've got here, you clearly put entries into many local shows, some I would imagine, quite big."

The head gardener nodded, then shrugged his shoulders. "Well

16

– yes, we do enter quite a number, I suppose. Have done so for a number of years – and many of them a fair way distant. As I said, Sir Henry is keen, so he doesn't mind footing the bills for travelling – and for staying away, in some instances. Amongst the nearer we do is the Devon County – we usually do the Royal Cornwall as well, which is not too bad travel wise. The Bath and West is a fair trip, of course, as is the big one, the Royal Show – which is usually held in the Midlands. And in the past few years, we have done the biggest of all – Chelsea. We've not had a major award there, but we have had a couple of highly commendeds – once for a collection of vegetables and another time for gladioli. Most of the trophies, rosettes and so forth have come from the Devon County and Royal Cornwall. We won half a dozen classes at the county show back in the spring, and three at the Royal Cornwall. I was a touch disappointed with that, mind you, as I thought we should have had a couple more firsts – but then, Deadeye, it's always as the judges see it; different judges look for different things, don't they?"

Deadeye Dawkins did not respond for several seconds, so stunned was he at the levels at which his host showed the produce grown by himself and his small staff. At length, he nodded his agreement that judges did indeed differ in that which they looked for and in their priorities: "Yes – yes – yes; they all vary, Maurice, quite a lot too. Having said that, boy, it seems it doesn't matter that much the way they look at things when it comes to what you show – you seem to get top spot no matter who the judge is. The fact is that quality generally will always come out on top. Clearly you win prizes in the top shows because your entries are the best."

The words he said flattered his host but were uttered in total honesty, for Deadeye Dawkins knew that the room in which they stood would not have been laden with these multitudinous badges of triumph had not those entries into these top ranking competitions been of the very highest standard. Inclined as he often was to put things into footballing terminology, he thought to himself at that moment, that if he was a tolerable semi-professional possibly of a standard to be a reserve for an average third division team, the man with whom he was sharing a bottle of whisky was Stanley Matthews. Briefly, he was a touch overawed. He had expected to be in the company of a fellow to whom he had been introduced because he was married to his wife's sister, but found himself in the presence – and with a relationship and friendship – of a man who was a leading exponent of the craft of gardening and the arcane art of the competitive showing of produce.

Deadeye Dawkins was a sharp, quick thinking man. Whilst he was stunned at the eminence of the man who was to be his host for the Christmas, his shrewd brain took over. The reality was that fate had given him a truly marvellous opportunity to, at last, gain that knowledge, learn those rare skills, indeed, have some insight into the tricks necessary to lift his performances as a grower of produce sufficiently to win that trophy which he had sought for so many years – not accolades at the Devon County show, for that was beyond his ability and far beyond his ambition; rather the fine silver cup presented to the competitor with most points overall at his village show. He would be the champion; it would be the proudest moment of his life – and his brother, Tiddler Tom, would know, at last, what it felt to be a runner up.

If there was one man in this world from whom he could gain such knowledge, then it was his new brother-in-law. Not that he aspired to emulate the achievements of Maurice Miller – he was not remotely in such a league. Men like this head gardener assuredly acquired much of their skills and knowledge thanks to experience, hard work, dedication, perhaps even study – but, essentially, such ability was in them from birth, rich seams waiting to be mined.

This was not the case with Deadeye. He knew that even if by some remarkable shaft of good fortune he had been able to achieve a position of the responsibility and status of his brother-in-law, whilst he might have been sufficiently "up to the job" to stay in such employment, his accomplishments would have been minimal in comparison. Thus did Deadeye target what he wanted from the head gardener – and it was not the knowledge and skills needed for him to change his employment from farm worker and gardener to working solely in a garden situation – he was perfectly happy where he was, working at Downside for Harvey and Sarah Martin, alongside a couple of other local lads beside whom he had grafted for many a long year, and whom he had known for even longer. Anyway, he was too old now to even contemplate a change of pursuit even if he had the ability and the desire. No, what he wanted to glean from Maurice were tips regarding turning a good collection of fruit, or plate of potatoes or carrots, or large, richly green lettuce, or vase of gaily coloured fragrantly perfumed pansies, from a quality entry into a winning one. He wanted his host to instruct him in the fine tuning – how to present produce to look their very best; when exactly to pick or gather it prior to the show – the very hour could have relevance.

He was convinced that often in the village show his brother was gaining top honours on produce which was no better than his – at times, in fact, possibly inferior. Tiddler Tom was, though, his brother had to concede, very adept in his presentation – and Deadeye could never readily see what he did to his exhibits which produced this advantage. Maurice Miller would probably know, however, without ever seeing them.

So Deadeye saw the following two days of their sojourn at the lodge as being an opportunity – completely unexpected – to make progress towards the hoisting in triumph, at last, of what to him was the 'Holy Grail', the Tamar Valley Cup for most points in the show. His initial objection to having to spend Christmas away had suddenly disappeared. A man who generally enjoyed Yuletide, he found himself very much looking forward to this one.

The following morning, the sisters busying themselves in the kitchen preparing Christmas dinner and getting up to date with family news and gossip, Celia's two sons by her first marriage – now close to their teens – playing on the small table tennis table they had been given, Maurice suggested the two men took a stroll outside to have a look around the gardens close to the big house – a proposal to which Deadeye agreed with alacrity.

It was a cloudy, raw, seasonal morning, but dry, so a walk around areas of mutual interest to the two men was no hardship, especially to the guest, for whom it was most instructive, and very impressive. For even now, in the depth of winter, with largish beds fallow and awaiting planting in the early spring, order, precision and professionalism abounded. Freshly turned beds, neatly clipped edges and borders, winter flowers standing vibrant, their colour bringing a touch of spring to the dourness all around, some sturdy, well formed winter root vegetables in the kitchen gardens (from which most of the veg they would be eating that day had been gathered) – all this and much more did Maurice Miller show his guest during the hour and more on their stroll.

Realising, ever more, just how privileged he was to be there on a personal level with a man of such ability and vision, Deadeye absorbed all that he could see; also, he asked questions, but in a way that was not overt. On the contrary, his probes were subtle – often entered into general conversation – whilst the answers were listened to by Deadeye with rapt attention; pearls of wisdom and experience which emanated from the head gardener's lips, stored away as would a wise squirrel hoard nuts. The questions went well beyond mere presentation of the produce grown – Maurice Miller and his team had not filled a large office with copious badges of success just because of presentation – clearly the produce was of the very top standard also. So Deadeye probed deftly as to how potatoes could be guided to a perfect shape, carrots to an impressive length, faint spots banished from the petals of roses and blemishes removed from shiny crimson strawberries. How so much fruit, flowers and veg could be guided to a standard sufficient to win first prizes in shows.

Maurice Miller's knowledge, naturally, was not total, but it was comprehensive. He did not know everything, he was not a magician nor a genius, but he was extremely good at what he did, being amongst the top exponents of his craft – and Deadeye Dawkins stored away in his agile mind every bit of information given, every tip passed on by the head gardener.

By the morning of the day following Boxing Day, as Harriet and he were being ferried by Maurice to the station to catch the train back home, Deadeye's enthusiasm for the New Year knew no bounds; for the first of January would see the countdown to July and the day when, at last, he would win the Tamar Valley Cup for accruing the most points in the show – of that he was completely confident.

Certainly he returned back down the southern line in far higher spirits than he had enjoyed on the way up on Christmas Eve – something noted by his wife. Indeed, she was most agreeably surprised – and assuredly delighted – at just how much he appeared to enjoy the Christmas with her sister and Maurice, after doing nothing but grumble and moan at the prospect of having to spend it away from home. However, she was not remotely aware of the reason, thinking it was the company of Celia, Maurice and the boys and their splendid hospitality which had brought about her husband's change of attitude, though he was soon to tell her (they shared most things) of all he had learnt, and of his plans for the show.

To be fair, Deadeye would probably have had to admit that he had enjoyed the company of his sister-in-law and brother-in-law, and that their kindness and attention to their comforts and needs had made it a memorable Yuletide. The knowledge, though, the wisdom imparted him by Maurice Miller and the fresh found confidence instilled within himself that he could, at last, be a winner, was what made this the best Christmas he could ever remember.

The beginning of a new year saw him do something he had ceased doing years – even decades – earlier; he made a resolution. Perhaps something even stronger than this, though, he made to himself a statement of intent, and it was simplicity itself – this was the one, this was the year. On the return train journey from Exeter following his so very instructive Christmas he had formulated his plans and with the coming of January he would put them into operation. His quest for the Tamar Valley Cup – and a successful one, of that he was confident – would begin in earnest.

Mind you, his preparation for the July show always did begin in the depths of winter so there was nothing radically new here; what was different, however, was the attention he gave to everything, the time he spent at it, his dedication to pursuit of glory on that Wednesday in July – far distant – when he began the laborious, detailed, at times, almost pedantic preparations.

Although over the years he had always worked towards the pursuit of the Tamar Valley Cup, and in single minded fashion, never before had it dominated his life as totally as it did during that winter, spring and early summer. Indeed, his life was none other than work at Downside Farm, eating, sleeping and labouring in his garden and upon his allotment in pursuit of perfection – or, at least, to get as close as it was humanly possible to achieve that unrealistic goal.

In all of it he was supported – in fact encouraged – by his wife Harriet; she too desperately wanted her husband to achieve this ambition of so many years and be 'top dog' at the show – not only would it please him so much, indeed, elevate his spirits and confidence to the highest level, it would give him a feeling of value, importance and self-worth in the parish, which she had always felt he lacked (in truth, which he did lack despite his unquestioned ability as a gardener). He would be, at last, the champion of the best show for miles both sides of the Tamar – and she, also, would gain status from it. Not that she was a proud woman or self-seeking – a member of the Woman's Institute and Townswomen's Guild, she was known and respected in the community already; it would, though, put her in a position where she could at last feel superior to her sister-in-law, Tiddler Tom's wife, Maureen. Harriet had always retained a reasonable relationship with her brother-in-law, even though her husband had not, but Maureen and herself had had a 'falling out' some twenty years previously and had not spoken since; what the row was about she had long since ceased to remember.

So Deadeye Dawkins went about his business of preparation for the show, not just with the dedication which had always been his way, but with a precision and adherence to detail which, probably, had not. He had not written down one single word of the advice Maurice Miller had given him – he had not needed to, as every tip, every suggestion, every word of insight and wisdom the man had accrued over the thirty years of rising to very near the top of his profession, which he had passed onto his brother-in-law, had been stored in that shrewd man's fertile brain.

During the bleak mid and late winter, Deadeye spent a great deal of time in his small greenhouse in the corner of his garden, nurturing seedlings in a way beyond that which he would normally have done – and never had he been tardy in doing this. Now, though, his attention was virtually constant, each small, fragile plant, each seed potato and so forth being treated with care and gentleness as if new born babies. Also he had purchased two paraffin heaters to augment the brace he already possessed, and these were giving out warmth constantly, the small glass house being kept permanently at a temperature higher than he had ever before achieved – indeed, ever thought necessary. Maurice, though, had advised that such a policy – one needing much vigilance and costing a sizable amount in terms of fuel – would give young life an early boost, one which was crucial in terms of raising the quality of his produce to the level where the prizes and trophies would come his way when show day arrived.

This, though, was only the start; come spring, then early summer, further painstaking, time consuming processes had to be pursued to elevate their fruit, flowers and vegetables from prize chasing entries to championship winning ones. It took much of Deadeye's and Harriet's money and a vast amount of their time, but as the show got ever closer they noted with much satisfaction the sheer splendour of what was being grown.

"You've always been good, Deadeye," opined his wife, "always produced quality in virtually all things; but this is the best you've ever grown – by a mile. I cannot see any way Tiddler Tom can beat you this time. I'm going to get a place ready on the sideboard for the Tamar Valley Cup. It's going to be ours, Deadeye – at last it's going to be ours."

The gardener, with his innate caution – and, indeed, natural pessimism – was a touch alarmed to hear his wife speak in such confident tones, but had to concede that if his brother was to beat him this year, then he would surely have to produce something beyond that which he had in previous years – most high though that always was.

As the weeks to the show got ever fewer, Deadeye's dedication and single-mindedness became ever greater. He had abandoned, temporarily, the loyal habit of a lifetime of going to Home Park, Plymouth on a Saturday afternoon, whilst the landlord of the Tamar View Inn commented – only half in jest – that his profits were well down because he had hardly seen the gardener since the New Year. Mind you, few others had seen much of him either with the exception of his employers and work mates.

He even failed to attend the annual social evening which the show committee always put on in the Parish Hall some six weeks before the show. At heart a sociable man, Deadeye felt that with the big day growing nearer at what seemed to him an alarming rate, he could not afford to spend even one evening away from the nurturing of his flourishing, potential cup winning, produce. Thus he eschewed an evening which had, since the committee had started doing it at the turn of the century, consisted of generous supplies of beer and scrumpy, a pasty supper plus various puddings with lashings of cream, all paid for out of show funds. All potential exhibitors in the show were welcome to attend plus spouses and family, along with the Parish Council and all connected with staging the show. Whilst it was primarily a social occasion, members of the committee were there to answer any queries regarding the upcoming show, to pass out schedules and point out the occasional small rule change and so forth.

Deadeye suggested that Harriet attend, he knowing that it was an evening she always enjoyed also, but she declined – although she wasn't totally sure why; perhaps she felt that as her husband was sacrificing a pleasurable evening in the pursuit of the dream, then she should show solidarity and do likewise.

So, that evening, and the next forty or so – now with maximum light as midsummer came and went – leading up to show day saw the intensity of their work and dedication reach almost the point of obsession, especially for Deadeye. At last, though, the day of the show arrived and although the Dawkins felt that the day had come upon them with almost frightening rapidity, both were confident they were ready for it; or to be more exact, their produce was ready. The quality of that which Deadeye had

24

produced had always been high, but never even remotely as good as that which lay before him that show morning in readiness to be transported to the village hall for staging, judging, then displaying to the large numbers from the parish – and with the show so highly regarded well beyond, goodly numbers coming, largely by train, from both the Plymouth and Tavistock directions.

Having borrowed Farmer Martin's old van, Harriet and he painstakingly loaded the fruit, flowers and vegetables aboard and carefully, very slowly, drove the half mile or so to the hall. Then, as the warm July sunshine beamed down from a cloudless day, the Dawkins carried the results of their unrelenting work for the past six months and more, from the van parked on the large patch of wasteland situated next to the hall. Upon this area showmen up from Plymouth were, in accordance with tradition, erecting a number of roundabouts and stalls offering prizes for the accuracy of throwing wooden balls at coconuts, darts at playing cards and suchlike, plus other traders, again mostly up from the city, selling goods, often at knock-down prices, the quality of which could, at times, be a touch untrustworthy.

The hall was alive with entrants carefully laying out their produce – the fruit, vegetables, flowers and plants, of course, but also the highly competitive baking and cooking section which sported a magnificent array of sponges, cakes, buns, pasties, pies, loaves, fruit tarts and much more; and the sewing, knitting and fabric classes with a wide array of garments, bags and rugs, some quite magnificent.

Deadeye and Harriet went briskly, but efficiently about their work, laying out the fruit and vegetables, arranging with immense care the flowers in their vases. And as they did so, they became aware, increasingly, of interest from other exhibitors – some pausing to gaze at the sheer quality of what they were laying out, a few making comments, the pick of which came from a real veteran, Rollo Rowlands, a man in his eighties who had been showing for over sixty years:

"I fancy, Deadeye, you'll be the man to beat this year."

Tiddler Tom's entries were, universally, of their customary championship standard but keeping as he always did, an eye upon

25

b

the exhibits of his brother, and, of course, being a man with a highly perceptive, knowledgeable view when it came to quality, conceded to Harriet when passing her as she was placing potatoes onto a plate:

"This could well be Deadeye's year, maid – it's the best he's ever produced In fact, it could be the best any of us has ever produced."

His sister-in-law smiled, then thanked him, aware, in view of the rift there was between him and her husband, just how generous and, indeed, conciliatory these comments were.

She had long desired a rapprochement between the two brothers, partly because she was by nature a woman who liked to live in harmony with family, and folk in general, but also she felt that her husband's enmity towards Tom did more harm to himself than to his target, and she was all too well aware that Deadeye was the main culprit in the long running estrangement of the two, his resentment – jealousy, in fact – regarding having to play, constantly, second fiddle to Tiddler Tom having got out of hand. Indeed, next to loyalty to Deadeye and a genuine desire to see his years – decades, in fact – of high standards as a gardener rewarded by attaining the championship of this prestigious show, she felt, certainly hoped, that if he did win the Tamar Valley Cup then the main cause of his resentment towards his younger brother would be removed – and a friendly, if not close, relationship between the two would be re-established.

Eventually all was staged and all entrants had to leave the hall, for the judging was about to begin. As Deadeye walked back through the hall towards the exit, his eyes devoured all that he walked past; he knew his own, of course, and he found it easy to pick out Tiddler Tom's. As always in recent times, overall the Dawkins brother's produce was in a class of its own.

Usually, whilst Deadeye's was invariably of high quality, his diminutive brother's would have, in a majority of categories, the edge – sometimes just shading things, but so often very clearly. This was something that Deadeye had been all too aware of. In previous years, walking back through the hall prior to judging, he knew that his brother and himself would be – by a margin – the dominant duo in the show; he would be aware, also, that Tiddler Tom would carry off the trophy, and would do so because overall, his fruit, veg and flowers were better. This year, though, as Deadeye walked to the exit he felt things were different, no – more than that, he knew they were.

Like most folk who lived by the land and tilled the soil, he was essentially a pessimist and whilst hoping for the best would automatically expect the worst. At the same time, though, he was a man who knew his craft – whose judgement of quality regarding that which came from the soil was of the highest order. By the time he passed through the hall door and moved into the fairground beyond, he felt a sense of elation which he had to fight hard to suppress. As always Tiddler Tom's entries were generally awash with excellence, but this time he, Deadeye, was at last matching him and, he felt – fighting desperately to avoid over confidence – that at last, at long, long last, he had possibly sufficient potential first prizes to shade it – to lay his hands, after all these long years, upon the Tamar Valley trophy.

All show competitors clear of the hall, a member of the committee closed, then locked the doors, leaving the judges to get about their work. There were ten in all, covering the wide range of classes which gave the show its eminence in the area – the grown (the bulk of the displays, naturally), the baked, the crafted, even the painted, as there was a section devoted to artwork. No judges were locally based; indeed, one came from as far afield as Barnstaple, 60 miles to the north, another from beyond Truro, 50 to the south. All were masters and mistresses of their trade, would all have been judging for several years, with the majority of them having judged at county level. None demurred, however, when invited to judge at what was on the face of it, just a village show, for they knew this was no ordinary parish exhibition – this was one set in, by far, the biggest community in the Tamar Valley amidst some of the most productive land possible to find, and contested likewise by many of the finest gardeners and commercial growers. If it was prestigious to win trophies here, it was also no small accolade to be invited to judge.

Deadeye and Harriet made for the tea tent to await the verdict of the judges which would he at least an hour away. Although it was now past noon and neither had eaten since an early and rushed breakfast at 7am, appetite escaped them both – but a few cups of strong sweet tea went down very well. Looking around the tent, Harriet was aware – as was always the case – the refreshment area was awash with a motley collection of exhibitors awaiting, nervously, the judges' decisions; tea was being drunk in abundance, but the hard working ladies doing the catering were selling little food. It was, though, ever thus; when the judges' verdicts were known, then the pasties, sandwiches, buns and cakes would go like snow before the sun, the victors eating in celebration, the vanquished doing so to settle nerves and smother disappointment, and of course, the large numbers who would attend to view the show, have some fun at the fair and side shows, generally relax and enjoy the biggest annual event on the Peninsula, would also partake in refreshments.

As the exhibitors whiled away nervous time by taking up residence in the tea tent, or by strolling around the fair, sideshows and stalls or just idly gossiping – intense activity was taking place in the hall, committee members and helpers busying themselves with final preparations for the official opening of the show by the local member of parliament, Sir Henry Blanchard, at 2 o'clock. Some of them were assigned to the assistance and accompaniment of the most important folk at that moment; as each judge decided on the destination of the range of awards in their gift – generally first, second, third and, on occasions, highly commended, so the official with him or her, would write the name of the relevant exhibitor on the different coloured cards (blue for first, red for second, yellow for third), then place it beside the entry. The result would then be entered into a hard-backed notebook which each carried prior to them all being put into a central register when judging had finished. It was then, of course, it would emerge who the trophy winners were for various sections – and most important of all, the overall champion of the show, and recipient of the Tamar Valley Cup, would become apparent.

Naturally the judges made their decisions on the excellence (in some instances the lack of it) of the exhibit before them with no idea of the identity of the person who had submitted it.

Accordingly officials would not know either, only able to confirm prize winners, when judging had been completed, by checking the numbers on the small card beside each exhibit against the comprehensive record of all entries in the show. However, old stagers going around with the judges (and most were) so often could not fail to know where the prizes were going in the fruit, flowers and veg sections – having seen the Dawkins brothers setting up, they were well aware that, as always, the two very local men (both born and bred in the village where they had lived their entire lives – except, in Tiddler Tom's case, for the four years he had been off fighting for King and Country) were dominating. The more astute amongst them – or, to be more accurate, amongst those who had seen the brothers setting it all up – had noted the perpetual excellence of Tom's entries but, more relevantly, the remarkably high standard this year of Deadeye's.

Veteran committee man, Albert Milton, commented to the chairman Gordon Simmonds, with most of the judging having been completed – only the slightly slower adjudicator of the vegetable section still to complete his work, with the turnip, carrot and potato classes remaining – giving voice to his perceptive perusal: "A Dawkins will win the cup as usual, boy, but this year it could be the other one."

The chairman, in a sense, disagreed with him: "I don't think it's a matter of 'could', Albert – almost definitely will win it, I'd say. I saw them earlier setting up the spuds – Tiddler Tom's were good, as they alway are, but Deadeye's were, well, outstanding, I've never seen spuds like it. From what I've seen and heard going around, I'd say Deadeye is out in front already – after they've judged the potatoes, he'll be a clear winner, I fancy. And I'm pleased to tell you the truth: Tiddler Tom's always won fair and square – always been the best; wonderful gardener. Deadeye, though, has scarcely ever put a poor entry into this show over the past 25 years, so no man deserves to win that cup more than he does – and no man has wanted to win it more than him, that I know."

Eventually Deadeye and Harriet left the tea tent and strolled slowly, in desultory fashion, around the stalls and sideshows.

"They're taking their time this year, maid," Deadeye commented to his spouse, though in reality the judges were taking no longer than normal to fulfill their difficult, laborious task – this was a big show with manifold entries. "I can usually take it all in my stride, but this year – well. . ." He had no need to say any more; this year was very different, and Harriet was as aware of the fact as was he.

Just after half past one, the news came that judging had finished, the hall main doors had been unlocked and the committee wished to see all exhibitors immediately.

Deadeye and Harriet knew what was coming – the routine had not altered in years – perhaps decades. They would enter the hall and be confronted with a series of boards, on easels, all with large sheets of paper pinned to them upon which would be written, by hand – and hastily – the results of every single class in the show and, on a separate board, the list of trophy winners, at the top of which would be the holy grail itself, the Tamar Valley Cup.

The numerous men, women and children who had submitted their produce, food and creations for the assessment of the judges, hastened into the hall – then divided into two groups; those with few entries and/or little expectation, went to the left to see if they had gained a prize, and those that were either always amongst the front runners – or hoping to be – moved to the right, nerves a jangling, to view the stark, large board, set apart from the others, upon which would be written the names of those who would carry off silverware.

Harriet Dawkins was fractionally in front of her husband as they rushed towards the 'trophy board'; also, she had slightly better sight, so she read the news a few seconds before Deadeye. She stopped in her tracks – almost as if she was Lot's wife, and had been turned to stone; Deadeye went past her a few feet so that he had a clear view of the board – then he too froze to the spot. Beside the Tamar Valley Cup, the name Dawkins was written – as it had been for years – but beside that surname again, as had been the case for so very long, was printed the Christian name, Thomas.

The elder brother shook his head – virtually in total despair. "I can't believe it, maid – I just cannot believe it," he stuttered to his wife, probably every bit as shattered as was her husband by this devastating announcement. "I saw our entries, and I saw Tiddler Tom's – his were good, as they always are – but overall ours were better, Harriet. They were better – and clearly so. Don't you think so, maid?" The last words were spoken to his loyal spouse in almost desperate tones – as if he was seeking, urgently, reassurance.

"Of course, they were, Deadeye – and, in many instances, far better," his wife retorted instantly – with anger in her voice. She was a lady who usually moved from dismay, even hurt, to anger with rapidity. She was, indeed, angry – furious, in fact. A dear husband of whom she thought the world and to whom she was intensely loyal, had been treated shamefully – even, perhaps, treacherously. "I'm going to complain, Deadeye. It's all a fiddle – they're a bunch of, of, of rogues – the judges, the committee. It's not right. – It's. . . it's disgusting. As I say, I'm going to complain, and I'm going to do it right away. I'll get hold of Gordon Simmonds – he's still chairman, isn't he?"

Before her husband could confirm that her identification of the chairman was correct, she had turned away and was about to hasten off to remonstrate with the hapless man.

However, Deadeye's intended plea to her that she made no fuss, there seemingly being no point as there would appear to be nothing tangible upon which to lodge a complaint (the quality of garden produce, like beauty, was in the eye of the beholder or, more relevantly, judge) was stilled in his throat as he became aware, suddenly, that the show chairman was standing beside him – but several feet away from Harriet.

"Deadeye – look boy – well, how can I put it other than to say that we all feel bad about you being beaten into second place again. Other years, Tiddler Tom's entries have had the edge. This year it was different – very much so. Overall, your entries were the better – in fact, some were outstanding and if it hadn't been for a. . . well a breach of rules. . . you would have won the Tamar Valley Cup."

By the expression on the chairman's face, he was finding his explanation to the distraught Deadeye stressful. The elder Dawkins' failure to, at last, land the trophy he craved so much induced in Simmonds increasing difficulty in terms of articulation, whilst his demeanor moved rapidly from sympathy, to sorrow, to a touch of bemusement, then clearly to embarrassment. He felt the need of back up: "It would be probably best, boy – better for you to, well, to appreciate what happened, if you spoke to the judge, Silas Flood. You know him, of course – he's been judging vegetable sections here for – for – well, perhaps thirty years or more. Comes down from Newton Abbot way every year to do it – knows his stuff, knows it inside out; he's judged at Devon County Show in the past, several times. I believe he was supposed to this year, but was down with the 'flu at the time apparently. What he doesn't know about veg – well, let's say, there's nobody in the county with better knowledge than him; very fair man, too – but a stickler for the rules."

The last six words were added as an afterthought, but the chairman had become aware they were so very relevant to the present lamentable situation and would perhaps be, to the clearly distressed Deadeye Dawkins, a clue as to why he was not destined to carry off the Tamar Valley Cup. The chairman opened his mouth to continue but was unable to speak, overwhelmed by a deluge of words from Deadeye's incandescent spouse.

"Nobody with a better knowledge of veg? How can you say such a thing, Gordon Simmonds? A child from the village school can see that Deadeye's veg are the best in this show by a mile. His fruit and flowers were good, but not as good as his veg – there's nothing he's entered this year that's not of the highest standard – I might not be a so-called expert judge, but I can see that, and I don't doubt all those who'll be coming in here this afternoon to look at everything will agree. He's been cheated, Gordon – and, he's been shamefully treated. If I had my way. . ."

What would happen if Harriet had her way would never be

known, for the chairman seeing, most urgently, the need to escape
from the tirade of words which threatened to overwhelm him,
returned rapidly to his plan of a few minutes earlier, seeing it as
a desperately needed means of escape:

"As I said just now, maid, perhaps the best thing," he
interjected loudly (a raised voice was crucial to make himself
heard above Harriet's harangue), "would be for you to talk with
Silas Flood himself – as judge, he is the man who decides, and
he's the man who made the decisions that led to the final result
today. He told me he'd be more than happy to have a chat with
you, Deadeye – in fact, in view of the fact that you entered such
high quality vegetables in the section he judged, but did not come
out on top, I fancy he would really welcome one. Will you come
over with me and see him?"

Deadeye nodded, looked at his wife, frowned and shook his
head as he saw she was about to recommence her verbal assault
on the chairman (nothing would be gained from Harriet's verbose
recriminations, he reasoned, justified though they were) and
moved slowly to where he could see the judges gathered, all
drinking tea. "It can do no harm, Gordon," he muttered.

Following the chairman, he approached the judges, was
introduced to Silas Flood – whom he had met on occasions in the
past – and looked at him expectantly, Gordon's purpose in having
introduced him being explained by a simple, "I feel, Silas, that
Deadeye here has a right to an explanation as to why he's ended
up in second place overall despite the so very high standard of his
entries."

The judge nodded, placed his cup and saucer upon a nearby
table, smiled gently, then said, "No man in England deserves an
explanation more than do you as to why, despite the outstanding
nature of your entries, you have failed to gain the champion's
cup. As you know, Mr Dawkins, I'm the judge covering the
vegetable section so I, in effect, am the reason you have failed to
win the Tamar Valley Cup. I have learnt since the termination of
the judging that if it had not been for a certain decision I made –
felt I had no option other than to make – you would have won the
trophy. The chairman told me just now that your brother had a

slender lead over you in the flower classes, but you just shaded the fruit section. Now, I have the fault, always, of being a touch slow in my judging – invariably, I'm afraid, no matter where I judge, the adjudicators of other sections and classes will have completed their business before I have. So it was here, with the results settled of the fruit and flower sections before – probably well before – I had finished judging the veg that with your brother and yourself virtually neck and neck, the destination of the Tamar Valley Cup would be decided on the results of the classes I was judging. As you know, obviously, I've no knowledge of the identity of who has put forward a certain entry. I just examine all entries, then award first, second, third and, occasionally, a highly commended. In most classes, two entries were, usually, superior to all others. Having judged here for many years, I suspected it would be the Dawkins brothers who were dominating – though, of course, I did not know for certain. At the end, though, I found out that I was correct. I found out also that whilst your brother Tom had, as always, done extremely well, you had done better, Mr Dawkins – until I came to the final classes to be judged, potatoes."

Deadeye seemed to shake off, suddenly, the torpor that shrouded him, and came to life. "Potatoes – but what was wrong with my spuds. Tiddler Tom's were good – yes, they always are – but mine were better, Mr Flood. I've been gardening all my life and I've never grown spuds like that before – and I'll say without – without – well without being big headed, that mine were the best in the show this year."

"And so they were," agreed Silas Flood – instantly. "I've been judging in shows now, in Devon and Cornwall – including country shows – for some thirty years, and I would say your potatoes, in all classes of that section, were quite possibly the best I've ever seen. I've certainly not seen better, not even at county level. As I said just now, with the subsequent identity of entrants revealed to me since my judging finished, you were ahead in the veg section before I got to the potato section; comfortably ahead, as well. Your brother was in second place – well in front of all other runners – but even if he won all sections of the potato classes, you would, I now understand, only have needed 2 third prizes to have sufficient points, overall, to be the winner of the Tamar Valley Cup – a trophy, frankly, you richly, richly deserve for the overall standard of all your entries in this fine show. As it was. . ."

"As it was, what?" interjected Deadeye, his previous desolation and confusion now replaced by a seething anger, an overwhelmingly destructive convulsion that somewhere along the line he had just been cheated of a prize he had coveted for so very, very long. "How – how – how in God's name could my spuds be so good as you yourself say, Mr Flood, yet I could not even gain a couple of third prizes – even one?"

"You gained no prizes, Mr Dawkins, because I had no option, sadly. In fact, this has been, frankly, my hardest decision in all these long years I've been judging, and most certainly, my worst moment. I had no other option than to disqualify all your entries in the potato classes, even though it grieved me to so dismiss such magnificent produce."

It was several seconds before Deadeye made reply. When he did so his voice was no more than a croak, seized as it was by a powerful combination of shock and bemusement.

"Disqualified? Did you say, disqualified?" – knowing full well that such was what the judge had said. "But why – why – for God's sake why? You said yourself, you've never seen better; certainly, I've never grown better – and I feel I can say this show has never seen better either."

"I don't doubt that, boy," agreed Silas Flood. "The problem is that quality doesn't come into it. I had no option other than to disqualify you because you were in breach of the rules. In every class of the potato section there were at least ten entries – all within the rules except for you, I'm afraid."

Deadeye shook his head, almost violently, in seemingly even greater bemusement. "In breach of the rules? Me – how? I don't follow you. I've been entering this show for just about thirty years – only missing the war years when there weren't shows, of course; and I've usually entered spuds – and I've never had any trouble before. I've followed the rules this year exactly in the same way as I have every year in the past – exactly."

"Which is the problem, Deadeye," interjected the chairman, Gordon Simmonds, "the rules changed this year, boy – in the potato sections, that is. All entrants seem to have been aware of them except you."

"How – how do you mean, changed? What can change? There are different varieties, with different shapes and colours – and as far as I can see, there's nothing different in that direction. I've done the same as everybody else – I've entered plates of potatoes. How could I be disqualified?"

"You had the wrong number on each plate you entered," replied the chairman.

"Five on a plate, Gordon," cried Deadeye Dawkins, reaching the very limit of his patience and tolerance. "What's wrong with that? It's always five on a plate."

"What's wrong, boy, is that this year the rules have changed – it's six on a plate," exclaimed Silas Flood in his customary measured tone and ever courteous manner. "And I am probably the cause of the change. For the past few years I've made comment to Gordon here, and to other members of the committee, that for some reason this is the only show in which I judge – including the county shows, Devon and Cornwall – which demands only five potatoes on the platter rather than six which the other shows require. Clearly the committee here made the decision this year that they would make a change to the rules and require six per plate in all classes, like everywhere else."

"Well, I didn't know that," came the sharp retort from the aggrieved exhibitor. "How was I supposed to know that?"

The weakness of his somewhat self-pitying complaint was exposed, instantly, by the chairman. "Clearly everybody else who entered did, boy – including your own brother. It was in the schedule, of course – but more to the point, all were made aware of it at the social evening last month. I mean, that's the main reason for that pre-show night, isn't it – to tell everybody entering of any changes to the rules and suchlike. It's for everybody to get together as well, but it's useful to give out information. There's usually little to tell, but this year I did announce this slight change regarding the number of potatoes on a plate – there was nothing else, as I recall, just that. Trouble was, though, Deadeye, come to think of it, you weren't there, were you? I've just remembered that – neither you or Harriet. I remarked on it to one or two others. It's the first time I can remember that you've not been there, both of you."

Deadeye Dawkins was silent – likewise his Harriet, standing beside him. After a few seconds he nodded: "We did miss it this year, true; and, like you say, it's the first time we've not been there for – well, probably since well before the war. It's an evening we've always enjoyed, both of us – but it's like you said, it's mainly social with little of any importance being announced. We both felt that, though we'd have liked to have been there, our time could be better spent, with the show so close, giving attention to the garden and allotment. Sod's law, isn't it, not to be there the very time when you were to tell of a rule change – not a big one, on the face of it, but one that's cost us the Tamar Valley Cup. Yes, Sod's law." He nodded towards the chairman and the judge, gave a wan smile – though it was a touch more like a grimace – then, Harriet still at his side, moved towards the exit. Not a word passed between them, but each were of like mind – and they had been together long enough to be aware of it; both were in need of the tea tent. Mind you, Deadeye felt in reality he was badly in need of the bar at the Tamar View Inn – and a long stay there as well, but that would have to wait.

A cup or two of strong, sweet tea would assuredly do no harm. Finding – fortunately, as it was busy – a small table in the corner of the tent, he slumped down upon the rather flimsy chair, whilst Harriet went off to get the tea. Eventually she returned (they were busy at the supply end of the tent) with tea and two Chelsea buns – she knew her husband's taste; he had the 'sweetest of teeth', and was particularly fond of cakes of this variety. He muttered his thanks, sipped the tea in desultory, perhaps somewhat distracted fashion, but ignored the bun – an action, or lack of it, which to Harriet spoke volumes regarding his deep despondency. Essentially a positive thinking, at times even ebullient fellow, the shroud of despair which appeared to envelop him would not be easy to evaporate, of that his wife was certain. And she sympathised; a prize which he had wanted for years – decades even – one, the gaining of which possibly suppressed all other ambitions and desires of recent times, had been snatched from him, and in such cruel fashion. His entries in the show had, overall, been the best; he would have been a deserving winner of the cup – none, she was sure, would or could dispute that. Yet it had been suddenly snatched from him – and, possibly to make things even worse, it had not been denied him through prejudice or injustice, rather for a small, but crucial error on his part. He was to blame – he knew it, she knew it and shortly the entire parish would know it; that, she knew fully, would be so very hard for him to take.

Silence reigned at their table, his Chelsea bun languishing upon the plate – though Harriet devoured hers, the traumas of the day having given her an appetite that a solitary bun would assuredly not satisfy. She was about to suggest to her husband that if he didn't want his culinary treat, then she would tackle it rather than allow it to go to waste, when she – both of them, in fact – were aware that there was a presence standing very close by. They both looked up, virtually in unison, and saw Tiddler Tom standing just a couple of feet from the table. For several seconds the two brothers gazed at each other, not a word being uttered. The silence was broken by the younger brother, speaking softly as was ever his way:

"Just to say, Deadeye, Harriet – don't go home before the cups are presented; you'll receive the Tamar Valley Cup."

His elder brother continued to gaze, silently, this time with an expression of bemusement upon his face. "I don't follow," said he, at last. "I came second – as you know. I was disqualified in all the spud classes."

Tom nodded. "I know that, obviously. But it's just a minor rule – a technical thing. Everybody knows you won today, Deadeye. Your spuds were the best I've ever seen in this show – the best anybody's seen for that matter. Even the judge said he'd never seen better. It was your day, today, boy – but you've been cheated of it. All these recent years I've won it, I've done so fair and square – but not this time. So I'm going to refuse it – in which case, as you were second, it'll be awarded to you. I've thought about it ever since I heard about the daft disqualification – about half an hour ago. My mind is made up – I'm going to refuse it. So as you're officially in second place, at last it'll be yours – justice'll be done."

Slowly Deadeye got to his feet and for what seemed an age, eyed his younger and somewhat more diminutive brother. Saying not a word, he slowly extended his right hand towards Tom, a touch of a smile about his lips, his face clearing, at last, of its taut, despairing, indeed angry, expression – to be replaced by one of acceptance and equilibrium, with his normal affability re-establishing itself; crucially, towards his younger brother, to whom he had been estranged for far too long, with the fault, he was well aware, being almost entirely his.

Tom took the proffered hand and shook it warmly – and a look of pure pleasure seized Harriet's features, she, for so long, having been upset – even possibly distressed – at the rift between her husband and brother-in-law.

"Tom – I appreciate this; more than I can say. What you're prepared to do is, is – well, beyond words really." Deadeye ceased talking for a few seconds, his voice a prisoner of his emotion. Getting himself back together, though, he stated his intention: "Boy – whilst I'll not forget this gesture of yours, ever, I can't go along with it. The cup's yours – you won it fair and square. You obeyed the rules – as did all the others showing spuds. It was my fault – mine and mine alone. The show's got rules as it has to – everything in this life's got rules, laws and suchlike. How could life go on if there were none? No – I was in the wrong, and there's an end to it. Even if you turn down the Tamar Valley Cup, I'll not be accepting it, so it'll mean a Dawkins won't win it – for the first time in God knows how many years. Father'll spin in his grave if we both turn it down; it meant as much to him when he used to show, as it does to us."

Their late father, George Dawkins, like Tiddler Tom, had won the cup several times right up until his premature death in the 1930s. Being a man very keen on his scrumpy, he had turned out late one evening from the Tamar View – very much the 'worse for wear' in the eyes of witnesses who had given evidence at the inquest – and had staggered into the path of a small lorry being driven by Sid Small, a local builder whom, many claimed (though it could never be proved) was also the 'worse for wear'. The fact that the builder died just a couple of years after, of cirrhosis of the liver gave some credence to the tale. On the evidence, however, the coroner had no option other than to record a verdict of 'accidental death'. Just a couple of years after George's demise, his younger son had won the cup – and had done likewise every single show since, a quite remarkable achievement.

"You've won it fair and square, Tom – and you've got to accept it."

Tiddler Tom nodded: "Yes, I see what you mean. It's just I feel I don't deserve it. I've earned it in previous years, mind you, but not this time. Still, if you won't take it – then I must. As you say, it's got to stay in – in our family."

Deadeye nodded. "Too right, boy – and it'll remain in the family next year, don't you worry about that – but it'll be in our house, mine and Harriet's, not yours, that's a promise I do make."

Tiddler Tom laughed, then nodded. "If you grow next year what you've grown this, then I've not the slightest doubt it's a promise you'll keep, as well." He raised his hand in farewell, and moved out of the tent and towards the hall.

Harriet Dawkins looked, searchingly, at her husband. "Well, Deadeye, despite the terrible shock and disappointment of not winning the cup, it has been, I feel, a good day – a very, very good day. It's time the rift between you and Tiddler Tom was healed – it's concerned me for so long. Now it is – thank heavens. And it must never appear again, Deadeye – never." The final words were spoken with, for Harriet, rare vehemence.

Her husband nodded. "You're right, maid. It mustn't – and it won't." He got to his feet and helped his wife up likewise. "Well, I reckon it's time we had a good look around the show. That's one of the advantages of being an exhibitor – you can get in for nothing."

II

The Sinner

The people of the parish had varying views on Jim Burnham –
though even the best registered very low on the popularity scale.

There were some – though it had to be said, not many – who
thought, "He's all right, really, old Jim – bit of a character, of
course, but no real harm in him." They would not have been the
victims of one of his 'scams'. Others, still on the generous side,
classed him as a "right beauty", though definitely not somebody
to remotely admire or respect.

A majority, though, whilst they accepted him being a true son
of the Peninsula, having been born there some fifty years
previously and having lived there all his life, had no illusions and,
in many instances, little tolerance regarding his character. Those
of a 'live and let live' nature might, on a good day, assess him as
being "A rogue, of course, but in many ways, a likeable one," but
a sizeable number of the citizenry dwelling on the land that lay
between the Tamar and Tavy would be infinitely more blunt –
"He's a scoundrel!" or, even more blunt, "He's a crook!" or, on
occasions, from a few, "The man's a menace – he should have
been banged up in Dartmoor years ago. The man's never lived an
honest day in his life, he's a scourge we could do without."

Such a judgment was perhaps a little draconian. Jim
Burnham was not a nasty fellow – not even an unpleasant one.
On the contrary, his was basically a friendly, even kindly nature;
never in his life had he committed an aggressive act, never

41

threatened anybody, never been rude or offensive. No, the problem with Mr Burnham was that, although he was a man not afraid of work, he had never in his life done, with consistency, any real job, never had a trade or craft; rather he had largely lived by his wits, and those sensibilities so often had about them a dishonest twist.

Not that he ever indulged in the more blatant forms regarding the acquisition of money or goods; he did not burgle or steal, shoplift or break and enter. Rather, his nefarious ways were based on cunning, fraud, deception and blatant lies. Some of such he had performed outside the parish; possibly his best remembered in this direction was that which he had attempted – and for a brief period seemed to have achieved – at the Pennycross Greyhound Track in Plymouth.

His father had always had a couple of greyhounds and so had Jim. Likewise, they both from time to time had raced them at the well patronised venue in the city, with some success – especially Burnham senior, who was a shrewd judge of the finer qualities of the speedy canines, often able to acquire them cheaply as pups (on occasions breed them) then train them up to be dogs able, at times, to win races which carried decent prize money. Also, had been canny in knowing when to lay bets. Like his son, he had never pursued any steady, regular way of making a living but had made a 'few bob' from his dogs (on a good summer's night at the Plymouth dog track his winnings from betting and prize money could possibly keep his family for a month); also, he sold logs and firewood in the winter, did – if things were a little tight – some fruit picking in the summer, and having 'the gift', made a bit from wort charming and other skills in the faith healing department. Unlike his son, though, Freddie Burnham had few enemies in the community, for whilst there might have been the odd time he would sail a touch 'close to the wind', he was basically an honest, trustworthy man who would never knowingly mislead, cheat or deceive.

Jim, though, whilst his somewhat mercurial, irresolute and quirky nature encouraged him to pursue the way of life of his father, did not possess the touch, the skills, the judgment to do it with success – legally. Thus had he, from an early age, pursued the confidence trick – cheated, lied and defrauded.

Like Freddie, he kept a couple of greyhounds which he would at times race at Pennycross. Lacking that judgment crucial to pick, as a pup, a winner from an also-ran, most of those he acquired would, in races, trail in well to the rear. By chance, though, he came across a greyhound of quality – one with a turn of speed which would win races; one which could, if handled correctly, make him some real money. In acquiring such a beast he had, as he would admit, "used up a year's good luck in a single day."

His next door neighbour, an elderly widow, Mrs Adams, had been given the dog as a pup by her son, Henry – born in the parish, but now living and working in Tavistock. He had found it wandering on Whitchurch Down while engaged in his work as a groundsman at the golf club. Nobody claimed ownership – nobody appeared to want the gentle creature – so he decided to keep it. His wife, though, no animal lover, had no desire to share her home with a "smelly, flee ridden dog," so he bowed to pressure and gave it to his mother, who loved animals. She though, whilst delighted to have it as company, died from pneumonia just three months after its acquisition. So Henry, as her only child, having to 'sort things out', and realising that the priority had to be the pet, offered him to Jim Burnham knowing he had always kept a couple of greyhounds.

Jim had just lost the better of his brace of dogs through distemper – a major blow as, whilst the animal was no champion, it had been capable of winning the odd race; the one which remained – named officially, and grandly, as Tamar Typhoon – showed no such qualities of speed and was, as his owner would say as it trailed in last in a race (not unusual) "a waste of good food." So he had nothing to lose by taking – for nothing – the young greyhound from next door.

Now fully grown, Burnham noted his ease and fluidity of movement, the shape and grace of a body built for speed. The following day, he took the dogs, as he often did, up to the council owned recreational fields and let them run across the football pitches to give them the exercise crucial for canines whose purpose in life was to race.

It was a moment he would not forget; for whilst Tamar Typhoon tended to, usually, be somewhat outclassed in his races at Plymouth, he was still no slouch. Jim's new beast, though, left the Typhoon far behind in their run across the field – "never seen anything move like it," he was to comment. Briefly, he distrusted what he had witnessed. Perhaps the young dog had looked fast because the ageing Tamar Typhoon was even slower than normal; but no, this was a dog who could surely 'motor' – a dog which would win races, a factor which embedded itself in his fertile mind, rapidly.

Giving thanks for his remarkable good fortune in having such a prize come his way, he wasted no time in exploiting it. Registering the dog as Tamar Terror, he started to enter him in races.

Quickly he appreciated the animal's strengths – and limitations. In the company of the top racers in the area, the Terror, whilst he could hold his own with the very good – beat them on his day – could not compete successfully with the best. Thus did the owner plan, carefully, and reasonably successfully, the races in which to enter the Terror – also the Typhoon, as well, as he still needed the occasional run. The Terror won more often than not, winning his owner modest, but welcome sums. He also showed a profit from the bets he made. The problem in this direction though, was that the more successful the dog became, the shorter the odds – thus diminishing returns from his bets. Most folk would have still been reasonably happy with the situation – a dog which often won, bets which showed a profit more often than not – but Jim Burnham was not 'most folk'.

His scheming and, as many would have described it, criminal mind began to take control. Thus was hatched a plan, clever in a sense, but totally fraudulent, which could, if it succeeded, make him some real, meaningful money. He had noticed how similar in appearance were his brace of dogs; both black and white, the Typhoon had more black about his body, though the Terror had a black smudge on his nose. It occurred to Burnham that if he was

44

to enter the Terror into a race not competing with the very best dogs – thus one where his chance of winning was extremely high – but disguised him to look like the Typhoon, then the odds against, being offered by the bookies, would have been long indeed (as opposed to possibly evens – perhaps odds on – if they knew it to be the Terror).

Thus did he, one June evening, use boot polish to black up the speedy Terror to resemble the sluggish Typhoon, take a paint brush to apply some white emulsion to the black spot on the nose, and enter his star turn in the name of his ageing also-ran.

The bookmakers, aware the Typhoon had won but a handful of races in his entire life, fixed the odds at 30 to one against; Jim Burnham put all the money he could lay his hands on upon his dog, taking care to share the investments amongst several 'turf accountants', aware a sizeable single investment upon a dog with such a poor record would appear suspicious.

The race was run – and won with ease by the Terror, whose disguise as the Tamar Typhoon appeared to fool one and all. An ecstatic Jim Burnham went to collect his dog from the winning post after the race, then he would – joyfully – make the round of visiting the bookies to receive his sizeable winnings. As he took hold of his dog, though, he was approached by Archie Hannaford, the veteran chief steward of the track.

"Well, Mr Burnham, your dog must have surprised you tonight. No great record in recent times, yet he ran beautifully. Just shows, you see, you never know what will transpire. That's the beauty of greyhounds – they can always surprise you." With that, he leant forward and patted Jim's dog on the back – then stood bolt upright, old soldier that he was, gazing at a right hand stained with black boot polish.

Jim Burnham collected no winnings that night; rather, he was banned from Pennycross for life, and was most fortunate to avoid the law courts.

The story, when it got about the parish – as it did with some rapidity – was greeted with mirth and little sympathy. Jim had tried once again to 'con' somebody and had failed. An original idea, though, folk conceded – one of his clever ones. And if he had succeeded, it would not have concerned local folk that much; a group of Plymouth bookmakers being hoodwinked would not have grieved many on the Peninsula.

Likewise the time he bought a horse – a youngish cob – from a gypsy near Callington. Burnham did not delve too deeply into how the 'didicoi' came by the beast (it was probably better not to know), but he bought it cheap as clearly 'Johnny Gippo' had not dug deep into his own pockets to obtain the animal and, also, showed signs, all too obvious, of not having had sufficient sustenance to maintain the well being of such a large creature. It appeared to Burnham, who had a reasonable knowledge of horses – farm stock as well for that matter – that if he could get some flesh on the cob, the chestnut mare would be worth probably double that which he paid for her. There were still farmers in the parish, whilst they had with varying degrees of enthusiasm embraced the benefits brought by the acquisition of a tractor, who had uses for a shire horse or cob.

Jim Burnham had travelled to Kelly Bray – adjacent to Callington – by train, paid the gypsy for the animal, then ridden the skinny, almost emaciated animal back to Gunnislake, then over the bridge across the Tamar into Devon. About half a mile further on from the bridge, he'd seen a field attached to a cottage – one he'd noted before as it was just that, a few acres which went with the small house, not part of any farm. The grass in the field – perhaps four acres – was lush; no animal had cropped in it many a month. Knocking boldly on the door, Burnham had apologised to the elderly gent who had opened it, explained he'd not have disturbed him had he not been burdened, suddenly, with a major problem. The fact was, said he, the mare he was riding had suddenly gone lame and could not possibly go any further; he was several miles from home (ensuring not to say where that home was, and doubly ensuring not to give his own name) and asked, seeing as it was already early evening, if he could leave the animal in the field next to the cottage overnight, then collect it in a horsebox the following morning.

The cottager was a touch taken aback at such an unusual request but, having nothing himself in the field (his custom in the past three or four years was to get a few pounds from a neighbouring farmer who would, within a month or so, cut the grass to hay), agreed to what seemed a reasonable request.

Jim Burnham did return to collect the cob – but not until over three weeks later, when the mare had feasted upon the grass, and restored many, many stones to her weight, and a shine to her coat.

During those weeks the cottager became bemused, then upset and angry at the equine cuckoo in the verdant nest, but was not sure what to do as he had no idea of the identity of he who had foisted the animal upon him. He had made up his mind to involve the police. Before he could, though, Burnham had returned unseen, in the early hours of a June morning – without a horsebox – caught the mare, then ridden her back to the Peninsula, leaving a field which would at best produce a decimated crop of hay.

Later that same day he sold the, by now, fine looking young cob to market gardener, Harvey Collins; he needed a beast to pull a 'scruffle' up and down strawberry rows to destroy weeds, his previous one having died, suddenly, just weeks before. For such work the hooves of a shire were too large; it had to be a cob, and in the era when, with so many tractors about, fewer were being bred, such an animal fetched good money – in this instance, virtually three times what the vendor had paid the gypsy.

The story of Burnham's nefarious escapades over the cob only became known a few months later when Collins, in a café with his wife in Tavistock one Friday, overheard the cottager who had been the victim of the villainy telling a friend – them sitting at a nearby table, drinking tea. The old gent described the events; he also described the cob. Harvey Collins knew instantly that he, now, was the owner of the animal. He also knew that little could be gained from telling the victim of the subterfuge, but ensured that he told one and all in the Tamar View Inn upon his visit to the hostelry the following evening, of Jim Burnham's most recent greedy and unpleasant trick. Again, though, this did not really affect anybody local.

Foolishly, however, Jim Burnham indulged in many acts of

dishonesty and deviousness 'upon his own doorstep' – acts not forgotten and often not forgiven.

When he had heard that Billy Gladwin – long established tenant of the Tamar View – wanted a dozen or so laying hens to fill a hen house which had, for some years, stood empty in his large back garden ('just as well put it to good use – and have some decent, fresh eggs every day'), Jim offered to supply them.

Thus it was late one evening, just before the landlord called 'time', Burnham appeared in the bar and informed Gladwin that a dozen 'first class layers' had been deposited into the hen house, and were well secured against the fox. The landlord, who was to say to himself later, that he really should have known better, paid his supplier there and then, out of the till; the latter, immediately, exiting the bar.

The following morning, Billy went to check on the well being of his livestock – and to collect the bounty which, he anticipated, would have been laid early that morning. He found the hens all present – all twelve of them; what he did not find, though, were any eggs. Furthermore, a farmer's son, he knew it was unlikely that this dozen would ever produce a solitary egg between them; virtually none had a full compliment of feathers – at least half had hardly any at all, due to moult or, more likely, old age. Where Burnham had got them the landlord had no idea. Being him, he would have bought them for very little but, as Gladwin was only too well aware, sold them at full price. So thin were the birds, there would be little on their bones to eat – and, anyway, they were so old it would be like chewing rubber.

Still, cheating Billy Gladwin had been a mistake on the part of the parish rogue; for the landlord ensured all and sundry were told of such despicable behaviour. More immediately, though, the irate pub tenant had gone around to Burnham's cottage and, finding him at home, demanded the return of his money – every penny. Billy Gladwin was a burly fellow, and when angry – not often – clearly not somebody to upset. He was repaid the cash instantly. The landlord also barred Burnham from the pub – though such a banishment did not last long; the fellow liked his drink and was thus a good customer, so the landlord reasoned –

when his better nature and judgment had returned – nothing was to be gained by depriving his till of Burnham's money.

This, though, was not the only banishment to come Jim Burnham's way – there were others, and they were permanent.

During the winter months, Jim, like his father, supplied logs. He acquired the wood, in principle, in the same way as had his father; he would agree with a farmer to pay a small amount for a wide, mature Devon hedge upon which grew many trees – some quite large – and chop them down. It was to the farmer's advantage in that there came a time when a hedge could be eroded beyond repair by the roots of ever growing trees (and they gained a few pounds from it) whilst to he who brought the trees to earth, though the work was hard with the felling and subsequent chopping into logs, such a hedge could usually produce a lot of fuel for the houses and cottages of the village. Logs were always in demand and a good profit could be made. Sometimes a farmer would let he who was doing the felling have a hedge for nothing as long as a goodly proportion of the wood – suitably chopped – was deposited with the owner to fuel his fires and stoves throughout the long winter months.

Burnham senior had always abided by this – his son so often did not. Variously he would take trees from hedges where he had no business to be, or go into copses and woodland and chop down timber which he felt the farmer would not miss. On occasions, when he had an agreement to supply part of a hedge to the farmer, he would deliver short of the agreement. Some farmers he fooled, but many he did not, and if caught in such nefariousness, would be turfed off the land and not permitted to return.

He often did not play fair with his customers, either. Many a regular, who trusted him, would believe him when he said he had delivered say, a quarter ton of logs into their outdoor shed, and pay him without checking – then find, when they did so, that the heap was vastly smaller than that which such an amount should create. Thus, usually a row would ensue and a good customer would be lost.

Jim was ever behind with the rent for his cottage and would surely have been evicted had it not been for the fact that he had

49

c

an exceedingly tolerant landlord and was able – somehow – when the patience of that good man ran out, as it did on occasions, usually to borrow from people who possibly did not know him too well and felt a touch sorry for him (he could tell a good, heart rending tale if he had to). When he failed to pay them back – which was ever 'par for the course' – they would join the ranks of the legion who disliked, distrusted, perhaps in a few instances even despised him.

He was still tolerated – because there was little else anybody could do. His natural geniality and affability, which in his earlier years brought him friends, availed him little now in the face of his inherent dishonesty and pursuit of the exploitation of those around him. In a sense, he was almost a tragic failure, increasingly isolated and shunned by his peers, but his wounds were self-inflicted.

Jim Burnham did, though, have one quality which was, whilst not a saving grace, a trait which even his most hostile critics had, probably grudgingly, to admit was to his credit – his deep, devoted love to, and care of his only child, his daughter Sally. Also he had been a loving and, in his erratic, slap happy way, caring husband to his wife, Esther. A lady delicate from birth, she and Jim had been childhood sweethearts and had married when both were twenty years of age. It was almost eight years before their daughter had been born – and an exceedingly difficult birth it had been, Sally having almost lost her life. She was told by her doctor, though, that it would not be possible, medically, for her to have any further children.

Theirs was a good marriage, based on deep love and mutual respect – for even though Esther had no illusions regarding her husband's often nefarious means of making a living, to her eternally he was kind, gentle, attentive, protective and loyal; it was truly a bitter blow to Jim and the nine year old Sally when Esther died. She had contracted tuberculosis and, due largely to her weakly constitution, was unable to fight it; within three months of the diagnosis she was in the churchyard.

Had it not been for his daughter who, naturally, relied on him for everything, Jim might well have lost the will to live, so great

was his devotion to, and love for, his wife. He rallied, though, and
had been, over the years, a marvellous father to Sally. Indeed,
many of his scams and fraudulent acts were directed towards
securing funds to keep his beloved daughter in decent food and
clothes – to give her some security in life.

A number in the village noted this laudable side to what was,
generally, a disreputable character – none more so than Mrs Celia
Maxwell, the rector's wife. She had no illusions regarding Mr
Burnham, but she commented often on what an admirable,
dedicated truly devoted father he was. Her husband, the Reverend
Luke Maxwell, who had long been successful and immensely
popular in the parish did not find it easy to agree with his wife
with any enthusiasm, but being a true Christian he did give the
fellow the benefit of the doubt, even though the great majority of
the local folk had no doubts at all regarding the character of a
scoundrel who had cheated so many of those amongst whom he
lived.

It was Sally, however, who brought to Jim Burnham a major
crisis. She, like her father, had had a sweetheart from childhood.
They had both attended the village school together, left together
and both worked in the parish. More industrious than her father
– and infinitely more honest and reliable – Sally, straight from
school, had obtained a job as a shop assistant at the chemists,
run by Roland Penrose. Rapidly – because of her excellent
attitude to her work, her efficiency and her courtesy towards one
and all – she became valued by her employer. Also, an
intelligent girl, she was soon being trained up by the chemist to
mix basic and simple medicines as well as carrying out clerical
work in the office.

Ernie Barnes loved the land, and all he ever wanted to do at
school was to leave it and work on a farm – as did his father
Bernard. The senior Barnes worked as cowman at Ridge Farm for
the affable Doug Jarrett but unfortunately, with Ridge being a
holding of little more than 70 acres, the farmer did not have the
work, or the income, to employ his son. Ernie, though, had, in a
sense, done very well in that he had managed to get employment
with Arnold Fuller of Brook Barton, the biggest farm on the

Peninsula and Fuller, arguably, was the best farmer. A difficult man to get on with, his strict Methodist beliefs making him quite puritanical, he was nonetheless very progressive – unlike many in the parish who, whilst good, efficient, hard working farmers and growers, were slow moving towards modern methods, machinery and technology. Fuller, on the other hand, had invested heavily in tractors and equipment to go with them. To a young fellow like Ernie Barnes, who saw steering a tractor as being vastly preferable to walking behind a horse, and the application of a milking machine as infinitely more desirable than having to extract the white bounty from an udder by hand, it was the ideal place to work and learn his craft.

An austere man, a stickler for time keeping, and an employer who expected a hard day's work from his employees, Fuller was still a worthwhile fellow for a young man to labour for, as he went out of his way to train a young employee, seeing it as his Christian duty to do so – "blessed is he who has found his work – let him seek no other blessedness," as he had been heard to say, often. Also, of course, it was to his own advantage to have a skilled, well trained workforce. A further trait of Fuller, which made him a desirable man by whom to be employed, was his custom of paying a higher hourly rate than anybody else in the parish; including to Ernie, who knew a youngster like him could earn more there than in most other jobs in the village – not a great deal more, but noticeable come pay day. It was earned, mind you, as no slacking – even to a minimal degree – would be tolerated. Somebody not pulling their weight, or indeed, not up to the job, would find themselves on a week's notice of dismissal.

In the January of that year, Ernie celebrated his nineteenth birthday and just two months later came Sally's; and the day following this, came the bombshell – one which she dropped upon her father just after she had come home from work in the late afternoon.

"Dad," said she, "there's something I need to tell you – a bit of news. I've known it for a few days now, but thought I'd wait 'til after my birthday was over before I told you. You're the first to know – except for. . . except for. . . well, obviously when you hear what it is – except for Ernie. Dad, I'm going to have a baby."

Jim Burnham sat as if turned to stone; he was beyond shock. He sat for minutes, saying not a word; he thought only of his beloved Esther – was there ever a time in his life he needed her more than now? She was not here though – and would never be. As he sat there he felt so lonely – so lost; his lovely Sally – so much her mother in nature and looks; just nineteen – not yet a woman in the eyes of the law; soon to be a mother. What to do? What to do?

"We'll have to get married, of course – Ernie and me. You see that, Dad, don't you? I'm sorry – so sorry, Dad, about this. It's. . . it's such a shock. People will talk, of course – say nasty things, some of them, but we'll be all right, Dad, Ernie and me. We love each other; and I know he'll look after me – and the baby, of course. You like him, Dad, don't you? You have always seemed to like him."

There was still no movement, no sound from her father. Eventually came a brief nod of his head: "Ernie's all right, maid – decent lad, hard working; from a good local family." Again he lapsed into silence.

"We'll need to get married in the next couple of months or so, Dad. The register office will be best – in Tavistock; just you and his mum and dad. Quiet – very quiet. Sadly, the way things are, that'll be the best way, with few knowing anything about it. I always wanted a church wedding – but it can't happen now." She said the words as a statement of fact, shrugged her shoulders, then shook her head – "No, it can't happen now," she repeated.

Again, seemingly, there was no response from her father, he just sat in his chair, staring straight ahead, his face an emotionless mask. Suddenly, though, he exploded into life. He jumped up from his chair, swivelled, looked intently at his daughter, then rasped: "It can happen, maid – a church wedding. It can, and it will. You and Ernie love each other, so you say – and I don't doubt you do; so why shouldn't you stand in church, in front of the Reverend Maxwell, and pledge it to each other – make your vows. Your mother and me were married in church and I know

53

that if she's looking down on us now – and she is, Sally, she is, make no mistake about that," (he spoke of Esther's constant vigilance upon her daughter and husband with absolute certainty) "she'll be wanting you to be married there too – so, so much. A church wedding, a bridesmaid or two, me giving you away – a reception after, perhaps in the village hall; speeches; an occasion, maid; you're our only daughter, Sally – our only child. It's got to be an occasion – it's got to be done proper, with some – some style, if you like."

His daughter looked dubious – unsure. "Well, yes, I see what you mean, Dad, the way you put it, yes, it would be lovely. And I believe Mum's looking down at us as well – and would love for us to be married in church as you were. But it's people, isn't it – in the village; what are they going to say? They'll know we've got to get married – a 'shotgun wedding' don't they call it? Some'll probably know already – that's the sort of place this is. They'll say hurtful, unkind things, Dad – and about you as well."

Her father laughed – defiantly, rather than in mirth. "They've been saying things like that about me most of my life, maid; and they've often been true, I can't deny that – I've deserved them, and still do. But most folk'll not say anything against you; you've done nothing wrong, either you or Ernie. You've only done what is natural. You'll be bringing new life into the world – what can be wrong with that? No, maid, your wedding will take place in the parish church. It's late March now, so I reckon early June'll be a good time. I'll do the arranging – see the vicar and set a date, book the Parish Hall, have a word with Billy Gladwin at the pub; he often caters for weddings – doesn't do a bad job either. You leave it with me, Sally – I'll get right on with it in the morning."

Thus did, the following day, the prospective bride's father set about the task of arranging his daughter's wedding. Sally and Ernie also had folk to inform. The latter had told his parents the previous day – as had Sally. They had taken the news tolerably well; for whilst, like so many others, their opinion of Jim Burnham was on the low side (very) they had a high regard for his daughter – "just like her mother" said Mrs Barnes, approvingly. A more difficult confrontation for Ernie was that

with his puritanical employer. He felt he needed to inform Arnold
Fuller before that unbending man heard it in the village – as
assuredly he would, sooner rather than later.

He received from that devout Methodist a disciplined lashing
from the tongue, the words 'shameful, immoral, godless, sinful'
being well to the fore. However, conscious of the fact the young
man had possessed both the courage and courtesy to tell him face
to face and unable to fault him in terms of his excellent work ethic
and determination to master the myriad skills required in the best
farm worker, he decided not to give him the sack – a thought
which had, fleetingly, skipped across the mind of this unbending
man. Sally's interview with her employers was far less fraught;
generally they were well-wishing, sympathetic and most
understanding. Also, Roland Penrose made a promise which
would be of far more value to her than all the kind words in the
world. He had said that whilst, obviously, she would have to
cease work as the baby's birth became more imminent, they
valued her so much that there would always be a job for her at the
chemists and dispensers – part time if that was what she wanted.
Even better from Sally's angle, she was told that as she had
mastered much of the office work and routine so well, it would be
of help to them – and an income for her – if she was to have some
of the clerical work brought round to her, enabling her to do it at
home. It would be of value to the chemists – and a major financial
boost for the bride, and mother, to be.

Unfortunately Jim Burnham's day was not as successful.
Firstly, he went to see the Reverend Luke Maxwell at the
rambling old rectory. The vicar extended to his rather notorious
visitor the same genial courtesy he extended to all. He absorbed
the information coming his way regarding Burnham's daughter,
her need for a quick wedding and desire for a church service,
without comment. There were those in the parish, Maxwell had
no doubt, who would make much comment on the matter – little
of it of a kindly nature – so he needed just to treat the interview
as a business consultation, not a moral judgment. On the business
front, the man promised to be a good customer: Jim Burnham
wanted it all – the vicar "saying the words," the organist playing

before, during and afterwards, the choir doing an anthem and the bells giving merry peals at the end. The rector agreed that all could be done, but it would not be cheap. The services of himself, an organist, a dozen, probably more, in the choir and four, at least, ringing the bells – and all needing paying. "Most of what we do here, Mr Burnham, is, of course, part and parcel of our regular duties. A wedding, though, is not; therefore the time on everybody involved including, I have to say myself, has to be paid for. If you give me a couple of minutes, I'll work out just how much it'll be."

Rapidly he jotted down the sums involved – something he'd done numerous times in the past, so knew them to the nearest penny, but felt always that the purchaser of the service had a right to view an itemised account so that they knew exactly what they would be getting and the cost of each individual aspect of that which they wanted. He totalled it all up, then turned the pad to face in the direction of his potential customer.

"There we are, Mr Burnham," said he. "It is not cheap, I'm afraid – but I can promise it will be a service and occasion your daughter and her groom will remember and treasure all their days."

The father of the bride glanced down at the sheet before him – then his face seemed to drain of blood to such an extent it almost matched it. For several seconds he said not a word, then muttered, "It's – well, it's a touch more than I expected. It's – quite a fair bit, isn't it? Dear me, it is."

"I'm afraid these things are not cheap. As I said just now, though, it will be a wonderful day – I cannot promise good weather, but I can guarantee all those taking part will make it memorable. But clearly you do not have to avail yourself of all the services I've itemised. Perhaps you'll not bother, say, with the bell ringers, for example; that will save you some money."

Burnham shook his head: "No Vicar, it's got to be done proper if done at all."

Luke Maxwell smiled: "An admirable, positive attitude if I may say," agreed he. "Well, there it is. I doubt you've the relevant amount on you today to pay this, Mr Burnham – though, of course, a cheque would be most acceptable. But as soon as you pay, then we can fix a date mutually convenient and set things in motion."

The visitor's face seemed even whiter – if that were possible. "You want the money right away, Vicar?" he croaked.

"Well, as soon as possible, Mr Burnham – so we can get things moving. We find, usually – well, it's better all round if the financial side of things is sorted out at the very beginning. It's out of the way then, isn't it – we can then get on and ensure that everything is in place for the day." The vicar tried to make it all sound as matter of fact and normal as he possibly could, but his rather 'hang dog' expression suggested it was most unusual for him to seek full settlement of the fees before anything had been done. In reality, it was more than unusual – rather it was the first time ever, in thirty years of ministry in the parish, he had ever asked for it. On occasions he had asked for a deposit when a touch unsure that a proposed wedding would actually take place, but never before the full amount. Yet, guilty though he felt in one sense, he knew it was the only fair course to take; if it was just him it might be different, but almost a score of others would be involved, giving up leisure time to make the wedding a success. They had a right to expect, and get, full and instant payment. Here, Jim Burnham's atrocious reputation had assuredly gone before him. For in this instance it was not a case of the wedding taking place – that, he felt, was a certainty. It was rather a case of having to wait a very long time afterwards for payment; sadly, that also was a certainty – if ever payment was made at all.

Jim Burnham arose from his chair, thanked the vicar for his time and help, said he would have to give it all a bit of thought – and work things out – but promised to return; and would do so. This wedding had to take place, it would take place, and it would be 'done proper' – his Esther, gazing down upon them, would never forgive him were it not. He had thought of money making schemes in the past – surely he could again. He had the feeling, though, that a lot would need to be raised; clearly this wedding would not be cheap.

Leaving the vicarage, he made his way to the neat bungalow on the edge of the village owned by Reg Perkins, long serving clerk to the council – and the fellow in charge of the letting of the village hall.

He expected, and received, a courteous reception when he called upon the Reverend Maxwell; he did not, though, anticipate a warm reception from the Parish Clerk – and assuredly he did not receive one. In fact, Perkins kept him on the doorstep. Brusquely he enquired as to what this unwelcome visitor wanted, and was told, by Jim, that he would wish in early June – almost certainly on a Saturday – to hire the village hall for a day; how much would it be? Again he was addressed in highly unfriendly fashion – but given the information sought.

Burnham's expression showed a modicum of alarm. "That much? That's a fair bit, Reg."

"Yes, it is – but the hall's an expensive place to maintain. Even with all the lettings we make, the damned place still has to be subsidised out of the rates. And, Jim – it'll be money up front too. Every penny will have to be paid before you get the keys to the hall – you understand me."

"All paid up front? That's new, Reg, isn't it? A small deposit, perhaps – fair enough. But all of it – come on, Reg, that's hardly fair. How long's the council been insisting on all the money in advance?"

"This is nothing to do with the council, boy – this is to do with me; I'm insisting on it – on their behalf. You've robbed and ripped off so many people in the parish for so long you've clearly forgotten you ripped me off once – in my capacity as clerk that is, not personally. Years ago now you hired the hall to run a whist drive – well supported as I remember; it wasn't cheap to enter and the prizes bore no resemblance to that which were promised – I know that because my wife, who's a good whist player, won a prize – a stone of spuds, which was ridiculous as all the prizes were promised to be poultry, spirits, chocolates and biscuits (though I remember wondering at the time where, the way things were then with rationing still in full swing, you were going to get hold of such things). And, of course, you didn't get hold of any of it, except a couple of scraggy old hens – you just conned people as normal. It was reported to Constable Barton but he never actually got round to doing anything about it – which is the way he often is, of course. If we'd had somebody sharper and keener in the parish as copper over the years other than old Claude, then you'd have been banged up long ago. But my grievance isn't over that specifically – it's over the fact that you hired the hall and never paid for it – not one penny. But if you want it again, you pay for it in full, when the booking is taken. Do I make myself plain?"

Jim Burnham nodded, then opened his mouth to say he had forgotten he owed the council money from years before – which was true as he had perpetrated so many devious acts, tricks and frauds upon those in the parish for so long, he had forgotten many of them, and upon whom they had been visited. Before a word had left his lips, however, Reg Perkins had slammed the door in his face; the consultation was at an end.

The prospective father of the bride was chastened, but determined to pursue possible arrangements for the marriage of his daughter. With such in mind did he enter the Tamar View Inn. Again he did not receive a warm welcome, Billy Gladwin remembering all too well the batch of featherless, egg-less, laying hens, for which he had paid good money. When asked by Burnham if he would be prepared to do the catering for the wedding, the landlord said that he would, gave him a price per head – quite reasonable – and said that he would have to know the date and the numbers attending. However, his final words were the most important: "It'll be cash up front, Jim – I'll want every penny before I've made a single sausage roll." With that, the landlord went to the far end of the bar to serve a customer.

Jim Burnham left the Tamar View Inn feeling as low, as completely despondent, as ever he had been during the many years since Esther had died. His dear daughter was to be wed – his flesh and blood, the one person in the world so very, very precious to him; yet short of robbing a bank, he was beginning to feel there was no possible way to fund it – or, at least, not the memorable church wedding she so deserved and which he so desperately desired to give her.

Going past the church on the way home, he saw a low wall and decided to ease the weight on his legs by sitting on it – though slumping upon it would have been a more accurate description. His head bent forward into his hands, thus did he sit there for some time trying to see a way forward; he shook that head – there was none, he feared. He had spent his life living by his wits, pursuing ideas, plots – yes, he had to admit, frauds and confidence tricks – and what had he to show for it; he was 50 years old, virtually penniless and friendless.

"Mr Burnham – is that you?"

He looked up – jerked up, in fact, unaware there was anybody nearby. Stood before him was the tallish, spare figure of Mrs Celia Maxwell, wife of the rector.

"Why, Mr Burnham – what is the matter; you look quite – quite – well, desolate is the word which comes to mind. What's happened – it's not your daughter is it? Sally's all right, I hope. Such a lovely, charming girl – she's always so kind, polite and helpful in the chemists."

"Well, yes, it is her in a sense, Mrs Maxwell. I'm afraid – well, I've just been told by her she's going to have a baby. She told me yesterday – a shock as you can imagine. She'll have to get married, of course, and soon – and I want it to be in church. She and young Ernie, it's important they marry in church; do it proper – the full service and ceremony; a good reception too, in the village hall – a nice number of guests. It's what her mother would have wanted, Mrs Maxwell – and expected. I'm not a religious man – probably not a very good man, either, but that doesn't mean I don't have my beliefs – my faith. Esther is always looking down at us – always – every second of the day, of that I'm certain – that I know. But it all costs so much – a decent wedding – and I don't have the money, Mrs Maxwell. I don't have enough for even a simple one in the church. I've seen your husband, and he's told me just how much it'll cost – and there's no way I can afford it; and he says he needs it before I can actually book the church – needs it up front. And the village hall, the catering by Billy Gladwin at the Tamar View; it's all so expensive – and they all want the money before they take the booking, before they've provided the food or anything else."

Celia Maxwell, momentarily, was taken aback, but after a few seconds, responded: "Yes, I know about Sally and Ernie getting married, Mr Burnham. I've just had a cup of tea with the vicar before coming round here to the church to sort out some flowers. He said about the wedding and how you'd been to see him – though he'd not mentioned about the baby, of course. He would never betray such a confidence, not even to me." This was true, but Celia Maxwell was an intelligent woman who had been married to a clergyman for a very long time, and knew that weddings arranged in haste were precipitated by the unexpected – and so often unwanted – imminence of birth. "I didn't realise my husband was asking for the money in advance, Mr Burnham. It's unusual for him to do that. . ." she ceased instantly, regretting what she had just said. The problem was it was true – in fact, in reality, she could never recall an occasion when Luke had requested the fees 'up front'. The reasons for him to do so were, mind you, obvious and understandable; likewise the reason for the others approached demanding payment in advance – this was the notorious Jim Burnham here, a man who had cheated and defrauded so many around him, for so very long. Not that he had ever committed such against she or her husband, but Luke would be so very aware of his nefarious ways plus his seeming lack of any repentance.

In his role as rector, he would, for the wedding, be committing the service and involvement of many others, who would have the right to expect prompt payment. However, her thought processes were moving towards 'having a word' with her husband to try to get him to relent a little in his stance regarding the payment. She was not without influence; and possibly there was another way she would be able to get Luke to help this, to her, broken man. Not that he did not deserve, in so many ways, his present misery, but she was never a woman lacking compassion. Also, constantly to the fore of her mind now – as it had long been with Jim Burnham – was his devotion, love, dedication to his Esther when she was alive, and to his daughter ever since, raising her on her own from childhood. Despite his manifold faults and what, to so many, appeared contempt for those around him – whom seemingly, he saw as being there solely for their exploitation by himself (his 'Mr Hyde' side) – she saw the 'Doctor Jekyll' aspect.

Celia Maxwell was a compassionate, devout Christian who believed, essentially, in the basic goodness within people; she believed that a sinner was rarely, if ever, beyond redemption. Jim Burnham, she felt, was certainly not beyond, and as she stood there talking to him she determined to try to do just that – redeem him; and it would help immensely in this direction in the wedding of his daughter, 'done proper' as he desired so passionately, desperately, were to take place in June. As wife to the rector, president of the local Woman's Institute and secretary to the Mothers' Union, she, assuredly, was not without influence, and she would use it. Firstly, though, this distressed man slumped on the wall before her needed to be 'verbally assaulted' even more before helping hands were extended.

"Mr Burnham, in the scriptures – which tell all – there are words which apply so completely to the ways in which you have lived your life: 'He that soweth the wind shall inherit the whirlwind'; yours has been the wind of deceit, fraud, lies and dishonesty for most of your life – and directed at those around you. Now you are inheriting their distrust, animosity, anger and, yes, contempt. Do you see this?" The question was asked sharply.

Burnham nodded. "Yes – yes, true, Mrs Maxwell," he mumbled.

"Despite all this, there are people in the parish prepared to help you. I am for one – and I can think of others, especially ladies I know, whom, whilst unsympathetic – in fact, often disgusted by your, your nefarious ways – do not, and will not forget your excellent qualities as a husband and father. I would have to say that on the Peninsula I know of nobody with greater attributes in this regard. Now, with my involvement in the church and other groups in the parish, I can possibly help you to actually make this wedding happen but there has to be some commitment from you. You clearly have little money, but you must raise what you can. How about Sally and Ernie – cannot they contribute a little towards the wedding?"

Burnham shook his head: "No, they've nothing really. Neither of them earn that much, and when the baby comes Sally'll have to give up her job – for a while at least. And they'll need a bit of money to rent a cottage or some such when they get married."

Celia Maxwell's expression showed surprise. "Rent a cottage – why? Surely they can live with you for a while, Mr Burnham. Your cottage isn't large, I know, but it's plenty large enough to house just three adults and a small child, surely."

For the first time, a fleeting shade of positivity passed across Burnham's face. He nodded again. "Yes, I suppose they could; I'd not thought of that. Good idea, that." He ceased briefly, then added, "But it doesn't alter the fact I'm her father, and it's my duty to provide and pay for a wedding – it's the way things should be done; it's what a father should do."

"In an ideal world, yes," snapped Celia Maxwell. "This, though, is not an ideal world. You do not have the money to provide such a wedding, and there's no way you can ever get it – except to rob a bank and I don't think even you, despite your sinful ways, would go that far, Mr Burnham. No, you need the help of others – and I feel that help could be there; I feel that I could be the catalyst to bring it about. It is though, down to you. I will lift not one finger to help unless, here and now, you make me a promise – the most important, meaningful serious promise you have ever made."

The fellow stood up at last and stared intently at this good lady whom, in just these few minutes, he had grown to trust – whom, he somehow knew, was as honest and straight a person as he was ever likely to meet. "What promise, Mrs Maxwell? What promise of such – such importance can I give? And would you believe me if I gave it? Would anybody believe me?"

"Yes, Mr Burnham, I'd believe you – and I would do so because if you broke it then it would involve your immortal soul. I believe in heaven and hell – if you broke this promise then I am certain your soul, for eternity, would writhe in torment and hell."

"What promise, Mrs Maxwell?"

"You have to promise me, Mr Burnham, that you will never again cheat or lie, extort from people, mislead or defraud. You will treat those about you – all, everywhere for that matter – with respect. It would be nice also if you came to church on occasions – though that is not essential. A change in your character is, though. You have to become the most honest, reliable and trustworthy person in this parish. Now, do you make such a promise – on your honour, and with your very soul involved – do you make that pledge?"

The words were not spoken to Jim Burnham – rather they were fired at him, like pellets form an airgun. He stood for many seconds rooted to the spot, then suddenly he brought his hands up to cover his face – and began to nod his head – then, his hands dropping away, Celia Maxwell could see tears oozing from his eyes and coursing down his cheeks:

"Yes – yes – yes. I pledge I will change, totally too. How I'll live I do not know. I suppose I'll have to get a job like everybody else; but I will change, Mrs Maxwell – yes, yes, yes I will. And I'll start to go to church. And thank you – how I wish I had spoken to you years ago."

On a lovely Saturday afternoon in early June, Sally Burnham and Ernie Barnes were wed, the service officiated by the Reverend Luke Maxwell, the bride given away in marriage by her proud father. The organ was at full throttle, the choir in full voice, the bells pealing the joyous tidings of a parish union across the verdant valley.

The redoubtable and, at times, irresistible Celia Maxwell had triumphed. Not only had she managed to get her husband to officiate without a fee and the choir, organist and bell ringers likewise, promising them all that they could attend the reception and eat their fill, she also persuaded the, basically, kindly Luke to make available the church hall – without fee (which as rector, was within her powers).

The only demand of Jim Burnham in this direction was that all the setting up of the chairs, trestle tables, and laying of such for the feast was carried out by him and anybody willing to help (not many, it had to be said). As to the food itself, that was provided in splendid – and generous – fashion by the ladies of the Mothers' Union. Celia had told them – almost verbatim – of her meeting with 'the sinner' outside the church. How, in her words, she saw him as a 'broken man', one ready – indeed, desperate – for redemption. She told of his pledge to lead a decent life – honest and God fearing. She reminded the group (a number needed no reminder) that despite the bitter harvest he had sown in the direction of others, he had never done so at home – being a truly exemplary husband and father. The rector's wife suggested he was upon the road to redemption and the stalwart ladies of the Mothers' Union, most of them reasonably regular churchgoers, agreed – and fell in with their secretary's suggestion that they cater, free of charge to Burnham, for the wedding of his precious daughter.

Thus it was a magnificent, memorable day – brought about by the practical, positive goodness of the rector's wife and the repentance of a previously recidivist sinner. As for that sinner, he did change his ways – instantly – getting a regular job bagging up coal at the railway goods yard, for distribution about the Peninsula, and becoming a regular churchgoer. Whilst few ever forgot the cynical dishonesty of his earlier life, most did forgive it – eventually.

III

The Pedigree Herd

'Pym' Harper had lived in the village all his life. He had been
born at Meadow Farm – as had his father before him – and had
lived and farmed there all of his, almost, sixty years (again, like
his father before him).

His real name was Sidney, but he had been known in the parish
as Pym since the 1920s when he had, for many years, played in
goal for the village team, getting his nickname from another
goalkeeper of good Devon stock, Dick Pym, who had gone on to
play at the highest level for Bolton Wanderers and England. He
was, of course, not quite of the same calibre but, nonetheless, was
held in high regard by his team mates, being an essential member
of a fine local side that won division one of the United Churches
League (covering large parts of west Devon and east Cornwall)
four seasons in a row, an accomplishment which was still talked
of, even though the present post-war side was even better. An
athletic figure he did not cut; some six feet, gangly, with less meat
on him than the proverbial 'butcher's pencil', he had feet as flat
as a bowling green (had he not been ineligible for military service
in the war, being in a reserved occupation and too old anyway, his
feet would assuredly have kept him out of uniform). He had,
though, large hands which rarely dropped the ball, an excellent
sense of positional play, and the heart of a lion. Naturally,
ultimately, he was replaced in the side, but not easily.

The farm from which he and his forbears had derived a living was small – little more than forty acres. There were many in the parish earning a living from smaller acreage, mind you (though often not a very good one), but invariably such precious land would be given over mainly, or exclusively, to growing cash crops.

Pym Harper, though, except for a few acres of mangolds, kale and turnips for winter fodder, grew nothing but grass. The name of the holding, 'Meadow', was a strong pointer in this direction. Predominantly gently sloping land running from the edge of the village towards the Tamar, the farm had some of the best soil in the parish. Also it was sheltered from cold east winds, whilst even in a dry period there was usually, retained in the rich earth, sufficient moisture to produce decent grass, and when conditions were particularly favourable, then the verbiage was lush, full of goodness – and most productive in terms of quality milk.

So milk was what Pym specialised in, again as did his father, grandfather and even the 'great' of that ilk. In theory there was not enough land to sustain a herd of cows, and their offspring, of sufficient number to turn a profit – yet he always managed to do so. In this he was aided by a number of factors. Firstly he did not employ help, with the animal husbandry, welfare and twice daily milking being done by himself and his able, affable spouse, Cynthia. A farmer's daughter, she was as adept at the practical side of matters as her husband, and a far shrewder, wiser business person. Indeed, all the 'paperwork' was left to her, a task which she quite enjoyed and at which she excelled. Also, the Harpers cut out the middleman, all their milk being bottled in their small dairy and then, daily except Sundays, being delivered around the village. Possibly, though, the third aspect of their operation was the one which really led to its viability – the breed and special qualities of the cows they kept.

Throughout the parish, just like throughout Devon, cows were predominately brown in colour – almost universally so. There were to be found a goodly number of a dark brown hue, the Devon, but the majority – a considerable one – were of a lighter brown shade, the South Devon breed, a large example of the bovine species. This was a cow which produced a reasonable amount of milk, per herd, with a highish level of quality butter fat and cream, plus calves – bulls being the relative gender here – which could be raised to be desirable to butchers, it being easier to put solid flesh upon sizeable frames.

Pym and Cynthia Harper also kept brown cows, but the only ones on the Peninsula – indeed, for very many miles around – of a shade slightly paler than that of the South Devon (also, with a small splash of white). Theirs was a pedigree herd, the foundations of which were set down by Pym's Great Grandfather at Meadow Farm as a young man, the greater part of a century before. The animal was more diminutive than the Devon breeds (considerably so) – thus its offspring would be far smaller, a minus with bull calves, their major financial asset being in terms of beef; they had faces and an appearance more refined, less bovine than the others, with, generally, a far more sylph-like body than the burly Devons. Jersey, was the breed – the only herd of such in the parish and one of only two in all of West Devon.

Selling the milk around the village was not, and had never been, a problem; in fact they could have sold far more than they produced, which meant they rarely took on new customers and often struggled to supply their regular patrons any more than their usual daily amount. The milk was valued for its rich, creamy taste, its goodness and the fact that anybody who wanted some quality clotted cream – usually to go with a dessert following the Sunday roast – only had to put a pint or two in a pan onto the hot plate of a stove, bring it to the boil, then skim off into a bowl the rich coat of cream which would be layered on top.

The Harpers' herd, thus, was much valued by the people of the village. Those whose health was a touch below par or had a sickly child or who did physical work and needed good, rich, natural food – or, indeed, simply those who enjoyed drinking a creamy, filling, flavoursome pint of milk – all relished the natural produce of Pym and Cynthia Harper. Indeed their herd of Jerseys were unquestionably the most famous, treasured and admired collection of animals in the large rural, farming and growing dominated parish.

It was the importance to folk of the Jersey milk which made them tolerant of Pym's somewhat erratic delivery service. The one certainty was that nothing would be put on doorsteps in the morning. If Pym, though, was in energetic mood – or if he planned a trip to the Tamar View Inn that evening – then the first bottles could be delivered about 3 o'clock. If his sense of urgency was even weaker than normal, however, then it could be past four before he started the round. Few complained about it, but on the rare occasions when anybody did and made adverse comment, he would make the point that his delivery was not late for today but, rather, early for tomorrow. Ever a genial, courteous, friendly fellow, the farmer still was well aware that, in a sense, he and Cynthia held the 'whip hand' – nowhere else in the parish, and well beyond could they obtain the harvest delivered by Jersey cows.

The Harpers, though, were not lackadaisical merely in their milk distribution, they were likewise in all aspects of their farming. Indeed, the tardiness of the delivery was, in reality, inevitable because their morning milking took place so very late. In fact, every other farm in the parish with a milking herd would have finished the process and had the cows back in the field before the Harpers, ever having a leisurely breakfast, would have arisen from their kitchen table to bring their herd in to the shippen to deliver the white liquid which had been brewing within them overnight. Part of the reason for this was that they were not subjected to the tyranny of the early calling lorry which collected the churns for the big dairy company north of Tavistock. Even the farms at the end of the driver's collection circuit had to have their milk ready to be taken away by 10 o'clock; thus, those slightly favoured by this would still have to start milking by 7am. In consequence the Harpers were their own masters in such matters.

So too, though, was Horace Blackmore with his herd of South Devons who farmed some 90 acres of steepish land – some of it a touch marshy – running down to, and alongside, the Tavy; the only other farmer in the parish to eschew the milk lorry, he also bottling it and doing a daily delivery. His cows, though, were always milked by 9 o'clock and his delivery around the parish –

unlike Pym, he would go to the far corners, not just around the village itself – would begin by eleven at the latest. Valued though his reliable, efficient delivery service was, however, it was not in essence a part of the structure of the parish as was Pym's – his product, though good quality, did not match the nutritional, health giving importance of Jersey milk. Thus if Blackmore had given up his daily delivery – he even delivered on a Sunday – it would be greatly missed, but if Pym abandoned his, it would be a calamity.

The Harpers' tardiness, as already stated, was not restricted to the milking of cows and the delivery of their bounty. In practically all matters relating to the running of Meadow Farm, they got round to doing things after – sometimes long after – the rest of the farmers of the parish had finished. Their small acreage did not give scope for anything other than a sparse acreage of crops. Except for the growing of a quarter acre of vegetables largely for themselves – mainly potatoes – everything else was for the consumption of their precious cows and offspring. Kale, mangolds and turnips dominated this, most of it for the hungry animals during the long winter months when even the generally verdant acres of Meadow Farm would produce little grass for the rough bovine tongue to sweep into a welcoming mouth. The sowing by Pym of the seeds for these vital crops would almost certainly take place later than anybody else in the parish. There was rarely any special reason why this was so – just a habit.

The fortunate thing from the Harpers' point of view, was that, except if an unusually prolonged spell of weather came along – weeks of drought, rain or lower than average temperatures – then their lateness was rarely punished, there being decent crops of the essential winter fodder to sustain the beasts, and produce their precious milk, throughout the short days.

Likewise, with hay; again the Harpers were not in a position to cut anything more than a small acreage of their grassland for vital winter supplies of the dried verbiage, but that which was put to the knife tended to be done in late summer rather than early (when it should have been). Indeed, many farmers were often as far forward as to be cutting corn when grass was being toppled at

70

Meadow Farm, but rarely did Pym and Cynthia have a poor harvest, despite being some two months late.

Some in the parish resented the fact the Harpers did everything far later than they should have, and generally got away with it, giving them the somewhat derisory description of being 'afternoon farmers'; most, though, accepted that this was the way they were, respecting the fact that in terms of what really mattered – their care for their stock, the quality of that which they produced and the overall maintenance of their small farm – they could not be faulted; more, they could not be bettered.

Their herd of Jerseys, some 22 in number – plus calves, yearlings and so forth – were sufficient for them to make a living from the direct sale of their milk, but not too many to prevent each having an individual name. Pym usually remembered each beast, though sometimes he would have to scrutinise a bovine face or body for its markings quite closely to be sure of its identity. Cynthia, though, knew each cow's name as easily and assuredly as if they had been her children – Mary had a blackish smudge under her left eye, Jane a tail a touch longer than any other, Sarah one horn a little shorter than the other, Judy a scar on her nose – and so on.

It was Molly, though, which took Cynthia's attention on that Tuesday morning in October. In a sense, the farmer's wife had felt for a couple of days that the cow – a very good milker coming to her peak – had been a little out of sorts, her yield down slightly, her demeanour rather sluggish. That particular morning, however, having finished milking her, Cynthia was concerned. The yield was well down, and the animal was picking with little enthusiasm at the cattle cake in the manger before her – most unusual, as generally it would be devoured with both enthusiasm and alacrity. She called the attention of her husband to it: "I've just milked Molly, Pym" – she always referred to him by his nickname, as this was used virtually universally in the parish those thirty years and more ago when they first started courting – "she's not herself. She was down yesterday, whilst today it's not half what she would normally give. We'll have to see how she goes – if she's no better tomorrow, then we'll have to call the vet."

Her husband nodded his agreement – there would certainly be no argument from him in that direction. Both of them took, generally, a 'laid back' attitude to most aspects of life (enjoying it the more because of that), but when it came to their valuable, valued – indeed, almost loved – herd, their approach was very different. Whilst some farmers were reluctant to go to the expense of have a vet even for a top quality cow until the creature was almost on its 'last legs', the Harpers summoned professional advice and assistance, pricey though it was, very early on in the animal's illness.

Thus it was the following morning, after milking, with Molly still looking very much 'under the weather', that Cynthia said simply and directly to her husband, "We need the vet, Pym, right away, too – I don't like the look of Molly. Good, young strong bullock like that should be looking a lot livelier than she is. Her yield's down again and she's eaten hardly anything."

Her husband nodded agreement, then without further comment, hastened into the kitchen to phone for professional advice and help.

Harvey Andrews was the fellow he contacted – a veteran veterinarian who lived in Tavistock, worked on his own, and who had, with his father before him, taken care of the health problems of farm animals in the parish for over half a century. A man now in his sixties, there was little in terms of illness and disease that came the way of farm stock which could ever be new to him, and he usually knew how to cure it – if there was a cure, that is. Harvey's wife answered the call – as was per usual if her husband was out on a case – said she expected him back within the hour and would get him to call at Meadow Farm that morning.

Clearly Mrs Andrews delivered her message, for the 'animal doctor' arrived just before one o'clock, as the Harpers were about to have their lunch prior to Pym – following his customary short nap in the early afternoon – making a start on his deliveries. The farmer explained their concerns regarding Molly, then led the vet out to the shippen where the ailing cow lay in her heavily strawed stall.

Andrews, as always, took his time. He looked into the cow's

eyes, her mouth, took Molly's temperature, prodded here and there, then listened to her heartbeat.

"I'll have to take some blood and get it tested, and I'll take a sample of her dung."

After a quarter hour, or so, he had finished his examination; thus did Pym invite him into the house for a "cup of tea and a bit of cake" – something of a ritual whenever Harvey visited. It was an invitation readily accepted – the vet had sampled Cynthia's fruit cakes many times in the past, and had never found them other than delicious.

The farmer noted the silence of his companion as they trudged from the shippen to house – unusual as Harvey was normally a chatty fellow. Also there was an expression upon his face which was not merely serious, but possibly grave. He took the proffered tea and large slice of cake with a smile on his face and an utterance of thanks. Biting into the heavily fruited delight, he said, as he always did, "Lovely, maid – superb. I know nobody who can make a cake like you can." He continued to munch, but his overall demeanour appeared to be somewhat downbeat, even despondent. The Harpers sensed this – Harvey was essentially a genial, communicative man not given to long silences even when eating.

"What's the verdict then, Harvey?" enquired Pym, apprehension clearly in his tone. Something was awry, of that he became more convinced as the seconds passed with no comment coming from the veterinary surgeon.

Harvey Andrews swallowed the last of the cake, put the empty plate back onto the kitchen table, looked towards Cynthia, said again, "Thanks, maid – delicious as always," then once more lapsed briefly into silence, a sombre expression upon his face. He glanced towards Pym, then Cynthia – then into the space between them, clearly very ill at ease. "I have to be honest and say I'm not sure what's wrong with Molly – that's why I'm going to have the blood and dung tested. I do feel though – sadly, with much certainty – that it is serious. I don't feel she will recover, I'm afraid. I'm fairly sure it's not any of the usual run of things which can come the way of milkers; a good, heavy milking cow, because

73

d

of the taxing nature of producing all that milk every day, is more prone to disease, illness – call it what you will – than steers and bulls. Most of these things though, are curable with the right treatment – drenches and, in some cases these days, there are injections you can give. The problem with Molly is, I fear, she's suffering from something far worse than this, though obviously I could be wrong. There are a few things it could be, but my money lies on it being one of two diseases, both of which, I have to say, can only lead to her death. It's probably a funny way of putting things but I hope it's 'John's Disease'. You'll both have had cows and bullocks with that over the years – in fact, I know you have. The animal is sick, goes into decline and there's no way to arrest it. Molly's symptoms take me partially along that route, but I'm far from certain; in a sense, she's carrying more flesh than would normally be expected with a cow suffering from that. They go to skin and bone very quickly – most times, that is. If she does have that then she'll have to be put down as there's no cure. It'll be a job for Don Colman with his knacker lorry. As I said just now, it might seem a very strange thing to say Pym, Cynthia, but I hope it is that. The one good aspect of John's Disease is that it is not contagious, so it is highly unlikely that any other beast here will be suffering from it. The other disease though, which I feel it could be, is very different – it's highly contagious, very dangerous and is immediately notifiable to the ministry."

"Good God, no – not foot and mouth, Harvey? Surely not. I've never actually seen foot and mouth, of course, but what I do know of it, Molly doesn't seem to show any signs of it." Pym Harper was gripped by far more than worry – rather terror.

"No – no – no, boy," the vet reassured Pym and his wife – hastily. "No – there's no way it'll be as bad as foot and mouth. That really is the very last thing anybody wants – that affects everybody. No, what I fear Molly is suffering from will probably only affect the stock here at Meadow Farm – but it could, I have to warn you, affect matters in a big way. You see, whilst I could be wrong – and I desperately hope that I am – your cow could be suffering from T.B."

There was silence for a few seconds. Cynthia recovered herself first. "And there's no cure? Molly will have to be destroyed?"

The vet nodded, an expression on his face mingling sorrow, anxiety, even despair.

"I'm sorry, Cynthia – so very much. The trouble, though, is it doesn't end there. The opposite – that's only the beginning. For if it is T.B. the ramifications can be very serious and far reaching. I emphasise that at present I do not know it is, and won't until I get the results from the blood and dung I've taken. I do have to say, though, that Molly's look and symptoms are very similar to that of a cow I treated five or six years ago on a farm the other side of Tavistock. She was found to have it – along with a number of others in the herd and their followers. That, of course, is the problem – it's contagion. Mind you, I'm looking on the black side as, I suppose, is my nature. Molly could be the only beast on the farm to have it – if that is what it is. I know, though, that where T.B. is concerned it would be rare for just one in a herd to have it. The reality is that cows and bullocks can be carrying T.B. yet never actually become ill; they live good lives, cows giving down their milk daily, and die in old age. A lot, of course, do become ill. The problem is that, whilst it's not as serious to a farming rural area as is foot and mouth, it is, as I've said, notifiable. If Molly is found to have it, then I immediately have to notify the ministry – that's the law. Ministry vets will come along and test every member of the herd down to the youngest calf – and probably within 24 hours. Any animal infected with T.B., no matter how minimal and no matter how well they appear to be, will have to be put down – immediately."

Briefly, he ceased, noting the look of horror upon Cynthia's face and that of incomprehension upon her husband's.

"I say right away, mind you, that it might not be that – it might not be John's Disease either. But it is only right to warn you both of such possibilities and, if it's T.B., the potential consequences. It's best to know the worst situation you could face, and hopefully my message of gloom and doom will prove either to be greatly exaggerated or, better still, without any foundation." He swallowed the last of a second cup of tea, then got up from his hard chair. "I'd better be off – I've got a couple of other calls;

testing these samples, though, will be a priority. As soon as I know anything, I'll let you know. Sorry Pym – Cynthia; truly I am; but all's not lost, it could be it's negative on the T.B. – and even if it's positive, it might not be affecting others in the herd." Saying his farewells, he left the kitchen, went to his battered old Morris parked in the yard and moved off in the direction of Tavistock, leaving an almost traumatised farming couple behind him.

Three days the Harpers had to wait for their results – "Three days of hell," as Pym was to comment for years to come. If said in the presence of Cynthia, she would add, "and a lot more days of hell to follow." Indeed there were, for when Harvey Andrews called upon them those three days after the tests, it was clear by just glancing at his demeanour that the news was not good. He alighted from his car just as the Harpers were leaving the kitchen following their breakfast. Slowly, silently he approached them.

Almost as if he wished to delay the vet from giving his news for as long as possible, the farmer rasped, "Will you come in, boy – come in and have a cup of tea; and – and a slice of cake. Cynthia only took one out of the oven yesterday, didn't you, maid?"

"Yes – that's right, Harvey; do come in – I'll make some more tea, and cut you a nice slice." Cynthia, like her husband, felt desperately the only way that day to avoid doom laden news was to hear no news.

The veterinary surgeon was, temporarily, a touch nonplussed; he rapidly took a grip of himself and the situation, accepting Cynthia's offer of tea but, a rare occurrence, he declined the offer of cake; this would be no occasion to be enjoying a culinary delight. He followed his hosts into the kitchen, took with muted thanks the cup of tea, rapidly made, put in three spoonfuls of sugar rather than his usual one (a sign of the stress he felt), then sitting at the table, looked at his hosts sitting opposite – Cynthia's expression fraught with fear, Pym totally impassive. He could delay no longer: "The news, I'm afraid, is not good. As I thought, and feared, it is T.B.; Molly will have to be destroyed immediately. Don Colman will be along this afternoon to do it – and he'll take her away, of course. Also along after dinner will be ministry vets down from Exeter; they could almost be on their way now. They'll test every animal on the farm – all except your dog."

A poor attempt at humour were the last four words, something the vet regretted immediately. There was assuredly not the slightest scope for levity in the situation, potentially calamitous, in which the Harpers found themselves. He continued hastily, trying to find words which might bring solace to the clearly distressed couple.

"The law demands everything be tested, of course – it doesn't mean to say that they'll find many more with T.B.; they might not find any. If Molly's been diagnosed early – and knowing the 'hawk eye' you both keep on your stock, there's no real way she could have been seen earlier – then it could be that none of the other cows or followers are affected; or, at least, very few," added he, feeling the need to temper his consoling words with at least a touch of realism. He would have been surprised, indeed, if Molly was the only victim to the insidious, cureless, wasting disease.

"How long before we know, Harvey?" The question was Pym's – terse and very much to the point; how long would the torture of uncertainty last. Upon hearing her husband's enquiry, Cynthia raised her head and gazed at the vet.

"Two, three days at the most. They don't take long." Harvey Andrews, though, was so very well aware that for the stressed farming couple, to whom their pedigree livestock was so precious in all senses of the word, two or three hours would be interminable; a similar number of days would be hard for them to bear. "As soon as they know you'll be informed. If any other stock are infected then I'm afraid they will be destroyed right away by the ministry vets, although Don Colman will probably be hired by them to take them away. You will, I'm pleased to say, receive compensation from the ministry, the current market value – though clearly there can be no compensation – or consolation – in losing quality, pedigree stock like you've got here, none at all." He added the words very quickly – to the Harpers their cows were almost like family; receipt of the crown jewels in their place could never be adequate compensation. There was little else the vet could say – so he made no attempt to do so. Rather, he told them he would be in touch as soon as he had news – but also that he was always there at the end of a phone, day or night, if they needed help or advice.

After he had spoken those words, the ministry men arrived to do their tests. Andrews immediately liaised with them, thus leaving the Harpers to get on with their lives for the next few days – as best they could. In that direction both Cynthia and Pym were of the view that it was essential to carry on as if things were normal – the fact they were anything but had to be ignored if they were to get through as stressful and difficult a time as either would have known in their lives.

Thus did they continue to milk their cows and deliver the milk around the village. Their loyal, ever appreciative customers completely unaware of the turmoil taking place within the lives of the Harpers – and the mind concentrating fact that each day could be the last upon which they would receive the rich, white liquid. Certainly Pym, upon the doorsteps, said not a word regarding the calamity which threatened and, most surprisingly, awareness of the tests which had taken place at Meadow Farm did not become common knowledge in the parish – much to the farmer's relief.

The Friday following the visit from the ministry vets found Pym, in early afternoon, loading up, as always, his battered old Commer van with freshly bottled milk from his pedigree cows. He was about to close the back doors when he became aware of engines; he looked round and saw two cars entering the yard from the narrow parish road beyond. Leading the way was that owned by Harvey Andrews, following a much larger vehicle with two men inside. They drew to a halt, then alighted, briskly in the case of the duo in the larger car, but much slower when it came to Harvey Andrews.

It was, Pym Harper knew very well, judgment time.

Cynthia, having heard the sound of engines, looked out of the kitchen window then, seeing Harvey Andrews and the duo who she knew had to be the 'men from the Ministry' came, immediately, out into the yard, gripped, like her husband, by fear.

One glance from the farming couple at the despondent

78

expression upon the face of the local vet saw their fear replaced by despair – total and absolute. The news was going to be bad – possibly exceedingly so.

It was Harvey who spoke, probably at the request of the two officials, feeling that the situation which appeared to be evolving would be handled better by somebody whom the farming couple knew well. The local vet introduced his two colleagues – "From the Ministry of Agriculture;" he then suggested they went into the kitchen: "We've got the results of the tests here. There's quite a lot to go through and explain, so it's probably better if we go into the kitchen and, perhaps, sit down at the table. It could – could take a little while." Harvey's expression and faltering words spoke of the very worst news it would be possible for the Harpers to be given.

Without a word, the farming couple led the way into the kitchen, followed by the three officials. Cynthia, her innate courtesy overcoming her crushing foreboding, pushed the heavy iron kettle onto the hotplate of the ancient range.

"I'll make some tea – the kettle's pretty hot already so it'll not take more than a couple of minutes. I'm sure we'll be needing some, especially Pym and me."

Harvey Andrews nodded. "Excellent idea, maid, I'll give you a hand – there's no point in me giving out the contents of the report until you're sitting down here with Pym." The vet had had so many cups of tea in that kitchen that he knew the whereabouts of all that was needed to make it and hold it. Brisk though was the making of the beverage, it took a few minutes – a period of time which seemed interminable to the three men at the table, where an oppressive silence shrouded everything. Eventually steaming cups were placed upon the roughish wood surface along with a jug of fresh, still slightly warm, Jersey milk and a bowl of sugar.

Cynthia and her helper sat down at the table. Silence still reigned as each helped themselves to milk and sugar – one of the officials, who rarely took it, putting two spoonfuls in his cup as he felt the need for sweetness; this was truly as difficult a situation as he had known in a very long time, experienced man though he was.

Eyes turned towards Harvey Andrews, as clearly he was about to be the spokesman, being the local man and, more crucially, having a good, quite close relationship with the farming couple. He cleared his throat, nervously and in a somewhat protracted fashion as if he wished he did not have to speak at all.

"Well, Cynthia, Pym," said he at last, "we have the results of the tests and obviously we're here to give them to you and to take whatever action is necessary – in fact, compulsory under the law. Regarding the cows, which are the most important, of course, the Jersey milkers. . ." He suddenly halted, emotion clearly getting the better of him, then stuttered, "I feel the facts and situation would be better coming from Mr Philips here, Mr Adam Philips from the ministry in Exeter. He is more used to this kind of thing than me – has more understanding of the procedure – and all that's involved." He looked pleadingly, almost desperately at the ministry man who, to be fair to him, was quick to take the cue from this good local vet who was finding the almost tragic nature of the situation too much for him.

"Yes, of course," agreed the official, urbanely but gravely. "I'll ask my colleague here, Mr Jennings, to give you the results of the T.B. tests on your cows and their followers, then I will explain the implications, plus the procedure for the immediate future." He looked to his right, to the very youthful looking Jennings, nodded, then leant back on his hard chair as the young official began to read, out loud, the report.

"I'll leave out the rather long preamble and get to the heart of things," said he briskly but softly. "Regarding the milking cows; there are twenty-two in total, all of which were tested and, I'm afraid. . ." He hesitated briefly, cleared his throat, then said even more softly, "I'm afraid – I'm afraid nineteen tested positive as being infected by T.B."

"How many?" cried Cynthia Harper, her voice pregnant with anguish, "did you say – nineteen?"

The young man nodded. "Yes, Mrs Harper, I'm afraid so. The situation amongst the followers, though, was somewhat better – amongst the young heifers, yearlings and calves, though a goodly number of those are infected also, the numbers there are. . ." He was not destined to say, his voice stilled by a cry of anguish from Pym – almost a shriek of despair.

"Nineteen – dear God, that's virtually the whole herd; there'll be only three left. And the heifers, calves, yearlings – most of them will be gone. Generations it's taken to build this herd – and it's going to be taken from us, in, in, well, taken from us in a day."

Harvey Andrews was aware that the distraught farmer had summed up matters in a most succinct fashion. He nodded, "Well, if you put it like that, Pym, it's hard to argue. That sadly – tragically – is the way things are. The infected stock will all be – be – be put to sleep today, and Don Colman will take them away. Dreadful, I know, but it's the law I'm afraid – as you know."

"There will be compensation paid, of course, Mr Harper – Mrs Harper," interjected Adam Phillips. "The ministry will pay the current market price, of course. I know," he added, hastily, "that no money can compensate you for the loss of such fine animals – the decimation of a quality pedigree herd – but the money will help you to restock, which you can do soon. I expect you would wish to do so – and I can assure you the compensation will be paid promptly."

"Restock, did you say? Restock?" The question came from the lips of Cynthia, tears streaming down her cheeks. "How can we, Mr Phillips? We're not replacing a bit of farm equipment that's broken – not replacing a rick of hay that's gone up in smoke. We're talking about a herd of cows it's taken generations of Pym's family to build up. We can't replace that ever – no money on Earth could ever put us in a position to do so. It'll be gone – forever. It's the end for us."

The ministry man, realising the brutal truth of the words, did the only thing he could do – remained silent. His young colleague, though, moved the conversation back to practical matters:

"I'm sorry at such a time as this to give more bad news, but when we came into the yard a little earlier I noticed that you were loading your van prior to delivering your milk – or so I assume, Mr Harper. I'm sure Mr Philips here will agree with me when I say that none of this milk can be delivered, as most of it, clearly, will have come from infected stock. When all the animals that have the disease are elim. . . are no longer part of the herd, then, of course, that produced by the remainder can be sold and delivered as previously." The young man made the statement in sympathetic and respectful tones – but firmly nonetheless.

"Three cows we'll have producing. We can't produce enough now – so that from just three will go nowhere; it won't be worth our while delivering it. And we'll be letting people down as well – good folk who've been loyal to us for years – decades, in fact, some of them. Letting them down badly," said Pym, largely to himself.

Suddenly Cynthia raised her head. Ever more practical, resourceful, resilient than her husband the tragedy of all that was happening about them was, temporarily, thrust to the back of her mind (though it would not remain there for long). "The round," she cried, "oh, dear me – I'd forgotten that with – with all that's going on. There are scores of people expecting a delivery of milk from us this afternoon, and they'll not get it. Somehow they have to be told – but how, I do not know. It'll have to be me, I suppose; Pym there's not up to it." One glance at the slumped, traumatised figure of her husband, leaning across the table, his head in his hands, confirmed her statement.

Harvey Andrews, though – aware the farming couple needed, most urgently, help and support in so many directions – came up with a solution. "One of your daughters, maid – Myra, isn't it – lives not that far away, doesn't she; over the other side of the railway line? I get over there now and again – not often, but when you've livestock there'll always be sickness at some time or other."

The Harper's younger daughter was married to Cyril Partridge, and they made a living from some thirty acres just a mile away from Meadow Farm. Some twenty and more of those acres were given over to that from which the Partridges gained the bulk of their living – the growing of daffodils, strawberries and potatoes – but on that portion which was both steep and cursed with poorish soil they had long kept store bullocks to which the vet ministered from time to time.

"Why don't you phone her, Cynthia, and firstly, tell her the results of the tests; she'll no doubt be desperate to know. Then perhaps, if she's able, ask her to go round to your regulars and explain what's happened. You'll have a list – she could just go from door to door and tell them, or leave a note if they're not there."

Cynthia Harper shook her head. "She'll not be waiting to know about the tests, Harvey – she knows nothing of them. I've not told her about any of this – nor Helen, her older sister, who lives in Tavistock. There was no need to alarm them, or anybody else, until we had solid news. Still, we've certainly got that now – with a vengeance. You're right, though; I'll tell her the – the terrible, terrible news" – she paused briefly, fighting the tears, but then continued, "and I'll ask her to go around as you suggest; tell folk there'll be no deliveries for the foreseeable future," again she stopped, then added, bitterly, "and the truth is, it's pretty certain we'll make no deliveries ever again."

"Well – well, it's very early days to be talking in that way, maid," the vet replied hastily. "No reason why in a few months time things can't be back to normal – reasonably speaking. I know they can never be the same as they are now. You will have lost the bulk of a top quality pedigree herd and we all know that cannot be adequately replaced, not in your lifetime, at least. But you've some good young heifers coming along that thankfully have not failed the test, some young calves as well. And if you buy in a few quality cows, then you can have a reasonably sized herd again – perhaps fifteen or so – which will be viable and enable you to supply most of your customers once more and it could be sooner than you think. One thing I fancy is you can be sure the majority of them will still want your Jersey milk. They'll have to go elsewhere for a month or two, of course, but most will flock back to you when you're up and running again."

Cynthia shook her head: "No Harvey – there'll be no way back for us. Perhaps if we were twenty years younger – but we're both nearly 60. I don't think I could face it – and I'm sure Pym can't; look at him."

The vet did so, noting the farmer still sitting at the table, his face registering nothing but utter despair. Harvey nodded: "Yes, Cynthia, I see what you mean; but the way he feels now – the way you both feel – may well be very different from what you feel in just a few weeks time; probably will be very different. The thing now is to get over today – and the next few. Can I suggest maid, you phone your other daughter as well – Hazel, isn't it? Tavistock she lives, doesn't she?"

The Harper's elder daughter lived on the edge of the old Stannary town, and was married to a jobbing builder, Tommy Jordan.

Cynthia nodded.

"Well, she'll want to know, won't she? She needs to know – and you and Pym need to have somebody with you for the rest of the day, at least – whilst – whilst, well, whilst everything is going on."

"The slaughter, you mean," Cynthia's words were sharp, and brutally to the point.

The vet nodded: "Yes; I've seen it before; rarely, I'm pleased to say, but just once is too often. Sadly it has to be done – but there's grief in it, and a great deal."

So there was. The early days were, as Cynthia put it, "What it must be like to be in hell," and the early weeks were little better. It slowly improved, though – or, more accurately, the Harpers began to adjust to it, even if possibly they would never accept it. Cynthia was the better at doing so, as she was always going to be – Pym finding it difficult to the point of impossible to understand why such a calamity had befallen them. So much had it shocked and disturbed him, he had started going to the Congregational Chapel once more. His parents being devout worshippers, he had been brought up to attend chapel at least once on a Sunday, but for many years he had rarely gone, not out of any lack of belief, or crisis of faith, but simply because he had got out of the habit. Cynthia, a Methodist – and, as such, like him, at home with the general informality, but perhaps more dour form or presbyterian worship – often went with him, though not always.

It was following the evening service at the chapel one Sunday, some three months after the devastation of the bulk of the herd, that they made their decision as to their future. Both knew they could not continue as they were, milking just three cows – and one of them about to go dry. Their delivery round was very short; it took about 20 minutes of an afternoon, covering a very limited clientele.

A week or so after Myra had gone around giving the urgent message of the, she hoped, relatively short break in the deliveries due to the dreadful calamity that had struck her parents' herd, Pym had gone around to everyone personally explaining the situation. He had received sympathy and understanding on every doorstep, with some 90 per cent saying that when he built up the herd again, they would want to receive his milk once more – as long as it was Jersey, of course.

The very limited amount of the rich lactation which was now available was being delivered to the handful of customers about the village with weakly children who needed the extra goodness of the rich product of the trio of cows. Even here there had to be rationing with customers receiving no more than a quart a day.

The die had to be cast one way or another; either large amounts of the compensation they had received from the ministry had to be spent on bringing in fresh, quality Jersey stock, or their existing cows and followers needed to be sold – and probably the farm along with it.

That Sunday evening, walking back from chapel, Cynthia brought up the subject which had dominated, increasingly, their minds, but which both had tended to skirt around in terms of making a decision – or even stating options.

"Pym, we can't go on like this," said she, "we have to make our minds up. Either we rebuild the herd or we sell everything – including Meadow Farm. Obviously we're understocked at the moment and losing money – which can't go on. Such a decision can never be easy – but for reasons for which neither of us is to blame, it's been forced on us; so let's make it – let's make it now. No more prevarication by either of us (and I've been avoiding it probably every bit as much as you). We either stay here and start to farm properly again, or we sell up, buy a bungalow, perhaps with a couple of fields, and largely retire. I've got my ideas on the matter – but what's yours? You're the farmer, Pym."

For a couple of minutes Pym Harper said not a word. Then, as they turned a corner of the road and Meadow Farm came into view, he looked at his wife and said, softly but resolutely, "We sell, maid. You're right – we've got to decide. I know it, and I've been thinking about nothing else for weeks now. Ten years ago I'd probably have said we should carry on; in fact, I'm sure I'd have said that, but we're both into our middle age, by the time we've got a decent herd together again, we'll be looking at old age, and even if we live to be a hundred we would never again have the quality of the beautiful stock put down three months ago. So we sell and move somewhere else in the parish, as you said. It's not as if we have anybody to leave it to in the working sense; there's nobody to take it over, is there? The trouble is, us bred a couple of 'heifers'; if they'd been 'bulls', then one of them at least might want to carry on at Meadow after us. But Hazel and Myra are married to men already well established in what they're doing. Mind you, I sometimes fancy Myra's Cyril would like to cut back on the growing side and do a lot more livestock farming, but with the small acreage he's got, he's no option but to grow fruit, flowers and spuds to send up the line. So – there it is; all things considered, we sell and get out. It'll break my heart, mind you – there have been Harpers at Meadow for well over a hundred years; but we've no option if truth be told."

They had reached the gate leading into the farmyard, but as they were about to turn into it, Cynthia stopped suddenly, looking at the small, compact farmhouse. She then turned to her husband and nodded.

"Up until very recently I'd not have agreed with you, Pym. But just this last week or two, as it's been clear to me a final decision has to be made, I've changed. I thought I'd be willing to take it all on – but I'm not. I'm too old – or soon will be; and like you say, we've nobody to take over from us. So we sell. It's not been in my family since early Victorian times as it has yours, but it'll break my heart as well. It has to be done, though – we have to sell. We must tell Myra and Hazel of what we've decided, then get the auctioneers involved. The remaining stock have to be sold – then the farm, of course. And we've got to find somewhere in the parish we fancy to live ourselves. More hard months to face – as if we've not faced enough of those; but it's got to be done."

Cynthia Harper, ever a woman of action, contacted her daughters with the news the following day. Both were surprised – though probably not shocked; Hazel especially had seen it coming, having commented to her husband Tommy for several weeks that whilst her mother had shown the resilience that was to be expected in a woman of her character, her father seemed to have had the stuffing battered out of him. She would have known though – as would Myra – that the decision to sell the farm lock, stock (what little there was of it) and barrel would have been joint. If their mother had set her face against it, assuredly it would not happen – quiet, essentially gentle, kind and unselfish though she was, Cynthia Harper nonetheless would generally have the final say in matters, not so much because her husband wanted a quiet life, but simply because throughout their married life he had been aware her vision and judgment were much superior to his own.

So both daughters heard of their parents' plan and pledged to help in any way they could. Selling up a farm, and all it had accumulated over a period well in excess of a century in the ownership of the same family, was a mighty and mind concentrating challenge.

Not only did Cynthia phone her daughters that day, she also contacted Denzil Latimer, senior partner of the long established Tavistock auctioneers, Colwill and Latimer (the second named being the great grandfather of Denzil), telling him of the intention of Pym and herself to sell up.

Knowing of the calamity which had befallen the old farming couple, Denzil, like the Harpers' daughters, was not highly surprised by their decision, but he was saddened – even though such a sale would put a decent amount of business his way. He hated seeing the old farming families move out of practical working of the land and into history. Rarely had it happened before the war – not even in the desperately difficult times of the thirties – but it was an increasing occurrence during the decade or so since 1945, though for what reason he was not sure. Not that

Latimer minded so much if farms were bought up by other local families who lived by the land, but increasingly fresh people were coming into West Devon and the Tamar Valley, many from far distant, folk who, in the eyes of the middle aged local auctioneer, did not always understand, or have sympathy with, the ambience, habits, customs, even foibles, of local life. There was nothing he could do about it, clearly, but he regretted it nevertheless. It was to be hoped that Meadow Farm would be bought by somebody reasonably local. The fact it was a very small farm favoured that possibility, as local folk could often raise the sort of money needed for a tolerably modest purchase of a holding under 50 acres. Larger farms though, throughout the area, were so often knocked down to wealthier clients from well beyond the borders of Devon.

It was just a couple of days after this – about mid evening – that the Harpers received a phone call from Myra, a call which was to prove to be of a significance well beyond that which would usually transpire between her and her parents to whom she had always been close. The call did not last long. After enquiring about their health, Myra asked of her mother if it would be convenient for her husband Cyril and herself to call upon them the following evening; not that they were asking permission as such – they would often drop into Meadow Farm unannounced (and vice versa) but, rather, she wished to ensure Pym and Cynthia would be at home as: "There's something we want to talk to you about – something very important for the future of us all."

Her mother said they would certainly be there – and a little later relayed Myra's final words to Pym – ". . .something very important for the future of us all."

The farmer appeared puzzled, then shook his head. "God knows what that means, maid," said he. "Nothing much I don't suppose. Then again, 'tis a funny thing for Myra to say – not one to go over the top on things generally is she? Always level headed – says it as it is, usually. Well, we'll see tomorrow night. I shan't worry about it."

Nor did he – but the words stayed in the minds of them both – indeed, dominated their thinking for the 24 hours or so before their younger daughter and son-in-law came calling. A large pot of tea was made, Cynthia produced a platter full of saffron buns she'd taken from the oven that afternoon and they all four sat in easy – though relatively decrepit – chairs in front of the kitchen range, eating their cake and sipping the steaming beverage.

It was Myra who brought the somewhat desultory conversation to heel. "Why I phoned last night to make sure you both would be in tonight is because me and Cyril have a few – well, a few ideas we'd like to mention to you. It was always likely you'd be here – it's rare you're out, except sometimes on a Friday night when you go to the pictures down the Parish Hall, or just now and again, Dad, when you go into the Tamar View for a drink. But what we've got to say could be of importance for us all – so I wanted to make sure we could talk about it, especially now as I know you've set the ball rolling with selling the farm – and everything that goes with it."

"Well, I've phoned Denzil Latimer, it's true dear," replied her mother, "but that's as far as it's got. He's going to contact us and arrange to come out and take some details. He'll bring somebody with him, of course, 'cause there'll be a mountain of things they'll have to list. Take them a day or two, I expect – even longer. So nothing's happened yet – and I expect it'll be a week or two before it does; Denzil's never a man to act quickly in anything, I fancy."

Her daughter nodded. "No, Mum, true. But clearly things will happen fairly soon, so that's why we felt we should come around and see you right away. It's about your future, the future of Meadow, here, and important to us, of course, our future as well. The fact is that you're selling the farm – a place that's been in the Harper family for over a century – because of the terrible business of losing those lovely cows, and your feeling, very natural, that you're both of an age now when you just cannot face having to build up your herd of pedigree Jerseys again. And I can understand that – both of us can. Put bluntly, if you had a son home here farming with you, then you might well be feeling different. In fact, I expect you would be – I expect you would decide to carry on, to bring in fresh pedigree Jersey stock, and

89

build the herd up once again; 'cause you would know that even if it wasn't fully achieved in your lifetime – and it possibly would not be – it would almost certainly be brought about by the son succeeding you. Well, Mum, Dad, what I'm saying is that although you don't have a farming son, you do have a farming daughter and son-in-law – both brought up to straight stock farming, and who enjoy that type of farming more than growing and market gardening (although we've made a reasonable living from it in recent years). We're here tonight to put something to you, a suggestion, if not as yet a proposal, for a possible way forward which would mean two crucial things when it comes to the future – you could once again have a herd of Jerseys and, in consequence, you would not have to sell the farm."

"Have a herd again – not sell the farm?" The words hurtled from Pym Harper's lips; then he stopped and shook his head. "That to me sounds like heaven on earth, maid," her father continued, "but I see no way it can happen. Your mum and me have fought the fight, long and hard; we're fought out – we've nothing left to give. Our lifetime's work has been destroyed – most of it, at least – and we know it's time to go."

"On your own, Dad, that's probably so. You and Mum are getting no younger and you probably have had enough. But what if you had a younger couple with you, fairly knowledgeable – though far less so than you two, of course – who wanted to be involved, who wanted to restore the Harper herd of pedigree Jerseys to their former glory. What if Cyril and me came in with you – if we joined our two small farms together. What then? What's to stop us from moving things back in the direction they were before the cows and stock were put down? It wouldn't be easy, clearly. In fact, it's doubtful we could in the foreseeable future get them back to the way they were – to the high standards admired in the parish and beyond. But we could have a try – a good try, and to some extent a successful one."

"Join our two farms together?" As always, Cynthia was ahead of her husband when it came to pinpointing the relevant. "What do you mean by that, Myra?"

It was her son-in-law who replied: "Well, Cynthia" – he always called his parents-in-law by their first names – "it's just that we've been talking about this ever since you told us you're going to sell the place; talked about little else. What it is, our place is too small for us to do what we want with it; thirty acres as you know. 'Cause of the size, we can only keep a smallish number of stock – store bullocks, no cows – and have to rely on daffs in the spring, and strawberries and potatoes as cash crops. Nothing wrong with that, mind you – and generally it serves us all right. We don't make a fortune but we do make a living, meaning neither us or the two children go short. And at least we have our own place and don't have to rent – my Grandfather Archie Partridge left me a bit some years ago, as you know, and the bank was a brave help; so we're land owners. But not enough land to be real farmers – which is what we want. Both of us probably enjoy keeping livestock more than we do tilling the soil – though, as I said, it's served us quite well, and we're happy to keep growing. What we'd like, though, is to have a herd of cows – Myra was brought up to it, and so was I. Mother and Father still run a small herd of South Devons over at Crossways; there's the followers as well, of course, and they keep about forty Devon longwool yaws. They do a bit of growing as well, but when I was home with them as a boy and young man before I was married, it was the cows I preferred. Since I've wed, younger brother Keith has left school and gone in with Mum and Dad – which is good; the farm will stay in the family for, hopefully, many, many years into the future. I suppose I'll feature somewhere in their will in years to come – there's just Keith and me so half the place – or it's value – will be mine, but that's a long way away; the longer the better come to that – I've got good parents and I'm in no hurry to lose them. But what I'm saying is Myra and me want to move towards having a milking herd – or involvement with one, if not full ownership. Pym, Cynthia, we clearly don't have money to buy into Meadow Farm, even if you were prepared to sell any of it – and I can't imagine why you would anyway; but we would like to invest what money we do have, and can raise, into helping you restore your – well, almost famed herd of Jerseys. Asking around the village, as we did yesterday – a bit of sauce, that, but we felt it made sense – people are very saddened by the loss of the cows and their milk, and the general consensus is that if it becomes available again, in the fairly short term, then the demand for it will be there again; increased, in fact, 'cause I know, Pym, you've always said you could sell more than you produce – you've, in effect, rationed people for years. If instead of just over 20 milkers, you had around the 30 mark, you'd have enough for everybody, and the income would increase in a biggish way – which it would have to, clearly, as Myra and me would have to get part of our living from it."

Cynthia, ever the practical, interjected, "But we've not the acreage, Cyril, to take on another eight, nine cows – it's as simple as that. We've always fretted we've never been able to fulfil demand, but any more than we've had would have meant we were overstocked; so the quality of beast and milk alike would have gone down."

Cyril nodded, "True," he agreed, "but that's because you've had to have room and keep for the followers – the heifers, yearlings, calves and suchlike. If we joined forces, the bulk of them could spend much of the time grazing our place. As you know, at present we keep several stores – mainly South Devon's, but a few crossbreeds as well – which graze what is mainly roughish pasture We sell them a couple of times a year and buy in younger to take their place. If we did what me and Myra suggest, and amalgamated with you to restore and increase your Jerseys, we'd get rid of all the stock we've got at present and our pasture would be there then for all your Jersey followers to graze, leaving several more acres here at Meadow Farm to support an increased number of cows. Also at our place, whilst we'd continue naturally with the growing side – on a good year, especially if the seasons are early, it can be well worthwhile – we could possibly put a few acres to growing fodder for winter feed, kale, turnips and the like. We've thought about this these past few days – thought of nothing else, talked of nothing else. It can work to the advantage of all of us – we're convinced of it."

"There's a money side, obviously," interjected the Harper's daughter, in some haste. Whilst she was fully in agreement with, and supportive of, all her husband had said, she was very aware that it was not that simple. "It's your farm, of course – and it will remain so. And if, heaven forbid, anything were to happen to you both then while I might have some expectation, Hazel will have an equal one. So initially at the very least, we would have to pay perhaps a kind of rent, perhaps draw up legally a kind of, say joint ownership of the stock and so forth. And, as I say, Hazel cannot be forgotten. So if we all decided to go along the path Cyril suggests, we'd have to get a solicitor's advice first, then formal agreements drawn up, signed and sealed. It's the only fair and sensible way – the only way to safeguard everybody."

Her husband nodded vehemently. "Oh yes, yes, yes – that would have to be. Everybody would have to know where they stand in all directions. If you decide to look at what we're saying Pym, Cynthia, then you'd need to have a chat with a solicitor as soon as possible; I suppose we all would. It'll cost a few bob, mind you. They never do something for nothing."

"I know one who might," Myra chimed in. "Alan Darwin; you know him, Mum and Dad; he lives at Crown Mine House up the top of the village. He's a junior partner in the solicitors in Tavistock, the ones halfway down Plymouth Road. You ought to know him – you've delivered milk there for years, and he's one of the few you still deliver to."

"Yes – of course," cried Pym. "He's got that poor little maid – crippled; calipers on her legs. Dear little maid she is. He's a nice fellow too, and his missus. I have a cup of tea there now and again. I don't know how the penny didn't drop when you mentioned him just now, Myra."

His daughter smiled. "Professional men like that live well because rarely do they do something for nothing, Dad. If he has to draw up formal agreements, after giving you the benefit of his professional advice, then he'll charge for it – and a fair bit, I don't doubt. But a casual chat with him when, say, you're delivering the milk – I feel he'd be quite happy to give you advice 'on the house'. I mean didn't he phone you just a couple of days after word went around that nearly all deliveries had ceased because of the loss of most of the cows – didn't he ask you, almost beg you in fact, to carry on supplying them with it if you possibly could, even if it was only a pint a day, because of their little girl – because in her fragile state, it's so good for her."

Pym Harper nodded. "Yes, he did – and grateful he was too when I said that I would be able to supply just a few customers in the short term – but, in effect, only those who, like him, really needed it for weak, poorly children; mainly, anyway. He has a quart every day. Now you mention it, he did almost beg me as you said. A couple of others phoned as well at the time, with strong requests, and we kept supplying them if we could. But none quite as desperate as him, said he had no idea where he could get it if we didn't supply it – though he could probably get it in Creber's in Tavistock, and he's in there most days to work."

"No matter, Dad – he asked you, and you've never let him down. If you feel there's things worth following up in what me and Cyril have been talking about, then ask him, as a friend, for a bit of advice – and promise him the business if you and Mum decide to take it further."

Myra and Cyril Partridge had said their piece, stated the mind concentrating business that had motivated their visit – and left Pym and Cynthia soon afterwards, the older couple promising to give the matter urgent thought, plus, what they knew was essential to one and all, a rapid response. And shortly after their daughter and son-in-law had departed, Cynthia stated that which her husband knew very well: "Well, there's a turn up, Pym – I never expected that, nor I reckon did you. There's much to think about, much to talk about – but it'll not hurt either of us to sleep on it – perhaps for a night or two. It's Saturday tomorrow, isn't it, you'll be delivering to Alan Darwin after dinner, and he should be about. It being a weekend, for sure he'll not be working. Have a word with him if you can – tell him we've made no decision – which, of course, is true; but point out the complications involved regarding the legal and money side of it all if we did agree to what Myra and Cyril are suggesting. He might say to let it be – to have nothing to do with such an arrangement, even though on the surface it might have appeal. On the other hand, he might see no problems that cannot easily be overcome. He's a legal man – and

94

whilst his need not necessarily be the last word, only a fool would ignore what he says – and we're not fools, Pym." The final words were said both as opinion and statement of intent.

The following afternoon Pym did indeed catch the youngish solicitor at home, and after delivering the quart of so valued milk, upon requesting a small piece of advice – "Not take more than five minutes of your time" – was treated to such, plus tea and biscuits by the legal fellow and his charming wife, Sharon, which, combined, took over an hour.

Pym returned to Cynthia and told all that the solicitor had said, but just as he was about to voice his own view on the matter, was stilled by her.

"Say nothing at the moment, Pym – let's sleep on it. Let's make a final decision in the morning. You've not been to the Tamar View for a while, have you – not with all that's been going on. And I've not been for many months – not that I've ever gone there often; so let's go along tonight – it'll do us both good. You like a drop of whisky and I don't mind the odd measure of port and lemon from time to time. In the morning we'll milk Jane, Susie and Bess, as has been our sole milking chore in recent weeks, then over a cup of tea following that, we'll make our decision – and it'll be final, whatever it is. Agreed?"

Her husband nodded. "Yes, all right, maid – that's fair; it makes sense. Tomorrow we decide."

This they did. And over tea and digestive biscuits, matters were weighed up. Both were of like mind. They were, when they really thought of it, too young to retire. More, though, they were the custodians of a rich heritage – a pedigree herd which had been prized for over a century, and whilst the bulk of that superb body of bovines had been destroyed, the means, the help, the desire to restore it had suddenly come their way, and it was a means which could easily be regulated and made fair to all in terms of the law. This, at least, was what Alan Darwin had said, and whilst clearly it was in his interest to ensure the long term future delivery of the rich, health-giving milk so precious to his daughter, he was a professional man of integrity; if he gave a legal opinion, it would be honest. Also, he said he would act for the Harpers in regulating all legal and financial agreements between Pym, Cynthia and their daughter and son-in-law, whilst at the same time ensuring that elder daughter Hazel was not a loser in the long term. And he promised any legal fees charged by himself would be, 'cost only' – whatever that meant.

So that Sunday morning, before they had nibbled a second digestive biscuit, Pym and Cynthia Harper made their decision – one which they knew would be irreversible; and already both knew in their hearts what it would be. Had not they, the previous evening – even though neither had spoken a word to each other on the matter – raised a glass to their lips, in effect at least, to celebrate and acknowledge the so massively desired rebirth of the Harper herd of pedigree Jerseys.

The discerning of the parish who desired milk and cream of the highest order could look forward to daily supplies for a very long time to come. Pym and Cynthia Harper could look forward to fulfilment, not failure, during the autumn and winter of their lives.

IV

The Poacher

Cuthbert Wells was the eldest member of a family who lived by their wits. Two sisters had married good, reliable, hard working men – one a plumber, the other in the ticket office at the local railway station – but his three brothers, like him, tended to go through life on a wing and a prayer, and also with a keen eye for the half-chance, for the openings and opportunities which do, on occasion, come along. Not all of these were within the law, but the only sin, as they saw it, was being caught and they never seemed to 'have their collars felt'. There were several reasons for this. To start with, they were shrewd, cunning and sharp. Also their offences were low level crime, something the local Police Constable, Claude Barton, worried little about. Not that he would have been greatly energised by high level crime – a quiet life was what he sought, and what he got. Physical violence he did not approve of and would take action against it (albeit at his own gentle pace), but a bit of pilfering and suchlike bothered him not at all.

The Wells' Father, Denzil – known as 'Moonlight', because it had usually been at night that he had done most of his work – had set the example and pattern for his sons' lifestyle, he never having had a real job in his life, beyond earning the 'King's shilling' in the First World War, coming unscathed through the Battle of the Somme where he had been mentioned in despatches. Moonlight had died of pneumonia after falling into the Tamar one chilly

e

night in the early 1930s, whilst poaching salmon, but his four sons – with his eldest the most able – had carried on his somewhat nefarious ways ever since.

That senior sibling, known as 'Cuffie' (the name Cuthbert having been abbreviated to that by school mates on the somewhat rare occasions he ever went), had for so many years lived – at times tolerably well, but ever precariously – by taking salmon out of the Tamar, rarely legally, and by catching rabbits, usually with the farmers' permission, but not always. On those occasions, it was, of course, poaching, but whilst he often knew about it, PC Barton never took action. The policeman reasoned that rabbits were nobody's property, and somewhat pretty creatures though they might be, they were vermin, very prolific and a menace to farmers and growers, especially in an area like the Tamar Valley where so much veg and fruit were grown. Also, they were good to eat – "Better than a chicken, a good young rabbit," and he had eaten a goodly number over the years, many supplied by Cuffie. The policeman was always given a sizeable discount (when not being given one free) by his wily supplier, and being very much a member of the 'let sleeping dogs lie' and 'where ignorance is bliss, 'tis folly to be wise' school of thought, asked no questions. During the forties, with the nation desperate for food, the policeman looked upon Cuffie, with his ability to catch rabbits in greater abundance than anybody else he had ever known, as almost a hero. "Cuffie's all right," he would say. "He's putting food on people's plates – and helping to rid the parish of a pest that's taking money out of farmers' pockets. When you think of the amount they eat, all the hordes of them – why Cuffie's doing everyone a favour, I reckon."

Unlike his brothers, Cuffie had seen no war service, having failed his medical. When a boy he had broken a leg, old Doctor Parkin, in liquor at the time, had set it badly, and Cuffie had walked with a slight limp ever since, his left leg being a little shorter than his right. Thus he had been free to rabbit to his heart's content and had become popular with many people in the parish in that he augmented, greatly and in flavoursome fashion, their meagre meat supplies – including the farmers who gave him permission to rabbit their acres, they always receiving each a brace of the furry beasts as was the custom (something which Cuffie, being essentially a man who believed in fair play, would never dream of betraying). Farmers also were pleased that the rabbit population was, in theory at least, being decreased by this shrewd man (though, in reality, they bred at such a rate it would have taken a score of rabbiters of like skill to make in-roads).

He was also adept at extracting salmon from the rich Tamar waters, usually with the assistance of one or more of his brothers – the navigating of the small, battered boat he owned plus the catching of the rich harvest always being more than a one-man job.

The taking of this valuable harvest without permission – more importantly, without a licence – was infinitely a more serious offence than the poaching of rabbits, and Constable Barton knew it. Certainly it was always the policeman's intention to take action against Cuffie and his brothers – as it had been to do likewise against their father – if the opportunity arose. The reason why such action had never been taken against the Wells family was down largely to the constable's inherent indolence, plus, he would say in his own defence, the incompetence of the River Bailiffs – whose purpose, amongst others, was to put a stop to poaching. In this he had some justification, though there were only a couple of part-time Bailiffs covering many miles of the long, broad river.

" 'Tis their job more than mine," the police officer would say in his defence on those occasions when law abiding folk in the parish (some of whom would, at times, buy from the poachers) complained that much of the river's rich stock of fish were being extracted illegally. "They've got the gear to go after them – boats and greater manpower and suchlike. All I've got is myself and my bike. I've got so much to do on the land, so much to look after and keep an eye on, there's no way I've got time to sort out what's going on down on the river." The fact he had no desire to do so, either, was never mentioned – but people accepted it as being 'old Claude's way' and, also, the Wells family were far from being unpopular in the parish.

There was one night, though, that Cuffie thought the 'judgement had come' when along with his brother Sam, he was cast into the chilly waters of the Tamar, their boat capsizing – an exceedingly rare piece of poor seamanship on their part. There was a problem in that neither of them could swim, and, in consequence, were mightily relieved to see a sizeable launch emerging through the dusk to rescue them. Both, though, felt somewhat less lucky when they noticed, painted in large letters on the craft's side, the mind concentrating word, 'Police'.

If they remained in the Tamar, they would drown, if they allowed themselves to be rescued, they would be in court. The options being clear cut, and the decision easy, though painful, they allowed themselves to be pulled aboard the launch by two burly officers, who promptly shrouded them in blankets, and gave each a generous tot of brandy.

Commiserations were spoken, with the opinion that, as it was not a stormy night and the river should remain calm, there was a reasonable chance they would be able to locate and upright their boat come daylight.

Cuffie who had said little except to thank the officers for rescuing and taking care of them, agreed with them that they might well be able to salvage their precious craft the following morning and insisted that, beyond being wet, he and his brother were fine and would be grateful if they could be dropped at the nearby quay on the Devon side from whence they came:

"You've been good to us – really good – and we'll not take up any more of your time."

Despite such utterances of gratitude and desire to cause as little trouble as possible, Cuffie was sure he and Sam would, at any moment, have their 'collars felt'.

It was, though, assuredly as fortunate a moment as they would know for many a long day. For, overhearing the conversation taking place around them, it became clear that the Police Launch was out on a jaunt – officially put down as testing the engines after a major overhaul. Whether or not they suspected the Wells brothers nocturnal activities were nefarious was never alluded to – though Cuffie felt that it would be a particularly obtuse police

100

officer who thought otherwise; a battered old boat catching fish in the Tamar with darkness all around. It was assuredly their lucky night, though, that the River Constabulary – up from Plymouth – had the same desire for a quiet life as their land-based colleague PC Barton. They were landed on the quay as requested – and the following morning did, indeed, salvage their battered but vital boat.

Although the war years were well past, Cuffie did not change his lifestyle, nor his means of making a living – nor, for that matter, did his brothers. They still did a fair bit of fishing in the Tamar, though less than normal as the bailiffs were more active than previously. And even when they did take to the water, they were able to harvest fewer fish, with the need for food during the forties having been so great, that more fish, legally, had been extracted from the waters than nature could possibly replenish. The rabbiting, though, went on as before, with demand remaining buoyant.

Still, Cuffie was not making quite the income he had in years past, so he, along with his wife, Edie, did seasonal work, usually for Harry and Sarah Martin at Downside Farm – picking daffodils in the early spring, strawberries in June and July, main crop potatoes, for storage (to be sold during the winter) in late September and October. Cuffie did not greatly enjoy such work, but its casual and irregular nature suited both his character and his lifestyle – and the money came in useful. Also, if he had to work for anyone – and essentially he was a man who liked to work exclusively for himself – then the Martins were as good as anybody in the parish. They were fair payers, though naturally expecting good productive work, and did not take exception to his occasionally arriving late at the strawberry or flower gardens – or, indeed, not at all.

There were times when Cuffie's nefarious activities – which, when they went well, could still be relatively lucrative – took precedence over the hard, repetitive graft of harvesting fruit and flowers, such as when the fish were biting in decent fashion or when the tides were not conducive to working both on land and water; at such a time, if the weather was fair, he would usually choose the water.

Sometimes Harry Martin would be none too pleased when Cuffie did not turn up of a morning – especially in peak season when the daffs were opening out far too quickly or when strawberries were ripening in the hot sun with such speed that it needed all hands – more, often – to gather them from the plants into punnets and baskets to be transported from the local railway station to markets around the country. Over-ripe, they would fetch a poor price at the wholesalers the following morning – even worse, much of the crop could be left to rot on the plants. The grower and farmer, though, put up with it, reasoning that Cuffie, if not there, was not being paid, and when he was there, he was certainly not afraid of work, and was a fast picker; mind you, Edie was even faster. Also, Harry valued the fellow's rabbiting skills, keeping he and Sarah supplied with a plentiful amount – a brace free every time he came to Downside with ferrets and nets – and also helping to keep down the abundant pests which laid siege to his crops.

Whilst the illegal extraction of far more valuable – and precious – salmon from the Tamar was infinitely more serious than his occasional poaching of rabbits from farms where he had no permission to be, it was the latter which was going to get him into trouble.

Brook Barton was a fine farm on the far side of the parish, high above the Tavy. It was the biggest in the parish, had generally good, productive soil, and had possibly a higher percentage of flat terrain than any other on the hilly, undulating peninsula. The owners, Arnold and Jill Fuller, had bought it just a few years earlier when Jill had come into a sizeable sum of money thanks to an inheritance from a wealthy relative. Whilst probably more than two thirds of their land was given over to livestock and sheep farming, they still grew a sizeable acreage of flowers, soft fruit, potatoes and carrots – and they grew it well, just as they farmed well. As such, they were highly regarded, especially by other farmers and growers, the majority of whom always had regard for those who were masters of their craft. They were not, however, liked. This was largely their own fault – though it is unlikely it caused them distress. For they never craved the approbation of others.

A solitary couple, they had never, since arriving in the parish some fifteen years earlier, made any meaningful effort to involve themselves with the wider community. None of the many women's organisations included Jill Fuller as a member, whilst her husband, likewise, 'kept himself to himself'. Certainly, the Tamar View Inn would never have enjoyed his custom, he, along with this wife, being a devout Methodist and, in consequence, teetotal. Indeed, it was through their local Methodist Chapel, up in North Devon, that the couple had met originally, eventually marrying in the same church. And the Methodist Chapel – well, two to be exact – was the one area where they were involved locally. Both did much work for the chapels, they were not ungenerous in terms of giving some financial support – especially when repairs to the building needed to be made – and Arnold preached on occasions, the Minister having a couple more chapels in the area come under his care. In fact, he had on one occasion, conducted a funeral when the Minister was down with the 'flu.

Thus they were essentially a decent couple – but austere, unbending, unyielding believers in absolutes of right and wrong, with no inclination for, indeed comprehension of, compromise. They were respected in the parish – and, to be fair, were respectful – but were aloof and not popular. Such an attitude towards them existed even amongst those attending (in very fair numbers) the two Methodist Chapels. The regulars there were aware of, and to some extent, grateful for the support and help given by the Fullers in so many directions, but found their coldness and repudiation of any overtures towards friendship somewhat off-putting – occasionally even repellant.

Cuffie Wells very rarely took his ferret and nets to Brook. Not unwisely, he concentrated his activities on farms where the farmers gave him permission to rabbit to his heart's content – expecting, of course, the traditional brace themselves as 'payment' for that permission. There were up to half a dozen farms which refused that consent – for reasons varying from a dispute between Cuffie and the farmers to the most reasonable desire of the land owner to keep rabbits on their property for the

103

sport of their workers and friends. On occasions when he felt his regular haunts needed a brief rest, he would wander on to some of the proscribed farms, choose a spot as far away from the farmhouse as possible, and, keeping a wary eye open, ply his trade. There were times, albeit few, when he did get caught, but up to now the worst that had happened to him was to be roundly abused by the farmer, and told to get off his land and never to return. With a couple of these farms, he had been banished as many as half a dozen times, always on the end of angry, perhaps threatening words, but nothing worse.

Only twice, though, had he ventured on to Brook during the fifteen or more years that the Fullers had occupied it. Neither time had he been apprehended, but they had been fraught, nervous hours – though well rewarded as some of Brook's distant fields, close to the railway line, sported, possibly, the most prolific rabbit warrens in the parish (and Cuffie knew them all). The problem was though, that he did not have the owner's permission to rabbit on his property, and never would. He had sought such consent from Arnold Fuller just a few months after he and his wife had moved in before the war, but had seen his request refused in blunt terms which held no ambiguity. Fuller had said in his customary, blunt, almost aggressive fashion:

"Any rabbiting on this land will be done by myself, my family and the men who work for me. I've been told already that some of the warrens produce the best sport in the parish. One of my men, Cyril Leyton, spends half of most weekends here with his ferrets and nets. He would be none too happy if I gave you permission, Mr Wells. I have to say that I have already heard that you have a reputation for going where you have no right to be. I have no way of knowing whether or not that is true, but I will say this, if ever I find you poaching rabbits on my land, I will immediately summon the police and have you charged with trespass and poaching. Do you hear me, Mr Wells?"

Cuffie did indeed hear him, and felt then – and assuredly had realised since – that he was the kind of man who would almost invariably do what he stated. If caught out at Brook he would, he had no doubt, find himself standing before the magistrates at

Tavistock where he could face, at least, a hefty fine. Thus, being a pragmatic man, he had only ventured to Brook on those rare occasions when the 'needs must' philosophy overrode sensible caution.

The previous occasions he had poached there were when, to fulfil a late order to the local butcher, he had needed more rabbits than normal and had very little time in which to net them. Both times had been successful, though not an experience the rabbiter had enjoyed. Though a wily man who did not lack nerve, he was not foolhardy – he knew very well that if Fuller caught him with his ferrets on his land, then he would be in court. His fate would also be likewise if any of the four men employed there saw him. All augmented their meat supplies from the Brook's bounteous warrens – as well as ensuring their employer's kitchen was well stocked – and were no friends of Cuffie Wells. If any of them saw him just one yard into Fuller's property then, he knew, they would report him instantly to their boss, and he would be in real trouble

It was in many ways, he would say long after, Ron Benton's fault. For one November evening the butcher called on Cuffie, in the small cottage Edie and he shared near the pub, with an urgent request. He sugared the pill a little by paying for the four prime rabbits dropped in earlier that day.

"Sorry I couldn't pay you there and then, boy, but as you saw I had a shop full of customers – a lot of them impatient. But you know, with me, you'll always get your money."

Cuffie nodded – the butcher could drive a hard bargain at times, but was a fair and prompt payer. "Thanks, Ron – you and I been doing business for so long now, I know you'll never let me down regarding the paying and I'll never let you down when it comes to supplying – well, where humanly possible, that is." He added this, aware that rabbiting was not an exact science. "Drop of Scrumpy, Boy?"

The butcher nodded. "Thank you, Cuffie, I will" – then took the seat by the fire proffered by his host, it being empty as Edie was in the kitchen preparing their supper, rabbit stew.

Within a couple of minutes, Cuffie would regret giving up a fine rabbit for their own consumption. The butcher downed half the large tankard of cider, nodding his approval of its quality – a bit of a connoisseur on the scrumpy front was Ron Benton – then looked directly at his host.

"Good stuff that, Cuffie – the best." Briefly he looked away, then glanced again towards his host, a somewhat uncertain, perhaps slightly embarrassed expression upon his face. "Cuffie – well, it's like this: To be honest, I'm in a bit of a spot, really. I had a busy day in the shop – well you saw yourself the numbers that were in there – like it for most of the day. I'm not complaining, mind you, not at all – it's good that folk are buying local and not going off to Tavistock Market every Friday. No – certainly no complaints there. The trouble is, I've sold all my rabbits – those you brought in this morning and a couple I had over from yesterday. So I'm out of rabbits. Now that wouldn't bother me much normally – it's not often I have a day like today. There's a lot of rabbits eaten, but there's a goodly number of chaps around the parish that catch them as well – generally for themselves but the odd one or two sell them on. There's nobody in your league, mind you," added he, hastily, "and that's one of the reasons I'm here now.

"The problem is that whilst normally I could go a day or so without any, just wait for you to drop a brace or two in, I now find myself in need of several – urgently. Just as I was shutting up the shop tonight, the phone rang. It was Liza, the cook up at the big house. She was full of apologies, 'cause she realised there was a big order she wanted and meant to put it in three days ago. For whatever reason, she failed to do so and gave it to me over the phone. It seems the Squire's got a big do on tomorrow night and, naturally, needs a fair bit of meat. Well, I say a fair bit – any amount really, so Liza's ordered beef, lamb, pork, sausages, even liver and hearts. Fortunately I've got enough of it at the shop to fill the order, though there won't be much left – I'll have to get onto the slaughterhouse in Tavi for more first thing. And when I leave here in a minute, I'll have to get right back to the shop and start getting their order ready. Jane said she'd come down to help me, thank heavens" – the butcher's wife, who often helped out in the shop, was a pleasant and very competent lady – "but even

106

with her help it'll take us half the night. It's got to be done, though
– they need it all by ten o'clock tomorrow morning. 'Course, if
we can't do it then it's their fault – well Liza's anyway. But it's a
hell of an order, Cuffie – and the Squire always pays full whack,
never quibbles, rarely complains, and is always very prompt
when it comes to paying. And he orders a lot over the year – or,
at least, Liza does. My best customer by a mile. So obviously I
don't want to let them down – in any way. Which is one of the
reasons I'm here tonight. Everything they've ordered I've got at
the shop, as I said – except one thing: rabbits. They want six
rabbits – and I've got none. So I'm here asking you, Cuffie –
begging you, in fact – to do your best first thing tomorrow to get
me those rabbits. The trouble is, as I said, that I'll need them by
ten – the order has to go off then, as clearly they'll need time to
prepare it all for the dinner in the evening. If you can get them for
me, Cuffie, I'll pay there and then – and above what I normally
pay – a small gesture to show my gratitude. It's a tall order, I
know, but if there's anybody in the parish – in Devon, in, in,
England who can do it, it's you."

That he had been elevated to national status in terms of his
rabbiting skills went unnoticed by Cuffie – he was stunned,
momentarily, by the demand which was just being made of him.
He shook his head for a few seconds, then looked at the butcher.

"But it can't be done, boy – it just can't. With the best will in
the world. It's – it's – well, it's nigh impossible. You want me to
catch six grown rabbits and have them in your shop by ten in the
morning. To start with, it's coming towards mid-winter; I can get
out to the warrens in the dark, but I'll not be able to see to do
anything until there's a bit of light – and that won't be until half
past seven at the earliest, later if there's cloud about. So I'll have
no more than a couple of hours to catch them, if you've got to
have them by ten. Ron, it just can't be done – really, it can't,
unless I have the most ridiculous luck. To net six rabbits in a
couple of hours or less – well it would be beyond anything I've
ever done."

"I know it'll not be easy, Cuffie – but I'd be so obliged if you'd
have a go. If you could only get three or four it would be

something. I reckon Liza would be happy with that seeing as it's her fault I wasn't told of the order before. So, Cuffie, have a go boy – please have a go."

The rabbiter shrugged his shoulders, then nodded. "All right, Ron – I'll try. I might be able to get a couple but I doubt any more – if that. Whatever I get, I'll see you have them by ten – but it will not be six; it might not be any. I can't order them out of the holes, boy – though old Chalky can be pretty persuasive, I suppose." He grinned as he said those final words in reference to his oldest, favourite and best ferret.

It was to Cuffie's mind a 'needs must' moment. Ron Benton needed six rabbits first thing in the morning. It would not be easy to achieve in such a brief space of time if he used dynamite and blew up a warren. With a ferret and nets, if he got a break, he would do well to catch a brace – three being a triumph. And even that could only be achieved if the rabbits within their burrows were abundant – and there was only one place in the parish which met such criteria as far as he was aware (and nobody else had greater knowledge of such matters as him, and probably nobody could equal it either). The risk would have to be taken – he would have to go to Brook Barton early in the morning, under the cover of darkness, then at first light put Chalky into a hole and hope he was in form – the form of his life.

The following morning, before half past six, saw Cuffie on the road with one sack full of nets and another containing two ferrets, Chalky and his son, Spider; he was not quite as good as his father, but he was reliable. He felt strangely light-hearted – almost elated. He had never been afraid of a challenge – and this was assuredly the biggest he had known in terms of making a living. Also, it was a joust against a man he did not like – in line with many other people in the parish – and also the four who worked for him, all of whom took advantage of their employer's insistence that only his workers could ferret the warrens on his land. Two of them, especially, were antagonistic towards Cuffie and had long been so, possibly aided by a touch of jealousy, as Cuffie did enjoy some minor fame in the parish – amongst many of the regulars at the Tamar View Inn, at least – because of his ability to coax salmon from the Tamar over many years, always managing to avoid the attention of the bailiffs, and the fact, generally acknowledged, that he had no equal when it came to catching rabbits.

Davie Walton certainly harboured such antipathy towards Wells for those reasons – plus the fact that he saw Cuffie as his rival, himself not averse to catching his employer's rabbits at which he was quite adept, and selling some to folk in the parish. If his employer ever heard of this practice, then for sure his strict Methodist principles – his intense belief in honesty in all, especially those he trusted – would make things very difficult for Walton. Farmer Fuller was happy for his men to catch as many as they wished for their own use – but not for sale. There was not in Cuffie Wells' mind the slightest doubt that if his employer knew that Davie Walton had sold just one rabbit, then that man's dismissal would be instant.

Dark though it was, Cuffie – who knew virtually every square yard of the parish – picked his way from the road, along a hedge close to the railway line, then cut across a field to a small patch of scrub where lay the warrens. Reaching them, he leant back into a hedge for some ten minutes awaiting the light. Fortunately there was only high wispy cloud, so a touch of daylight sufficient for him to locate relevant holes then shroud them with nets, came just after half past seven.

The choice of holes to cover – seemingly a multitude – was made by a man who had been honing his skills for over thirty years (since childhood, in fact) and could judge, usually successfully, the holes which led to the burrows with the largest number of residents. He was not always right, but if he was not usually so, then he could never have kept himself, let alone a wife and two children. Whether or not he had it right this time would soon become clear. Mind you, he could not give exclusive attention to Chalky and the nets – there was a hostile farmer and his four workmen to watch out for. If caught, he would be in trouble, especially if seen by Farmer Fuller, Davie Walton or Cyril Leyton who, having been called up in 1940 and serving five years in the Tank Regiment, resented Cuffie's lack of service –

the fact that clearly his lameness made him unsuitable for the army being ignored by a man who, like his employer, had few friends in the parish, unlike Mr Wells, who had many.

Chalky had been in the hole for less than a minute when suddenly there was a burst of action to Cuffie's left – a net flew from off the back of a hole, a fine rabbit writhing within it. Rapidly did the rabbiter move to the ensnared creature, pick it up, extract it from the net – then break its neck with a single powerful blow from his right hand: Death was instantaneous. A good start – only five more to go.

Chalky came out of the hole and gazed about him. Instantly he was grabbled by his owner, then thrust into another. Cuffie awaited developments. It took a while longer this time – over twenty minutes – but eventually a sizeable prize hurtled out, threshed in the net and was immediately seized and dispatched by the poacher.

Again the ferret was put back, this time into the same hole, Cuffie having a feeling that there were more to be turned out. So it proved, for within a few minutes another fine beast hurtled out into a net – again to be rapidly put to death.

The poacher was elated – three already, in little over half an hour. These warrens were, indeed, a rich source – like nothing else in the parish, of that he was sure (and he doubted there was any better in any other).

He took hold of Chalky, returned him to the sack, took out his son, Spider, and quickly put the younger hunter into a hole. The fearsome Chalky had done a first class job but, a ferret by its very nature, was an animal which, whilst happy to chase a quarry, was even happier killing it. If he did that, and in the hole – which was quite likely – he would almost certainly indulge himself in a decent breakfast, then get his head down. It could be hours before he came out again. Spider, though was fresh to the game and would, hopefully, be happy for a while with the chase – though, like his father, he would soon see his quarry in terms of a potential meal.

Cuffie looked about himself – nervously. Whilst these warrens were some way from the farm house, buildings and barns, there clearly could be no guarantee that Farmer Fuller or one or more of his employees would not pass by about their work. All, though, appeared to be quiet – including activities within the warren. Precious time passed – half an hour, then thirty-five minutes, then forty, and not a sign of a rabbit or, indeed, Spider.

Cuffie pulled a battered fob watch from the pocket of his well worn waistcoat – a timepiece which had belonged to his father and was much older than he was. Five to nine – in another half hour he would have to be off if he was to get his harvest to Ron Benton before ten o'clock. Spider did not have quite the instincts of the veteran Chalky, but he was still a touch disappointed the ferret had neither turned out a rabbit or, at least, reappeared.

The poacher paced, anxiously, up and down beside the netted holes, like a guardsman. Occasionally he would glance around to ensure he himself was not about to be hunted. He looked again at his watch – ten past nine. Rapidly he was coming to the conclusion that not only was his haul of rabbits going to remain static, he could well face problems recovering his ferret. If Spider did not come out soon, then he would have to be left with his owner returning later in the day – probably at dusk, to try to find him.

Suddenly, though – action: A net just to his left flew out from the hole, full of rabbit – two of them. Cuffie moved with surprising speed for a man with his leg impairment. He thrust his hand into the net, grabbed the legs of one, promptly snapped his neck, then just as the other was about to shake itself free of the mesh, he again managed to take hold of its legs, rapidly dispatching it to oblivion with a chop from the side of his hand. Fortuitously, Spider himself just then came out of the hole, to be grabbed by a highly delighted Cuffie.

"Well done, me beauty," he enthused. "Just right – just in time." He moved to collect his nets – then halted. He told his Edie later that the Devil was in him. He could have gathered up the nets, the ferrets and the brilliant effort of catching five rabbits in just an hour and a half and made off for Ron Benton's shop. He had no doubt the butcher would have been delighted with it – but the poacher was conscious that the order was six. And, Cuffie said

111

to himself, "He'll have six." Though all too well aware that he had less than ten minutes to get the final beast, he felt it could be done.

Spider turning out a brace suggested to him that there were several more rabbits in the burrow, that they would be in a state of terror, and thus could easily be persuaded to bolt. So he threw caution to the winds and thrust the beast back into the same hole. To save time a bit later, he strung together the rabbits already harvested then moved towards the net furthest away from where the ferret had entered, to remove it and pack it away. Just, though, as his hands moved towards it, astonishingly a terrified rabbit hurtled from the hole, taking the net a yard into the field. Again Cuffie reacted quickly, grabbing the hapless creature and dispatching it. Clearly his brace of ferocious, tenacious ferrets had instilled such utter terror into the inhabitants of the burrows that some were trying to escape though not actually being chased – there was no way Spider could have been within many yards of this creature.

It was time to go. With luck Spider would appear very, very soon – but if he did not he would have to remain in the warren to be retrieved later – hopefully. He picked up two further nets – then, once more was called into urgent action. Another fine beast hit one of the three remaining nets, to be followed instantly by the highly efficient Spider. Cuffie grabbed, and killed, the seventh member of his crop then took hold of the ferret, and returned him to the sack with a rapid smoothing of his back and a terse, but heartfelt, "Good work, boy." He gathered up all he had brought, plus his haul – then heard a dog bark.

He looked up to see, less than a couple of hundred yards away, two men running towards him – accompanied by a dog, for which Cuffie would say later, again to Edie, he would be eternally grateful. For the Collie's bark alerted him of the danger he was in. Approaching him, speedily, were – other than Farmer Fuller – the very two men he least wanted to see, Cyril Leyton and Davie Walton. The Collie, though, had given him a chance. Despite his short leg, he could move at a fair pace when he had to – and assuredly there had never been a moment in his rabbiting (and poaching) career when he needed to move as quickly. He realised he had to make the neutral territory that was the road.

Scampering over a nearby hedge, heavily burdened by baggage and creatures, alive and dead, he headed for a nearby copse. As he gained it, he saw his pursuers were now little over a hundred yards behind, and shouting absurdly for him to stop – an order he assuredly would not obey.

This was truly bad luck – another five minutes and he would have been away. He had noticed a flock of sheep in the field next to the warrens and had hoped that nobody would come out to check them until later in the day. Such hopes, clearly, had been dashed. However, he knew this copse well – if he went off at a right angle, which his pursuers might not anticipate, he would drop down into a type of gully which would put him, temporarily at least, out of sight of his pursuers. This he did, and was, indeed, invisible to the pair, and their dog. He then made for a hedge nearby, scrambled over it, then keeping low, somewhat uncomfortably, down behind it, moved along towards the railway – a moment of inspiration having seized him. For some 300 yards along, the hedge ran into the embankment which led up to the line. Reaching the steep escarpment, he began, laboriously, to scramble up it. He heard the shouts of his pursuers but, looking behind, saw that he had increased his lead over them – clearly his copse ruse had been successful.

Hopefully, likewise, would be his sudden decision to make for the railway rather than the road. If he could reach the top and cross the dual pair of tracks, then he would be well away from Brook and within a hundred yards of a parish road. He gritted his teeth, forced air into his lungs, and scampered on, upwards, ever upwards on the high embankment. At last, his lungs aching, he reached the lines. Looking both ways to make sure no trains were going either north or south, he staggered across, then stumbled down the embankment the other side. Within a couple of minutes, he had made the road – and safety.

A quarter of an hour later he was standing before Ron Benton, laying not six, but seven rabbits upon his counter. "There you are, Ron – that do you?" Cuffie spoke the words in as casual a manner as was possible, giving no hint of the somewhat manic, traumatic few hours which had passed since he had arisen from his bed first thing.

The butcher looked down at the rabbits, then up at his supplier, then down again. Seconds passed before he made comment – then words flooded from him:

"Cuffie – this – this – this is, well I don't know how to put it. It's remarkable – just, amazing. I thought you might come up with a couple, even three if things were going really well, 'cause you're a master of your craft if ever anybody was – the best in the parish by far, as everybody knows – perhaps the best in the district. But seven, Cuffie – seven. Boy, that's brilliant! That's genius. It means I can keep the Squire happy and still have one to sell in the shop. I can't get over it – nor will Jane when I tell her."

He turned away, went to the till, took some money from it, came back to the counter and put it down before the 'rabbiting genius'.

"There you are, boy, more than usual as I promised, just to show how much I appreciate your efforts – not that I'll be making it a habit, mind you," added he, rapidly, being a shrewd businessman as well as a knowledgeable butcher.

Cuffie gathered up the welcome cash and pushed it into his trouser pocket. "Thanks, Ron – I've earned it, the morning I've had."

"You have that, Cuffie, thank you. Tell you what, though, I could do with a few more for the shop – as soon as you can, really. Thursday today – if you could drop in whatever you've got tomorrow, boy, I'd be obliged. There's always a sale for them around the weekend – people making stews, even having them to bulk out a roast if there's several to feed."

"I'll see what I can do, Ron – but I'll not be going out again today; I've got a few things to do at home – and it's not been an easy morning with people – well, with one thing and another." Nothing was to be gained by telling him, or anybody else, of his lively first hours to a working day. The fewer who knew, assuredly the better.

After saying his farewells to the butcher, he made his way

home, and had a quietish morning, drinking a few cups of tea, smoking a couple of pipes of tobacco, and generally getting in Edie's way – except when he went out into the back yard to check the health of his ferrets and change the bedding in their hutches. Truly they were the tools of his trade, and adept though he was at using them, their relentless hunting qualities were essential to his living – and his reputation.

As the morning passed, his skirmish with – or rather, his flight from – the malevolent pair from Brook receded, rapidly, into memory. He was almost as pleased with his decision to go up over the railway embankment (contrary to what the chasing pair would have anticipated) as he was with the remarkable success of his hunting. He was, he was about to discover, far too premature.

He got up from the kitchen table early that afternoon, following the devouring of one of his wife's excellent pasties, intending to have a brief nap before, contrary to what he had said to the butcher earlier, going out with Chalky, Spider and the nets for an hour or two. He had not anticipated doing so, but feeling relaxed to a degree he had not expected a few hours earlier – following his intense, fraught, though successful start to the day – felt that as Benton, a very good customer, was in need of rabbits, then it was to the benefit of them both that he made attempts to catch them as soon as possible.

He was moving towards his battered old chair beside the kitchen range, intending to rest his eyes for half an hour before going out about his business, legally this time, when there came a loud knock at the door.

With Edie out the back, he opened it himself. Stood before him was the burly figure of Constable Claude Barton – in uniform.

"Afternoon, Claude," he said affably. "What can I do for you?"

The normally genial Policeman looked serious – and a touch embarrassed and uncomfortable.

"Cuffie – sorry to bother you, boy – and Edie, of course – but could I come in and, well, have a word?"

The rabbiter nodded. "Course, boy – come in by the fire. It's a bit raw out there." As he closed the door behind the entering officer he was assailed by the feeling his day was about to take a turn for the worse. "Sit down, Claude."

An equally shabby chair the other side of the range was indicated and was promptly occupied by Barton, muttering his thanks.

"Cup of tea?"

The policeman turned down the offer of beverage about once a year and was reluctant to do so on this occasion – but felt that the news he was about to deliver to his host would not be conducive to accepting such hospitality at that particular time.

"No, I won't, Cuffie, thank you all the same – just – just had dinner." He placed his helmet upon the lino beside his chair, then glanced across at Cuffie who had just sat down. "I'm sorry about all this, boy – it's none of my doing, but I have to tell you that you've been accused of poaching. Farmer Fuller, out at Brook, came to see me about half past ten and reckons you were poaching on his land early this morning. He didn't see you, but two of his men, Cyril Leyton and Davie Walton did – and he says they will testify to it if need be. I don't like doing this, Cuffie – in fact, I hate it. Now you've got a bit of a name for poaching the odd salmon out of the Tamar – and if you were caught doing that, then I'd not have that much sympathy with you. There's not that many fish in the river these days. But that's a matter for the bailiffs, not for me. It's up to them to catch you – if that's what you do," he added, hastily.

"I've got plenty enough to do here on land. Rabbits, though, that's different. There's thousands of them in the parish – and they're a menace to farmers; And they're good meat – where would we have been in the war if there hadn't been rabbits to eat? Even now, for that matter, there's not that much good meat about. And men like you have provided it. I told Fuller that I could see nothing wrong with somebody taking the odd rabbit or two – fewer to eat his crops to start with. He doesn't see it that way, though – funny devil, always has been. Has never made any effort to get on with folk, nor has his missus. The law's the law as far as he's concerned – and he'll never give an inch. I've had several run-ins with him over the years, but there's not much I can do this time. The trouble is, his two men, according to him, are as keen to prosecute you as he is. And the speed at which he came to report it suggests that's true. After seeing you – or alleging they saw you," added he hastily, "they must have told him the instant they got back to the yard – and he must have jumped in his car and come straight into the station."

Wells nodded, a somewhat bitter expression upon his face. "Oh yes, they'd love to see me in court, that pair. I've no love for Arnold Fuller, but at least he has always been consistent and is straight. He's never taken prisoners, but Leyton and Walton – they would string me up if they could, for different reasons. Anyway, what exactly are you telling me, Claude – that I've got to go to court, something like that?"

"Well, yes, boy – I'm afraid so. You'll be summoned to appear at Tavistock Magistrates' Court, probably next Friday. You can plead guilty or not guilty. If guilty you'll be fined there and then – or probably fined, though technically you could get a week or two in Exeter Prison. If you plead not guilty then it'll take longer because the prosecution will put forward Leyton and Walton as witnesses. That'll be their case – two people claiming to see you there. Just one, it would be very different – it would be just his word against yours – that's if you claimed you weren't there, of course."

"Nor was I," rasped Cuffie. "Nowhere near there. Do you think I'd ever be so daft as to go poaching on Brook? Years ago I asked him permission to rabbit on his place, not long after they'd come there. I'd have seen him all right with the odd brace or two, as I always do, and always have. Not only did he say no, he also said in that nasty sort of way he's got, that if ever he caught me or even saw me on his land, then he'd put me in the hands of the law. I could see he meant it, and the way he's behaved with others over the years proved just that. Do you think I'd be so daft as to poach on the land of a man like that?"

Cuffie Wells was well aware he was telling the village policeman a pack of lies, but he was not under oath, and he was angry. He would have expected no other than such action from Farmer Fuller, but for his two workmen, a pair he had known all his life, to create such trouble for him offended him greatly; it brought out the cussed side within him, and assuredly there was one.

"I'll fight this, Claude. I'll fight it all. I'll deny everything – they'll have to prove it."

"Well, I shouldn't say this, Cuffie – but good for you. I hope you do – and I hope you win. I'm sorry to be involved in any of it – but I've no option. Arnold Fuller has insisted charges of poaching and trespass are laid against you, and it's my duty to see they are. But I told him straight that I disagreed with it and that I would do just the minimum the law demanded of me, and I would take no part in gathering evidence."

"Thanks, Claude," said the rabbiter, fully aware that indolent and, at times, somewhat incompetent though the village policeman was, he was essentially an honest and fair man. He would not deviate from what he had just said.

"So I'm sorry about all this, boy, but as I've said there's nothing I can do about it. But, I say again, there's nothing I'll do to help it." He got up from his chair, and moved towards the door. Opening it, he turned and looked at Cuffie. "If you'll take my advice, you'll get a solicitor. It'll cost you a few bob, but you'd be wise to get one. There's all sorts of legal tricks they've got up their sleeves – well, a good one will, anyway. Do you know Gerald Mason? Well, you must do – he lives at Halton House, overlooking the Tavy on the far side of the parish. He's the head of Matthews, Oliver and Mason – their offices are in Plymouth as I reckon you know, but he's lived in this parish for years – before I came here. He's the man to get hold of. Mustard in court is Gerald; knows all the legal tricks. It'd pay you to get hold of him as soon as possible. I should phone him in the morning – even this afternoon – and make an appointment to see him. His advice will be good, you can be sure of that."

Cuffie suddenly smiled. "I know him, Claude – and I know his missus even better. A real lady – knows how to treat people. I've been supplying them with rabbits for years – in fact, I've promised to drop a brace into them early next week. They've got people visiting, apparently, and amongst other things, she wants to serve them rabbit pie. Mind you, they eat any amount of rabbits themselves – love them, they do."

"First class," said the policeman with some enthusiasm. "Well, if I were you, boy, I'd catch those rabbits as soon as you can and drop them out to them on, say, Saturday. He'll be about then, and if you know him personally I reckon you'll be able to have a chat – and perhaps get a bit of advice. Not that you'll get it for nothing – solicitors don't give free advice. But knowing him personally could help a great deal. Yes, boy, get hold of him as soon as you can."

The rabbiter took the policeman at his word. Immediately Claude left, Cuffie found his wife and told her of all that had transpired – news which brought an angry response from the, at times, fiery Edie. She knew Leyton and Walton, as did her husband, liked neither and absolutely detested the wife of the former, Maureen – a gossip with, often, a mischievous tongue.

Cuffie then fetched his ferrets and nets, went out to Farmer Martin's farm, sought, and got, permission to have a couple of hours rabbiting and returned home half an hour after dark with two rabbits, having given one to Sarah Martin. He returned there early the following morning and, by mid afternoon, had turned out a further five. Again, one was left with the farmer's wife, whilst the other four were laid upon Ron Benton's counter just before he closed his shop at 5 o'clock.

The Saturday morning saw him walking the mile or so out to Halton House, a brace of fleshy young rabbits over his shoulder. On reaching the large, imposing Victorian house, he turned into the short drive – and found himself in luck. Raking up some leaves in front of the house was the solicitor himself. He looked up, hearing footsteps upon the gravel.

"Why, hello there, Cuffie," he called in most friendly fashion. "Good to see you – and those two fine rabbits you've draped over your shoulder. Laura will be delighted to have those – so will I, for that matter. No meat I like more than rabbit; it's better than steak in my view."

"Morning, Mr Mason; I promised Mrs Mason a brace and am just dropping them off."

119

"She's in the kitchen. If you'll take them round to her, and ask her to put the kettle on. A bit chilly this morning – I could do with a drink, and I expect you could as well."

"Right – yes, thank you, I will." He made his way to the kitchen as instructed, knocked upon the door and was admitted promptly by Laura Mason.

She looked pleased to see him, and was delighted with the brace of rabbits. "Oh, well done, Cuffie; I didn't expect them today, but it works out just right as I can get them ready for cooking here and now, and put them into a pie."

The rabbiter gave her the meat – then delivered her husband's message.

"Right," said she, pushing the heavy kettle onto a hotplate of the large Aga stove. "I'll get some money and pay you, then I'll make the tea. You'll join us for a cup, of course – and a few biscuits."

He smiled and nodded, then took the hard kitchen chair proffered by the lady of the house. "Thank you, Mrs Mason – that would be very nice."

No sooner had she returned with the money than her husband came in from the garden, washed his hands and sat down.

Tea made, and biscuit barrel produced, Cuffie was provided with a glorious chance to tell the solicitor of his present parlous position. He took it. Firstly apologising for raising the subject at such a time, he told the solicitor that he was in need, urgently, of legal advice. Mason instantly asked him to tell his story – which he proceeded to do; or at least told of the accusations made against him and the identity of those who were making them.

Although at core an honest man, despite his occasional poaching pursuits, the rabbiter was so incensed at what he saw to be vindictiveness by the farmer and, even more so, by his two men – one, of whom, Davie Walton had been a classmate at the village school – that he omitted to tell the solicitor that actually he had, indeed, been where they alleged – he had been poaching. If he said that, he knew that Mason would have no option other than to tell him to plead guilty. As it was, he made it sound as if Leyton and Walton were bearing false witness against him.

Whilst this troubled his conscience a little, it was not enough to make him tell the full – and very relevant – truth.

Whether or not the solicitor believed him he could not know. It was possible he did not – but he did not ask such a question directly, possibly exercising the 'where ignorance is bliss' principle. As it happened – which was good for the poacher – the solicitor himself had no love for Arnold Fuller. For the first five years after he had moved into the area, Gerald had been the farmer's solicitor. He had found him difficult and demanding, but he had always had such clients – it went with the profession. However, some ten years previously a bill had been sent by Mason's office to Fuller, for services rendered. Unfortunately, an error had been made and the farmer had been over-charged. Fuller had complained, the genuine error had been acknowledged, apologised for and put right. The farmer paid the correct amount, but wrote a quite unpleasant letter to the solicitor questioning his competence and that of his entire staff – and terminating his business with immediate effect. Gerald Mason was a genial, mild-mannered man, but such behaviour and slur on his ability offended him greatly – and he had not forgotten it.

Cuffie Wells told his tale – or, at least, his heavily weighted and abridged version – and requested that the solicitor, if it was possible, gave him advice. "I'll pay, of course," he said finally.

The Solicitor laughed. "Don't worry about that, Cuffie – you can pay me in rabbits should the matter actually come to court. Mind you, it's hard to see any way in which it can really fail to do so. I suspect that our friends Leyton and Walton will already have been to Tavistock Police Station – the attitude displayed by dear old Claude Barton making it a reasonable bet that they, under Fuller's guidance, will avoid all dealings with him, the local policeman. The problem is – there are two of them. Constable Barton it seems, summed it up by what you've told me he pointed out – there's two of them telling the same story. Just one and they would have no case, as nothing could be proved, his word against yours – case dismissed. If only one of them was to have second thoughts about testifying – but it seems rather unlikely. Still, what I'll do, Cuffie, is to contact Tavistock Police on Monday, tell them

121

f

I'm representing you, and have them send me details of the case against you. I do not promise I can get you out of this – but certainly I will try."

"Thank you, Mr Mason. I cannot tell you how much this is appreciated." And it was. He had always thought of the solicitor and his wife as being people to respect and like and this, to him, proved his judgement was accurate.

As he walked back to his cottage he mulled over Mason's words: "If only one of them would have second thoughts about testifying." That, of course, was the key – one of the vindictive pair would have to be cajoled by whatever means possible to withdraw his statement. One of them never would, that was fairly certain; but the other – that could be a different matter. Regarding the first, Cuffie could think of no pressure he could bring to bear, but the second – perhaps? He, the rabbiter reasoned, was vulnerable. That weak spot had to be attacked, and only he could do it.

As he approached his cottage, a plan had formed in his agile mind, and that very afternoon he would put it into practice. It was not something he relished doing, being basically an easy going man of a strong 'live and let live' turn of mind, but extreme circumstances call for courageous action, and he needed to take it before he lost his nerve. He would have his dinner – rabbit stew, something which he enjoyed winter time even though he spent so much of his life catching them – then, that afternoon, he would make for a row of cottages on the edge of the village. It being a Saturday the man he wished to see would probably be at home.

So just after 2 o'clock, his resolve fortified following the consumption of a large bowl of stew, he set out on his mission, walking, despite his limp, quite quickly. Reaching the brick built dwellings he turned in through the gate of the second one, went to the front door and knocked loudly. Several seconds elapsed with nothing happening, but just as he was about to knock again – even more loudly – the door opened.

Davie Walton stood before him. Momentarily he looked nonplussed, then an expression of alarm engulfed his face. "Go away, Cuffie, go away – I've got nothing to say to you. I can see you've come to cause trouble. Well, I don't want trouble; all I want is for you to go away and leave me in peace – if you don't, I'll fetch Claude Barton."

"That'll do you no good, Davie – Constable Barton is disgusted the way you're prepared to go to court and tell lies about me," Cuffie rasped – with a considerable amount of exaggeration. "And it'll be lies under oath – you could go to jail for that, swearing on the Bible to tell the truth then telling lies, saying I was down at Brook the other morning poaching. Lies and you know it." Cuffie was amazed at his own vehemence – and at the way he had convinced, almost, himself that he had not committed the crimes of which he was accused.

"But they're not lies – I saw you. As did Cyril. Both of us, we saw you there beside the warrens in the outside field. You saw us, gathered up the nets, ferrets and the rabbits you caught, then made off. We chased you but you went up over the embankment and got away. That's what I said in my statement to the police in Tavistock so there's an end to it – now go away and leave me in peace."

"Well, if you're not willing to withdraw your statement, then I'll have to make one of my own – to Farmer Fuller."

Walton's expression changed from one of angry defiance to one of uncertainty – even fear. "What do you mean – what's Farmer Fuller got to do with it?"

"Well, knowing the sort of man he is, he would not be very forgiving if he found that a man he trusted was, was, well betraying him. He keeps everybody away from the warrens on Brook so that he and you blokes that work for him can catch as many rabbits as you wish – for your own use, and that of your families. If he heard, though, that you regularly sold several of the ones you catch, he would not be a happy man – and you, I fancy, would be out of a job. He'd sack you on the spot and you know it. With all his faults, he's got a good name as a boss. The four of you who work for him have been there for years and, I don't doubt, would be happy to stay. You don't want to be sacked from there, Davie."

"Who – who – who says I sell rabbits?" The tenor of the voice was dominated by fear.

"I could write out a list of folk you've sold to, Davie – and I will do if I have to, and I'll give it to Fuller. Only a couple of weeks ago I went to drop one off to old Mrs White up in the council houses – I'd had a good catch and she's often pleased to buy one if I've one spare – her Sid lives on rabbit stews in the winter, or so she says. She didn't want it, though, because she'd bought one from you the day before. She quite often buys from you she told me. Likewise Mrs Penrose, the Chemist's missus; she has a fairly regular supply from me – and from you. There's others too – as I said, I can make out a list, and it won't be that short."

Consternation, clearly, gripped Walton. For several seconds he said not a word, though his face spoke volumes of his inner turmoil. "You wouldn't, Cuffie. You wouldn't, would you?"

"Oh yes, boy, I would – like a shot." The words were directed at Davie Walton with unusual venom, especially as they came from an even tempered man.

But Cuffie, when in anger – as now he was – could be an intimidating figure. A strong, square jawline to his face, a thickish neck on top of a body built like a granite outhouse – albeit he was on the short side – physically he had the appearance of a man who, when upset, one had to handle with care.

Eventually Walton gave his response: "But if I go to the boss and tell him I'm not going to give evidence, then he'll sack me anyway – for, well, for letting him down."

"No he won't – especially if you say you've got to withdraw your statement because you cannot, in conscience, place your hand upon the Bible and swear to its accuracy – to its truth. You thought it was me that morning, but you cannot be certain. You were a fair way away – you didn't have a clear look at my face. You assumed it was me but you cannot swear on oath that it was. Farmer Fuller is a strict, rigid Methodist, guided totally by what he believes to be right. He, of all people, would not expect you to swear by Almighty God to something you were very uncertain of – and you know he wouldn't."

Walton looked away, then back at the formidable poacher. All defiance had gone from the man. His body sagged visibly, his

124

expression of truculence replaced by one of defeat, alarm, even misery. "What can I do? I mean – I just can't change it all now – surely I can't? It's too late, isn't it?" The tone was little more than a plaintive wail.

" 'Course it's not too late. On Monday morning you go to Farmer Fuller and tell him that having thought long and hard about it you can't in conscience swear on the Bible it was me you definitely saw that morning – and you ask him to phone the police in Tavistock and tell them you want to withdraw your statement. The easiest thing in the world, Davie. And I reckon you'll have no problem with your boss. As I said earlier, whatever else he might be, he's as honest and straight as they come – and he expects that in others; and heaven help them if they are not."

Cuffie turned to go, then looked back at the crushed Walton. "I'll expect to hear by Wednesday, at the latest, that you've withdrawn your statement, either direct from the police or from Gerald Mason who's representing me. If I don't hear, then on Thursday I'll be round to see your boss with my list." He gave his adversary one final, malevolent glare, then turned away, heading for home.

For the rest of his life, Cuffie Wells was to muse that the visiting that afternoon of one of the men who could have put him in jail, was the most inspirational – and, in a sense, successful – moments of his life. On the Tuesday morning Claude Barton called round, genuinely delighted to tell the poacher that all charges against him had been dropped.

"Davie Walton withdrew his statement – said he couldn't swear on oath it was you. A pity he hadn't said it before, as it would have saved a lot of trouble and grief. So there's an end to it, Cuffie. But, boy, promise me please – don't go poaching round at Brook again. As long as Farmer Fuller is there it's always going to mean problems and trouble. I'm happier with a quiet life, Cuffie – as I'm sure you are. So no more, boy, right?" He fixed the rabbiter with a searching look – no fool was Claude Barton; Nobody knew the ways and habits of the people of the Peninsula as did he.

No time for words was this, as Cuffie knew. He just smiled,

nodded – but did say a courteous and grateful, "Thank you, Claude."

Late that afternoon, there came a further knock on the door. When opened, Cuffie was confronted by Gerald Mason.

"Good evening, Cuffie," said the solicitor briskly and politely. "I thought I'd drop in on the way home and tell you that the cases against you have been dropped. Davie Walton withdrew his statement, saying that he could not be certain the man he saw that morning was you, he did not really have the chance to make sure. They were a fair way away, and he never really saw your face. Strange he should have such doubts as in his statement, like Cyril Leyton, he was certain it was you. But then, perhaps you already know all this."

"Well, yes, I do, Mr Mason, to tell you the truth – Constable Barton dropped in a bit earlier and told me. I appreciate you coming by, though, and all your kindness and support. It's a relief, I have to say. I've perhaps sailed a bit close to the wind at times, but I've always managed to avoid the courts – up to now."

"Well, I hope you continue to do so, Cuffie – though if everybody avoided them, then Laura and I would be on the streets." He laughed, briefly, as was his way. Then a serious expression came to his face. "I don't know why Walton backed off, though. I've seen his statement – in it he had not the slightest doubt it was you. It could be, of course, that somebody – well, how can I put it – somebody encouraged him to withdraw it. As I said to you on Saturday, without the two statements there would be no case. Very good news, indeed, that now there is only the one." He fixed Cuffie with a quite serious look, then smiled – "Well, I must be getting home, Cuffie. It's good to bring somebody good news, even though you already knew it. So often it's bad. Good night."

"Good night to you, Mr Mason – and thank you. I'll drop in a brace of rabbits on the weekend as, well, as a way of saying thank you."

"Most acceptable, Cuffie, thank you. But we'll pay for them. How can I charge for my services – I've not provided any. The case was over before it started. But certainly we will look forward

126

to the rabbits." He turned away and moved towards his car. Then, looking back, said: "A satisfactory end to an annoying, unnecessary affair."

And so it was. An episode which saw Cyril Leyton's antipathy towards Cuffie get ever stronger – along with irrational resentment. One from which Davie Walton escaped reasonably unscathed – Cuffie's prediction being accurate that whilst he was disappointed not to be able to bring a Godless miscreant to some sort of judgement, Farmer Fuller accepted without demur his workman's decision to withdraw his statement when he could not, on oath, swear it was accurate.

There was a winner, though – Cuffie Wells himself. He became, in the parish, something of a living legend. Ron Belton saw to that. For years to come he never tired of telling of the rabbiter's prowess in providing him one morning, with seven freshly caught rabbits. The number caught remained the same in the Butcher's story, but the time it took to net them, ever shorter. Indeed, most times he told the tale in the Tamar View – not infrequent, especially when he was 'in his cups' (again, not infrequent) – the time Cuffie had taken to accomplish such a feat got so brief eventually, that the rabbits must have queued up awaiting execution!

As for the poacher himself, he never changed his lifestyle – nor did he ever see the inside of a court, which was a relief in so many ways, not the least being the fact that had he ever been indicted, and had to stand in the box and give evidence, he could never have lied under oath, his occasional visits to the Methodist Sunday School as a young boy staying with him all of his life.

V

The Postman

Alfie Spooner was a walking local newspaper, gossip, soothsayer, philosopher, wit and sage. There was very little that went on in the parish which he did not know about; happy and positive, sad and calamitous – especially the latter. Not everything he imparted was totally accurate, but rarely was it without a modicum of truth. He was, it had to be said, not averse to the odd bit of exaggeration, seasoned with a soupçon of surmise, but he was on the whole sufficiently accurate in his tidings for folk about the parish – especially in the farms and cottages outside of the main village – to heed the news he brought to their doors, generally believing it to reflect events on the Peninsula. And it was to their thresholds he went, along with his standard issue GPO bicycle, delivering the mail.

Born and bred down by the Tamar, he had joined the Royal Navy in 1915 – lying about his age as he was only sixteen at the time – had seen action at the Battle of Jutland, and had remained in the Service following the end of the Great War. He served twelve years before leaving to get married, settling back in the parish of his birth.

He had a small service pension, but had pointed out ever since – when a few rums and pints of scrumpy were within him (quite often) that if he had done a further ten years then he would have had a full pension. Granted he would receive a small pension from the Post Office when he retired at sixty-five, and granted that he had always enjoyed his work travelling the lanes he knew so well, delivering His Majesty's mail, but he was ever bitter that he had abandoned the Senior Service – sailing the oceans, seeing the world – for a desperately unhappy marriage.

Had he and his spouse, Avril, had a good relationship then it is possible contentment would have been his. He would still have missed the travel, the comradeship and the somewhat carefree life of the Navy, but the fulfilment of a happy married and family life would have compensated – and more. He and Avril, though, were as unsuited as any two people could be. Essentially he was an easy going, very sociable man – in fact nobody enjoyed company more than he. Avril though, was quite a solitary person. She hated social gatherings and the like – even had little to do with neighbours. She was not an unpleasant woman, and to her few friends she was loyal and kind, but she had a sharp tongue and a quickish temper. Alfie could, at times, 'fly off the handle' himself, and assuredly he could be most stubborn. The problem was that these two faults manifested themselves most when in the company of his wife, their home quickly becoming a battlefield.

They had met at a dance in Plymouth when he was on leave from the Navy. It was a romance of whirlwind pace, with Alfie being somewhat captivated by a young woman of, if not beauty, certainly exceedingly good looks. Within six months of meeting they were married, and Avril left her native Plymouth to come and live in Alfie's native village, with a husband who had come out of the Navy, turning down the chance to sign on for another decade. "I must have been daft," he would spit out with venom, after a few had passed his lips.

Village life being very different to that of the city, Avril did not take to it in any way. To her immense discredit she made no attempt to. In fact, she tended to look down on the people in the parish, one of her more frequent comments to Alfie being, "I've heard every village has an idiot – but they're all idiots in this place."

Their marriage lasted just five years, ending abruptly in a tumultuous quarrel between the two, she packing her bags that very same day, and returning to Plymouth to live with her widowed mother, taking their son, three years old Oliver, with her.

He was never to see her again – but assuredly she was not destined to go out of his life, desperately though he wished she would.

After a few years they divorced, she citing mental cruelty on his part. This was not so – and most of the village knew likewise – but so keen was he to get rid of her that he agreed to it. He would have agreed to anything to erase her from his life.

Sadly, from his point of view, whilst the divorce freed him to get on with his life (he could marry again if he wished, though in reality, he did not, and never would, citing "once bitten, twice shy"), it did not free him of a considerable liability to an ex-wife and a son he never saw. Regarding the latter, he had to concede he was partly to blame, as during the years of Oliver's childhood, he the father, not being the paternal kind, did not particularly wish to keep in contact with the boy and, thus, never made a serious attempt to do so. Had he done so, assuredly no court would have refused access to a son whom he unfailingly supported financially.

It was not until the boy was in his teens that Alfie felt regret – and no small measure of shame – over, in effect, his repudiation of his flesh and blood. So many men who desired a son were never gifted one – he had been, yet he had spurned him. Whilst some bitterness and anger was directed towards himself, it was mild in comparison to that he felt towards his ex-wife, whom he saw as a vampire sucking his blood.

He accepted he had a commitment to maintain his son until, at least, he left school, even though he never saw him. With reluctance, he accepted he had, possibly, an obligation to maintain Avril herself as long as she was his wife, though a youngish, good looking and able woman, who had worked in one of Plymouth's main shops before their marriage, could easily have returned to the working world, he mused to himself.

However, after the divorce he had assumed that whilst he would continue to pay maintenance for his son, there would be no expectation of him also keeping an ex-wife. The judge disabused him of this notion. He ruled that until Avril returned to employment, or remarried, then she had a right to receive maintenance from her former husband. Whilst this did not alter Alfie's basic affability, sociability and kind nature, it did, within him, create something of a Jekyll and Hyde. Ninety percent of the time he had the former, but mention of Avril, or reference in general to the purloining of money by authorities, councils or governments, brought forth bile and bitterness – if he had downed a few, even strong language.

Not that he gave in to the monthly paying of this 'ransom' (as he put it) without resistance. Never was he late paying the sum for Oliver's keep, but regularly he would fail to pay into the Court Office at Tavistock – that being the nearest – the larger sum due to Avril. Of course, he would not get away with it, he knew that very well, but it would keep the money in his pocket for a few extra weeks and, more importantly, it would keep it from the clutches of the woman he so hated. And this routine had gone on now since the day they had been divorced, some twenty years earlier.

The Court Office would realise after a week or so that they had not received Avril's monthly due, they would write to him in the name of the Clerk to the Justices, demanding payment within seven days. They would not get it. Another letter would be sent by the court telling him that if payment was not made by a certain date in the future – always a Friday, when Tavistock Magistrates sat – then Alfie was summoned to stand before them to explain his inability, or refusal, to fulfil his obligations. The day before the hearing, in the afternoon, following the completion of his post round, he would take the train to Tavistock, go to the office and pay the money due, to the very penny. Usually four or five weeks would have passed since the cash was due; a month or more when this fiendish woman from Plymouth had not been able to get her hands upon his very hard earned, and none too plentiful resources. Then the entire process would start again.

Over these many years the court had sent him hundreds of letters – many of which he had delivered to himself. He had, though, always managed to avoid actually ending up in court for non-payment as this was a place he needed to avoid if at all possible. The problem was that he had been told by a fellow victim not long after the divorce, that some magistrates – who usually took the part of the ex-wife – would look at the monthly amount being paid, decide it was not enough, and order the sorely tried ex-husband to pay more. Over the years Avril had made requests to the court for the payments for her son and herself to be put up, to 'cover ever-rising prices' and he had been summoned to stand before the magistrates. Unfortunately, not once had they refused her request, he always leaving court poorer despite his plaintive – often blatantly angry – cry that she should be supporting herself, a fit woman like her.

Always the magistrates would give answer along the same line – the terms of the Court Order were that payment would have to be made until she either got a job or remarried. She had done neither. She was destined never to do either. The postman could not find fault with the fact she did not marry again (even though he desired it greatly) – after all, there were few in this world so bad that they warranted the punishment of being married to Avril, he reasoned. But that she had never sought employment disgusted him.

Whilst not popular with court clerks, and assuredly not with Avril, Alfie was well liked, indeed, valued in the parish. Arthur Courtenay, who ran the village Post Office, thought the world of him. He had two other posties – Jimmy Smart and Molly Jordan (though she was only part time, doing usually a couple of days a week and covering for sickness and the odd week's holiday). Jimmy, like Alfie, was local, whilst Molly had come to the parish during the war, along with her parents, having been bombed out in Plymouth. The latter had returned, but she met Don Jordan, the Baker's son – and latterly, partner – and they had married just a year or so after the war. They had a little girl, but Molly found she had ample time to help out with the post. Also being, like Alfie, a sociable person, she enjoyed the contant involvement with people. It was Alfie, though, upon whom the Post Master relied the most. He knew every nook and cranny of the Peninsula, could decipher and make sense of the most ill-written or inaccurate address and seemed always to know the names of folk who had only been living there a 'dog's watch'. If an error had been made – the wrong post delivered, or late or, worse still, lost; if somebody had been offended in any way – in the diverse fraught situations which could, and so often did, arise in providing such a vital service as did the Post Office, Alfie Spooner was the man Courtenay would despatch to heal wounds – pour oils. With his courteous demeanour, quick wit, shrewd judge of people's character, he, so often, was able to make life easy for the Post Master, and that wily man was very well aware of it. Also, he was very reliable, rarely going sick, even more rarely making any mistakes.

The postman had been a friend of Harry Martin at Downside Farm since childhood, they having been in the same class at school and Alfie having spent many hours playing on the farm with the present owner. For very many years – since before the war – Spooner had delivered the mail to Downside. It was his penultimate stop, only a small cottage some 300 yards from the farm, towards the village, remaining. The time he arrived at the farm would vary according to the amount of post to be delivered, and the number of places receiving it. Usually, though, he would get to the farm round about one o'clock, when he would always be given a cup of tea and a bun or slice of cake by Sarah Martin. Occasionally, he would be invited to join them for a full dinner if his timing was right and she had prepared enough.

Certainly there were few delivery days when he did not call, they receiving a fair deal of mail – as farms so often did, with many official forms, bills from agricultural merchants, circulars and the odd cheque for produce or stock sold. Harry, Sarah, their son Graham, if he was about, and Alfie were always easy in each other's company. Whilst, generally, there was an exchange of conversation, the bulk usually came from the postman. News of what was happening in the parish – deaths and births first of all, who was ill, who had suffered calamity, and less often news of someone who had enjoyed triumph – daft decisions just made by the Parish Council, occasionally tidings of who was leaving the parish or who had just entered in – and, of course, rumour and plain gossip, gathered like daffodils in spring from the folk he would have delivered to, or over some scrumpy and rum the previous night in the Tamar View Inn (most evenings would find him in attendance, though by no means all).

He would comment often on the mail he was delivering – not so much on personal matters which he deemed to be none of his business, but regularly on official looking letters, particularly those bearing 'On His Majesty's Service'. If the words 'Inland Revenue' should also appear, then his fury would know no bounds.

"Tax, again, Harry – thieving devils, take the shirt off your back they would. What with them and that woman, it's a miracle I've enough left to put a crust of bread on the table." Avril, always was referred to as 'that woman', though occasionally he varied it by adding an expletive after 'that'. It was clear why she came in for condemnation, but the Income Tax Authorities also received his abuse because he was taxed, in his view, far higher than he should have been.

Harry and Sarah usually mouthed sympathy, but kept out of it. Harry had always found the Inland Revenue tolerably fair and could see no reason why they would pick on the hapless postman. The best thing to do when he exploded in such a way was to steer him off the subject – not always an easy thing to do.

At Christmas – or, to be more exact, on Christmas Day morning – a certain routine had been established; certainly it was one which had not varied during the previous ten or more years. Alfie's popularity, his reliability, dedication to duty, acts of kindness and thoughtfulness, his almost constant geniality was rewarded on the days leading up to the Yuletide but on that day especially he would receive gifts of money, cigarettes, cigars and chocolate – and, significantly, liquor (whisky, beer and, his favourite, a few rums).

Alfie refused most drink, except tea, right up to Christmas Day morning, but with the mail he delivered then usually being quite light, and mainly cards – the knowledge that it would not take that long to deliver, encouraged him, always, to stop for refreshment when invited. Such sustenance took many forms – Christmas

134

cake, Yule Log, mince pies (all of which he loved), plenty of tea, the odd cup of Camp coffee (of which he was not so keen) and, naturally, liquor.

A couple of the farmers he called upon were serious drinking men – both on holdings fairly close to the Martins. Before he got to that brace of whisky drinkers, he would be a touch worse for wear (and a goodly amount needed to go down his gullet to achieve that), but after he left, he would be seriously inebriated! Accompanied by his trusty, sturdy bike, the purpose of which at this stage was assuredly not to ride, but rather to prop him up – not always successfully – he would stagger along the narrowish lane to Downside.

This, for years, had been the Christmas pattern, with Alfie stumbling into the farmyard whether he had a delivery or not – usually between noon and half past twelve. He would be welcomed by the farmer and his wife – but there would be nothing alcoholic awaiting him. Harry was a moderate drinker, and at Christmas would see off a fair amount of Scotch; Sarah, though, rarely drank except, on occasions, for the odd glass of port. They both, though, whilst drinking mainly tea, did enjoy a percolated pot of strong coffee, Sarah buying the ground beans from the quite wide range kept by Crebers of Tavistock.

Thus when Alfie Spooner meandered his drunken way up to the kitchen door at Downside, strong, black coffee would always await him. He would flop into one of the battered, but most comfortable easy chairs either side of the big Aga stove, gulp coffee and talk nonsense. Well much of it was, but virtually always somewhere along the line he would launch into a tirade against his hated ex-spouse. "Bled me dry, she has – year, on year, on year she's bled me dry. That woman – that woman. God knows what I ever did to deserve it. Treated her well, I did. Treated her like a queen. Gave up the Navy for her – I could have done another ten years and had a full pension. She ruined my life – that – that woman did. And there's Oliver, my son – my flesh and blood. Not seen him since he was three – all these years, and I've not seen him, even though he's only in Plymouth. He'll be grown up now."

Whilst the Martins, like many others, had sympathy with him regarding the way his ex-wife had siphoned money off him over the years, such feelings were far less prevalent when it came to Oliver. Folk had pointed out to Alfie that he had rights regarding his only son. If he wished access, then he had a right to it. Never, though, had the postman made the slightest effort to make contact with the boy – the teenager – now the man. He had, of course, continued to pay regular maintenance for his upkeep, although this had ceased when Oliver left school at the age of sixteen and had gone into Devonport Dockyard as an apprentice – or so his father had heard via the courts when advised that no more payments, in this direction, would be required.

Having got the Christmas morning routine off to a fine art, Harry and Sarah would wait until the postman had downed a couple of cups of coffee – and had finished his tirade against the bain of his life – then act with some alacrity. The danger was, if the timing was not right, Alfie would rapidly descend into deep sleep and be with them for the rest of the day, and to have a snoring, drunken postman in the kitchen whilst they were eating their Christmas dinner was not a prospect that appealed. Thus would Harry take control, he saying, regularly, words to the effect: "Right, Alfie, it's time I got you home. The van's outside. I'll load your bike aboard, get you in, and I'll drop you off at your house." He would then go out the back door, put the big, heavy bike into the back of his van, go back into the kitchen, help the suffering man to his feet, support him across the kitchen then out the door and into the yard.

Alfie would mouth a slurred: "Thank you, Sarah and – and – what is it? Christmas – a Happy Christmas, maid."

His hostess would smile benignly – she did not at all appreciate the way the postman drank, at times, and she certainly disliked intensely the constant abuse he flung in the direction of his former wife – though, being a most diligent, conscientious woman, it appalled her that Avril Spooner had been happy all these years to live off an ex-husband she detested, rather than ridding herself of him totally by earning her own living. The estrangement of Alfie and his son, Oliver, though, upset her.

136

Clearly the Postman was much to blame in that he had never attempted to establish a relationship with his only child – he had paid, dutifully, the monthly amount due for his maintenance, but apart from that he appeared to behave as if his son did not exist. With her strong belief in the sanctity of family – as well as marriage – she saw this as a tragedy. In this direction she was probably more sympathetic to the postman then he deserved, but she could do no other on Christmas Day than see him for what, probably, he was – a lonely, somewhat unhappy middle-aged man.

As the farmer got behind the driver's seat, he would glance into the large postbag which usually would lay on Alfie's lap as he sprawled in the passenger seat. Generally some letters and, or, cards would lie in there. "Those for the bungalow, boy?" he would ask. He would receive a grunt and a nod in response, so would pull the mail from the bag, and lay it on the dashboard in front of him. With that, he would start the engine, drive the van into the lane, stop in front of the bungalow a little further up, thrust the letters into the post box outside, then deliver a largely inert postman back to his cottage in the village.

Being a creature of routine, Harry Martin approached that Christmas morning as he had the previous score and more. He got up before 6am, had a quick, strong, sweet cup of tea, then put on an ancient, but thick overcoat, a battered trilby hat, slipped on his wellington boots, and went out into the raw, dark morning to the outhouses and the shippen, firstly to check all was well with the stock, then to carry out the feed round before beginning the milking. He would be joined by a couple of his workers by the time he had started the feeding, as everything that day always started sooner then normal – it being the one day of the year when the lorry from the dairy, collecting the full churns, came earlier. It meant as well that the two good, reliable fellows who always turned out to fill the beasts' stomachs and empty their milk sacks, could themselves get away home earlier to join their families; that applying especially to the cowman, Herbie Parsons, who was in charge, and who had two youngish children. A plus when time was of the essence, was that the milkers that time of year were inside at night, away from the rigours of winter nights – thus they did not require bringing in from a nearby meadow. The minus was that being in for so many hours, chained in their stalls, there was much dung to be cleared away into the yard, fresh straw bedding to be put down, and large amounts of hay, cattle cake, turnips, kale and mangolds to be put before the big South Devon cows to satisfy large appetites – and produce valuable milk.

That morning all went well, with a trio of men very used to one another, all at ease in each other's company, all masters of their craft. The milking was finished, the churns put on the platform by the road for collection, the cows turned out into a nearby field for the daylight hours, to be brought in again for milking later in the day – then, again, to spend the night in their stalls. The cleaning out was done, bedding put down, mounds of fodder put in their mangers as provender for when the cows came in again a few hours later, and the two men – who would have received from the Martins their Christmassing a few days before (food, drink, vegetables, potatoes and such like, delivered by Harry in the van) were driven up to the village, and their homes, by the farmer.

Returning to the yard, Harry parked the van close to the kitchen door for the inevitable passenger who would need it later in the morning. He went into the kitchen, smelt – a glorious aroma – the percolator of coffee which Sarah had made, poured himself a beaker, before so much of it would be consigned to the task of sobering up the mercurial postman, then sat down beside the Aga. He glanced at the rather battered, but still imposing, grandfather clock standing in the corner: "Half past eleven – not bad at all. We've got half an hour before Alfie gets here – more, I expect."

He was to be proved wrong. Within a few minutes there was a knock on the door. It was opened quickly by Sarah – and Alfie Spooner was standing their grasping in his hand what was clearly a Christmas card.

"Morning Sarah – Harry. Happy Christmas to you both – and many more I hope."

For a few seconds the couple were transfixed. It looked like Alfie Spooner – and clearly it was him – but this man was stone cold sober. Sarah gathered her wits quicker than did her husband.

"And to you, Alfie – a very happy one, I hope. Come in – as you can probably smell, we've got a pot of coffee on the go. Can I pour you one?"

"Yes, that'll be nice, maid, thank you – but just a small one if you would. I've got to catch the train to Plymouth just after half past twelve. I've nothing to deliver to the bungalow, so when I leave here I'll cycle straight home, get changed and get to the station. I should be all right for time."

The farmer's wits returned to him at last – "Have a full cup, boy – I'll drop you home as I usually do. So you've a fair amount of time."

The postman nodded. "Thanks, Harry." Suddenly he laughed. "I see the van close by, there. I don't doubt, to cart me home as you've so kindly done now for many years – though most times I can hardly remember it. I reckon I might well have given you both something of a shock turning up this morning in this state. To be honest, I've shocked myself a bit."

Harry nodded. "Well, yes, Alfie, it is a touch unusual. Clearly you've not had many this morning."

The postman shook his head: "It's not a case of not having many – rather one of having none at all. I've had some cake, yule log and a few cups of tea – but that's all. Not one drop of liquor has passed my lips."

The farmer looked puzzled – "What, you've signed the pledge or something? You're one of the last people I would ever have expected to do that. If you have, I admire you – it takes some willpower. I could never do it."

The postman shook his head. "Nothing as dramatic as that, boy – certainly nothing as final. I like my drink too much for that – especially rum and scrumpy. No – it's just that today I need a clear head. Probably never in my life have I needed a clearer one, or more luck."

Seeing the puzzled expressions upon the faces of his hosts, he hastened into an explanation. "I'd just got back to the Post Office after my round yesterday – I don't always go back, but I had to drop off a few letters I wasn't able to deliver. I'd only been there a few minutes when Arthur Courtenay told me there was a phone call for me from, of all the people in this world, my boy Oliver. As I've said before, it's over twenty years now since I saw him, spoke to him – or had any contact with him at all. I can only think he phoned me at the Post Office because he knew I was a postman so there was a chance he would find me there. He couldn't look me up in the phone book because I'm not on the phone. It was strange speaking to him – for both of us, I expect. He gave me news – big, very unexpected and important news. His mother, Avril is dead – buried as well, come to that. Died of a massive stroke nearly a fortnight ago. He wasn't sure whether to contact me or not but finally he thought he ought to – or, by the way he was talking, his wife did; called Barbara, apparently – and they've got a little nipper just six months old; Brian." He stopped briefly, the suspicion of tears in his eyes – "A Grandson – it's good to know that. Another generation of Spooners. Still, he felt I should know – which was thoughtful of him, and her, clearly. I'd have been told eventually, of course – the court would have done that, told me that I didn't have to pay any more maintenance ever again. Mind you, I reckon it would take several weeks for me to hear officially. If I owe them money, I soon hear about it – one way, it is, always has been. Why. . ." He stopped abruptly, realising he was on the verge of a tirade – and this was not the time for that.

"Well – we had a bit of a chat, me and Oliver; I suppose you could say we've a lot to talk about – a vast amount to catch up on. Then out of the blue, he asked me what I was doing for Christmas Day – Christmas dinner. Well I told him I had to do my post round in the morning, then I'd get together something at home for dinner. Not true, as you know. I regularly get so drunk out on my round, it's years since I ate a proper dinner Christmas Day. It was then he said that he and Barbara would like me to join them down Plymouth today for dinner – Ford, they live, so it's not much more than twenty minutes on the train. Again, I fancy, it's more her than him that's inviting me – she feels we should get together then I can meet her and my grandson. And Oliver, clearly, he's like a stranger to me – and it would be understandable if after all

140

these years of me making no effort to see him – contact him, even – he wanted nothing to do with me. I get the feeling, though, that now his mother's gone, he wants to perhaps have, at least, some contact with his father, even if it's not a close one. So there it is – I'm off out for Christmas dinner, with my son, daughter-in-law and grandson. It would not do to go there drunk, though, or even smelling of liquor – so I've been teetotal all morning. I need to make a reasonable impression."

Sarah Martin's face was almost showing joy. As the postman ceased his talk and tackled his coffee, she could contain herself no longer. Though not remotely of a demonstrative nature, she could not stop herself rushing forward and embracing him – quite to the astonishment of her husband.

"Oh, Alfie," cried she, "I'm so happy to hear such – such wonderful news. After all these years. At last the chance for you to get to know your son, grandson and Barbara – she clearly wants you to be part of their family. And, of course, you are part of their family. Oh Alfie – such good, good tidings at Christmas, which is the time for family. That really was a wonderful phone call, Alfie – the start of a new era for you. You must feel so, so . . ." Her voice tailed off, and an expression of embarrassment clouded her face. She glanced at her husband – sitting quietly and somewhat detached – then looked again at their guest. "Alfie, I'm sorry – I've been very thoughtless. I felt so pleased over you and Oliver getting together at last, that I forgot the other part of the phone conversation – the death of Avril. Very sudden, and quite young. She could hardly have been fifty. I know you had your differences, Alfie, but it must have come as a shock to you, nonetheless."

The postman drained his coffee cup, then looked across at his hostess. "Yes, in a sense it was a shock, maid – certainly a massive surprise. Something I can scarce believe. But if you feel that whilst the chance to make my peace with Oliver is good news, the death of Avril is bad – then you are so very wrong. There was no bad news in that phone call, maid – not an iota. I'm many things in this life, many possibly bad, but I'm no hypocrite. I'll shed no tears for Avril. She sponged off me for well over twenty years – fit, able woman, yet she refused to work. And she never married again – which is surprising as, to be fair to her, she was a good looking woman; that's what I fell for. I sometimes feel she avoided marriage just to spite me. Certainly, to live off me. I know you shouldn't speak ill of the dead, but there is no way I could speak well of her – and I'm not going to attempt to. No longer has she got her hand in my wallet – and for that, I am so very grateful." He put down his empty coffee mug, and arose from his chair. "Well, I'd better be off – time I get home, change, and get to the station, I'll not have much time to spare. Than you, Sarah – as always."

Harry Martin also arose, went across to the back door, put on his coat and boots and ushered the postman out. Collecting his bike, and loading it into the van, the farmer was about to make a round trip of less than a mile; but the postman was set to make the most significant journey of his lifetime.

VI
The Vicar

The Reverend Luke Maxwell was regarded by many in the parish
– indeed, possibly by most – as being 'a bit of a case'. The
important aspect, though, was that such a description came with
affection and warmth – even admiration – never with a sense of
criticism or disapproval.

The son of a small builder in North Devon, he had won a
scholarship to a local grammar school where he had prospered.
However, he had left full time education with not the slightest
idea as to what he wanted to do, so briefly worked for his father
in the building trade. His short term career, though, was easily
decided for him. Having left school at Christmas 1913, within
eight months he had enlisted in the Devonshire Regiment and set
off for Flanders Fields. Being intelligent, personable with
leadership qualities, he was soon commissioned and by the time
of the armistice, had risen to the rank of Acting Major and had
been awarded the Military Cross for Valour.

Demobbed in 1919, he made a momentous decision. Having
been in the front line of fighting for over four years, and having,
whilst seeing so many comrades slaughtered and maimed (in
mind as well as body), come through without a solitary scratch,
he followed a conviction which had slowly come upon him – that,
somehow, God was watching over him, giving him protection.
Why he should be so chosen he did not know, but one day in late
summer, 1918, that conviction became absolute. Suddenly, in

'no-man's-land', coming under intensive machine gun fire, he saw two soldiers immediately to his right shot – one dead, the other badly wounded – whilst the corporal to his left was also mortally wounded. Yet he, who as the Officer in Charge would have been the principal prize – thus the main target – again escaped unscathed. He had always, since a small boy, had quite a strong faith – partly instilled in him by his devout mother – and even though he had never refrained from enjoying the myriad pleasures life had to offer (especially in the brief periods of respite during the hell of war, in the bars and taverns of France), he found faith had grown ever stronger, unlike that of so many of his comrades. The barbarities and carnage about them, day in, day out, had weakened belief – often destroyed it, in fact, even amongst many who, like himself, had come through intact in both body and mind.

Thus within just a month of his demob, he had made positive moves to be ordained into the Anglican Church, managing to enrol to study divinity at Exeter University. Though not essentially an enthusiastic person, he approached the study with positivity and determination – and in the fullness of time became an ordained minister in the Church of England.

Firstly he was appointed as curate to a parish in Devonport, close to the dockyard, staying there almost three years. During this time he met and married Celia – who became the rock upon which he built his life. In 1924 he had been offered the living on the Peninsula, and he took it with alacrity and gratitude. A country boy by birth and inclination this, to him, was the perfect posting – in theory, at least. And it proved to be so in reality, he and Celia having been there in the sprawling, draughty, damp old vicarage (built before Victoria came to the throne) ever since – almost thirty years. In that time both had become central to the life of the community. Celia had been for some time a deep thinking, proactive member of the Parish Council, President of the local Women's Institute and Secretary to the Mother's Union whilst Luke had fulfilled, in unique fashion, his job description in that he had become the undisputed spiritual leader of the area. Although a representative of the established church this was a major achievement, one not attained by any of his predecessors for the previous hundred years and more. For, like most rural areas of Devon and Cornwall, the Peninsula was non-conformist territory – the influence of John Wesley and others who had spurned the rituals and formality of Anglicanism was much to the fore.

The parish had two Methodist Chapels and one Congregational, and when Luke Maxwell had first set foot there as rector, each of them had probably more than double the congregation of the Parish Church. A difficult situation had been made worse over the years by Luke's predecessor, the Reverend Rollo Cartwright – and many years they had been, more than thirty-five, the elderly rector dying in office. A basically decent, kindly and devout man, Reverend Cartwright was of a dour, almost taciturn disposition. Whilst fulfilling his primary function of conducting weddings and baptisms plus, most important of all, burying the dead, he had little charm, a personality which deterred rather than attracted and, unacceptable in the spiritual leader of a community, an aloofness from, and lack of interest in, the people whom, in theory, were his flock. Add to this the fact his sermons were often of interminable length and could induce sleep within five minutes, it was little wonder that at the time of his demise those worshipping in the Parish Church were but a hardy, exceedingly loyal rump. Some Anglicans attended occasional services in the chapels, others just spent their Sundays at home.

Thus when Luke Maxwell took over he faced a daunting task – one of which the Bishop of Plymouth had, in total honesty, appraised him prior to his taking up the post. He was there, he was told, to restore to a degree the image of the established church on the Peninsula and to increase numbers of worshippers.

"You will never match the chapels, mind you, no matter how hard you try, or how hard you work. It's non-conformist country and they will always have greater numbers in the chapels than we will in the church. But a young man like you should at least be able to bring some back into the fold."

This he did – remarkably effectively. It was not a rapid process

g

– initially he found it tough in the extreme. In any pursuit in life, folk were usually easier to capture than to recapture. After about five years, though, the attendances at the church showed noticeable improvement. After ten they had more than doubled since the latter times of Reverend Cartwright, and by the time the Second World War had run its course, none of the chapels hosted the numbers, remotely, of those who turned up to worship at the Parish Church. This was down almost entirely to the vicar and his unparalleled popularity amongst the people, a populism not connected with any lack of regard or respect for the two non-conformist ministers in the parish.

The Congregational Chapel was presided over by the Reverend Cuthbert Kenny, a good, hard working Christian of high moral calibre, very diligent in such matters as visiting the sick and lonely. Luke Maxwell had chipped away considerably at the numbers frequenting that chapel – set right in the middle of the village next door to the Tamar View Inn – no mean achievement seeing as Kenny himself was long serving, coming to the Peninsula about three years before the rector's arrival.

The greater loss though, in terms of those attending the services, Sunday School and other associated events was felt by the Methodist Chapels – both, in size, larger than the Congregational, one set in the heart of the village, the other on the very edge, green fields running away from it. The Reverend Godfrey Jennings had taken over from the popular Maurice Roundtree upon that good man's retirement during the early days of the war. He was a clergyman of admirable qualities – highly principled, devout, a tower of moral rectitude. However, whilst it could not be said he was unpopular, and most certainly it would have been most unfair to say he was not held in some regard, he was neither admired or loved. An austere, unbending man, devout to the point of obsession, he was capable of kindness but not understanding. He would visit the sick of his congregation and the vulnerable with regularity and reliability but gave, always, the impression he did so out of a sense of duty rather than compassion – or love. Being a man of such character, he disapproved of all frivolity and so many of the pleasures of life –

and the consumption of alcohol was to him a major sin. He assuredly would have been at home in the ranks of the Puritans who set sail on the Mayflower. Whatever, whilst he was respected by, and held the loyalty of those who were generally the older followers of Wesley in the parish, many of the less committed drifted away, some staying at home on a Sunday, but a significant number going to the Parish Church, and to the Ministry of the Reverend Luke Maxwell. For he was all that Jennings was not – come to that, very different also from Cuthbert Kenny. The rector's early life had assuredly shaped the rest of it – including, very much, his Ministry. Brought up in a Christian home by parents who lived by the basic tenets of the faith – tolerance, compassion and respect for others – he had lived, within the bounds of morality and the law, a full life as a young man, and had, of course, experienced the traumas, horrors and, to a young country lad, brutally mind stretching experiences of war, of life and the world. All this he had taken to his Ministry, so as a young rector, he could bring a wide vision and knowledge of life, good, bad and raw, the like of which the two non-conformist ministers of the parish never could, both having been raised by strict, somewhat narrow-minded, though loving parents, and neither having served in the war – Godfrey Jennings, because he had been too young, Kenny due to his being an asthmatic.

Maxwell, though a man of the cloth, lived his life very much as he had done since coming to adulthood – certainly in terms of the same habits or, some might say, vices. Whilst not quite a chain smoker, rarely during his leisure time would he not have a cigarette between his lips. He was quite a regular in the Tamar View Inn, always going in there for an hour following the evening service on a Sunday. Rum was his favourite 'tipple', developing a taste for it thanks to the tots he consumed – standard rations – prior to 'going over the top' in the war. Seeing as he had always survived these terrifying stumblings across 'no-man's-land', it was clear, he reasoned, that the powerful liquor had done him the world of good. He enjoyed the occasional hand of whist, and rarely missed the Christmas Whist Drives held for various local organisations in the village hall. Here he always hoped to win fare for the Yuletide dinner table; liquor as well and, being a shrewd, experienced player, often did. Also it was well known he did the football pools. Famously just before the war he had won five hundred pounds and, promptly, given half to local charities.

All this tended to endear him, generally, to his flock. True there were some who disapproved of such 'shameful Godless pursuits – the ways of the Devil', as was stated by the rigid Methodist, Arnold Fuller, who farmed Brook Barton, and it was probable the brace of non-conformist ministers thought likewise though both had sufficient sense, and courtesy, to keep their feelings to themselves. They were all too well aware just how popular the rector was and suspected that much of his popularity was down to what in the eyes of the more puritanical folk in the parish, were his 'dissolute ways' – which included his regular visits with Celia to Chemist, Ronald Penrose's, Friday night film shows, including the latest (or most definitely recent) Hollywood Blockbusters, in the Village Hall. Even more sinful to them was the couple's occasional attendance at dances in the hall, both enjoying the odd waltz and quickstep, and being reasonably good at them – especially Celia.

Whilst all these pursuits of pleasure and relaxation endeared him to the parishioners, it was, though, his professionalism and mastery of his brief as a clergyman which elevated him to a status no previous occupant of the village Rectory, surely, would have surpassed – and few would ever have equalled. For Luke Maxwell was a master of the spoken word; Erudite, original, highly articulate, with a voice and tone which many a Shakespearian actor might well envy. When conducting a wedding he made the special day of a bride and groom even more memorable by his seemingly effortless invoking of the joy, the hope, the precious promise of the occasion – and he would enjoy, afterwards, the reception to which he was usually invited. Regarding funerals, he was sublime. Clarence Langton, the Undertaker, whilst acknowledging that the Reverends Jennings and Kenny always "handled funerals well enough", considered they were not in the same league as Rector Maxwell – "but then," he would say to put matters into perspective, "nobody is;" or, certainly as far as the experienced Funeral Director was concerned, and he had paraded his coffins before a very wide range of clergymen over the years – sometimes in churches and chapels in other villages and towns in West Devon and East Cornwall. The Vicar of the Peninsula, however, was unassailable. His strengths went well beyond his faultless delivery, his mastery of the orders and subtitles of the service. No matter whom he buried, he always spoke of the deceased as if he had known them for years, highlighted their strengths, their value in the community, the good they had done, referring to any well known faults or weaknesses in a gentle, often humorous way – if at all. Some of these deceased he had known well, but there were many he knew little of – some he knew not at all. But what he did not know of people, he took the trouble to find out – sometimes an exacting, time devouring exercise. Under his ministry, the dead were laid to rest with dignity and compassion, their families' grief partially neutralised by the balm of his soothing, caring and usually perceptive words. His reputation was such that many folk in the parish, though brought up to be Methodists and Congregationalists, chose to have 'the words said over' their loved ones by the Reverend Maxwell, and virtually all those who rarely attended any house of worship – and had no loyalty to any – chose to have their 'nearest and dearest' carried into the Parish Church, as long as it was this most charismatic man who conducted the service (and as there was no curate, it would be rare in the extreme unless he was on holiday, for it not to be him).

Still, the excellence with which the Rector 'matched and dispatched' people, important and appreciated though it was, paled in comparison to that which was his over-riding strength – the gift, the talent which had over the years brought Anglicans back to the hard pews of the church from the comfort of their homes, even on the foulest of Sundays. That, even more significantly – possibly even remarkably – which had drawn so many non-conformists from the Methodist and Congregational Chapels, some just occasionally but a number semi-permanently (though, if asked their denomination, they would immediately state allegiance to John Wesley and the like). As many would say,

"The vicar can cuff a good tale." Whatever, they came, one and all, from the far corners of the parish – a few, even, from Tavistock – to listen to, to enjoy, indeed, to immerse themselves in his sermons.

Reg Perkins, Clerk to the Parish Council, an old, and maimed soldier of the First World War (who ever since the conflict had needed a stick to help him walk), a cynical, rather world weary, though basically genial man, became a regular at Parish Church on a Sunday evening; not, he would say because of any deep belief or conviction – unlike the vicar, his experiences in the trenches had shattered his faith beyond repair – but just to hear the rich tones of Luke Maxwell, to feast on the power and beauty of his words. Whilst always basing his sermons on biblical texts, the rector varied them greatly, bringing in many aspects of local and modern life, articulating the problems, challenges, opportunities of the world around them. Sometimes they were gentle, positive homilies of the love of God; and of Christ, and of the essential goodness of mankind. At others, though, he would preach what Perkins would describe as a brimstone sermon, full of 'Hell fire and damnation', a chilling warning to the 'ne'er-do-wells' of the world to change their ways or face savage retribution.

Being a season ticket holder at Plymouth Argyle – along with his Celia – such diatribes of doom usually followed a particularly bad home defeat, it invariably upsetting him for days to come, though never his wife. Whilst she enjoyed the football, if she had witnessed a disaster at Home Park, she would merely shrug her shoulders, say, "It's only a game, for heaven's sake," and forget all about it. The rector, though, once said to Reg Perkins, when they were sat in the Tamar View Inn one evening talking of their experiences of the Great War, the grotesque horrors of which had clearly destroyed the parish clerk's faith, yet had had the opposite effect on the clergyman: "It's a daft thing to say, Reg, and probably a shocking one, and I'd say it only to somebody like yourself, but a defeat of Argyle at home can shake my faith far more than anything that happened in the trenches." Perkins fancied the vicar was being totally serious.

150

Still, if the rector did not lack faith in God, he – and his loyal wife – certainly did in the Church Authorities. When they moved into the old vicarage back in the 1920s, they had found the rambling building – ". . .more than half the size of Buckingham Palace, or so it feels," as Celia had said so very many times over the thirty-plus years they had been there, run down, damp, cold, the roof leaking, some rot in the window frames and internal paintwork peeling. It had been promised by an official in the Bishop's office in Plymouth, that measures would be taken – "in the immediate future" – to rectify matters. They never had been. Rather, they had got worse. Granted, over the years small, urgent repairs would have been made by builders under contract to the church, but these generally were emergencies – a burst pipe, slates blowing off the roof in a gale, a broken window and such like. The basic structure of the house had not been touched, and in consequence its condition had deteriorated to such an extent it was now barely habitable.

Over the years, the Maxwells had closed up rooms, and in recent times, with their son, Duncan, and daughter Ellie, having long-since flown the nest, were living in probably less than a quarter of the house – that made reasonably habitable and comfortable due only to them spending their own, limited, income upon it, something which Celia especially railed against.

"Shameful, Luke, the way they treat us. When I think of what you've done for this parish – what you've done for the church in this parish. Hardly anybody was going when poor old Rollo Cartwright was here, and now you get a bigger congregation than Tavistock. And the Bishop knows it. Yet he's done nothing to make us comfortable here. We've not a great income – nobody enters the ministry to make money – yet we've got to spend some of it to make this place even habitable. It's not fair, Luke – and it can't go on."

It had gone on, however, even though the vicar, essentially an easy going man, had made major and regular representations to the church authorities, in ever more strident tones. He was constantly fobbed off with promises that major work to the Vicarage was on their priority list but it was doubtful there would be sufficient funding this year – though things would probably be sorted out during the following one. Luke and Celia were all too aware it was unlikely anything, barring emergency repairs, would be done in the next decade, let alone the next year.

The Maxwells had also, over many years, suggested to the Bishop's office that the Vicarage be sold and a much smaller house, even bungalow perhaps, bought from the proceeds. Their argument – a sound one – was that an old decrepit house, far bigger than any clergyman could possible need, would be off the hands of the church (which always appeared short of money). A reasonable sum would come their way despite the dilapidation, and even after the purchase of a far smaller Rectory in the parish, money would be left to swell beleaguered financial assets.

In recent times such a request – and suggestion – had been made increasingly by the couple, especially following those ever more regular times when some calamity or other afflicted the Vicarage – and, in consequence, the Maxwells. Always, though, it was rejected. Not that the argument in business and financial terms did not make sense. On the contrary, in that direction it would have very much been in the interests of the church; something their accountants and administrators were most aware of and regularly brought to the attention of the Bishop's office – and to that good man himself. He, though, like his immediate predecessor, who had been in office for the first twenty or so years of the Maxwell's occupancy of the old ruin, preferred to eschew financial wisdom in the interests of image – of creating the right impression. He reasoned that as the Anglicans of the parish had long fought battles against the non-conformists in terms of gaining, and retaining congregations of size (in previous times, usually, losing ones), it was essential that the Rectory was big and imposing – even though it might be, he had to concede, 'a touch run down'. It was crucial to these senior clerics that the Rectory exceeded in size and basic grandeur, which it did, the manses of the Congregational and Methodist Ministers.

There had, possibly, been some validity in that argument prior to the arrival of the Reverend Maxwell, but it certainly did not apply after a few years of that effective man's occupancy of the parish ministry. The present Bishop could see this but was still reluctant to change the policy of his predecessor – though he was aware that a time might come when it would make sense in all directions for the Rectory to be sold and a smaller dwelling in the parish purchased for the same purpose.

Luke's frustrations with the deterioration of their living conditions had increased over the years, but they were nothing compared with the seething anger within Celia. Throughout the late 1920s she had been annoyed, during the thirties she became very annoyed, and by the time that war had broken out she was incensed – and increasingly so. During the early years of the conflict Celia had made to her husband the radical suggestion that they bought a bungalow or small house in the parish and forsook the shambolic Rectory.

"We would have somewhere pleasant and comfortable in which to live and, possibly even more importantly, we'd have a place of our own when the time comes for you to retire. Then we'll have to vacate this dreadful barn, of course – it's a tied house, after all. It goes with the job. We've not a great deal of money, clearly, but you're still young enough to get a mortgage, Luke."

Her husband saw, totally, her point of view, and in many ways agreed with it. He put to her, though, after much thought, a point of view relevant and powerful. "You're right in so many ways, my dear, but as I see it, we do not, as you say, have a great income. When you don the dog collar you condemn yourself and, I'm afraid, your spouse and family to, if not poverty, certainly a frugal life. One of the few bonuses, though, is that a rent free house comes with the job. If we left here and bought our own place, the church are not going to increase my stipend at all, even though it would leave them a big property to sell if they wished. So whilst in a sense I am more than sympathetic to what you say, I feel we've got to see it out here as, income wise, it makes sense for us to do so. What I'll do, though, is to push harder, and more often, to ensure something is done to improve this house. I'm sure I'll get somewhere in the end."

This was not really true – he was far from certain that, having failed to make any progress with the Bishop's office in the past, he would make a breakthrough in the future.

The reality was that he did not – and by the early 1950s he knew he never would. Also, relevantly and worryingly, it was too late to pursue the option of buying their own dwelling on the Peninsula. He had turned sixty and clearly was far too old to take on a mortgage – more to the point, perhaps, too old to be offered one. There was, too, no way in which he and Celia would ever be able to raise sufficient to purchase even the most humble of abodes. Reasons for this were not complicated. Quite simply, the ministry was no profession for anybody who wanted to make a good living. Having said this, many a clergyman still managed to put by sufficient to buy a residence for their retirement. Neither Luke or Celia, though, had ever had ambitions in the direction of savings. Not that they were profligate, but in the directions in which they wished to spend a bit, they did.

As responsible, loving and visionary parents they were ever supportive of their two children. Both Duncan and Ellie had won scholarships from the village school to Tavistock Grammar, then gone on to enter training – their son as a surveyor, Ellie as a teacher. Both subsequently obtained good, well paid jobs – thus their parents' support and 'investment' had assuredly not been wasted. In their personal lives, the vicar and his spouse both worked hard within the church and community, and felt they deserved some comfort and modest indulgence in their leisure time. They enjoyed good food and Celia, being an excellent cook, created delicious, often unusual dishes, and within reason, was not deterred by the price of ingredients – though their availability had become a problem (at times, a major one) during the wartime years and the late forties.

A woman who liked to look smart, and be reasonably up to date fashion-wise, she did not stint on her clothes. Her Husband ran a small car – useful for his duties of ministry, but not essential – and never stinted on his cigarettes and drink (where he drank little other than rum, assuredly more pricey than beer and scrumpy, the liquors most commonly drunk). Also, the Maxwells had for decades taken a fortnight's holiday every summer, originally with the children, since their growth to adulthood, just the two of them. Liking the sea, their destination had always been the South Coast of Devon – the 'English Riviera' – or that of North Cornwall with its magnificent cliffs and walks. Their accommodation was habitually in decent hotels and they would ever ensure they had a relaxing and reasonably indulgent vacation.

Thus, did Luke Maxwell celebrate his sixty-first birthday on a stormy March day knowing he and his loyal wife would have to remain in this Victorian relic for a number of years to come. It would be four years before he could draw his old age pension, and nine before he could access the full one which the church would pay to him. The two together would probably be sufficient for them to maintain a tolerable standard of living, but if he retired then – if still alive, of course, as he would be seventy – there would be a major expenditure in a direction new to them, the rental of a dwelling, almost certainly in this parish which neither wished to leave.

Not that Luke had any problem with the prospect of filling the pulpit of the Parish Church for a further decade – the opposite applied. For he had enjoyed every day of his ministry, the involvement with the men, women and children of the parish, the knowledge – or, at least, feeling – that at times he could, and did, help folk in their time of hurt or need. To be central to local events in such a way had been the kernel of his life for so long he found it difficult to imagine any other.

Celia, also, derived fulfilment from her vital role as the rector's spouse, a position which inevitably involved her in parish life and affairs. Her own pursuits in the WI and so forth were also very central to her life, and she had no desire, for the foreseeable future, to see them change. Only the Vicarage posed a problem – having to live in what was little more than a damp, cold slum, albeit, a large one.

Luke enjoyed his birthday, as he usually did – the fact he was growing ever older fazed him not in the slightest. He had gained much fulfilment from his life and hoped it had a fair number of years still to run. If it had not, however, then so be it – he would commit himself to the Lord's keeping.

They had a contented evening with a few drinks (following the devouring of a splendid meal prepared by Celia), listening to music on the radio – or, at least, listening as best they could, as the wind, gale force throughout the day, moved up a notch to severe gale, hurtling up the Tamar bringing heavy rain which beat against the windows, much of it seeping in, whilst there was a constant howl as if the house was being besieged by a gigantic pack of wolves. It did not affect their contentment, though, and they retired to bed at eleven o'clock, the vicar thanking his loyal wife for a meal fit for a gourmet, and a delightful day – then both proceeded to sleep deeply.

It was a slumber, though, which was not destined to last until dawn. For at four o'clock, or just thereafter, they were awakened violently, perhaps even terrifyingly (though both said long after, they were fortunate to awaken at all). Suddenly, through the midst of their deep doze, they were aware of a roaring sound, louder, much nearer than that of the wind which had harried the house, and the Peninsula, for the greater part of 24 hours. Then there was an even louder tone, harsher, more alarming. Before either could respond, their bed was being bombed by what appeared to be masonry. Had it been that, the chances of survival for either of them would have been remote; Plaster from the ceiling though, whilst heavy, did not carry the menace, quite, of granite or concrete blocks. The ceiling of their bedroom, however – or at least half of it – had descended from its correct place and was living in huge chunks on and around their bed, whilst looking upwards to where it had been, they could see the relative light of the wild night sky.

Despite their deep shock, both realised rapidly what had happened – the treacherous wind had removed a portion of the roof, the rain had hammered in and the sagging ceiling (it had been that way for years) finally gave way to the laws of gravity. They were a couple alike in that in most situations they were able to regroup – pull themselves together – and react quickly. This they did, pushing aside the heavy rubble – no easy task – then struggling out of their bed. Without a word, they went down to the kitchen, where Celia put the heavy kettle onto the ever hot hob of the massive, and ancient, range. The kettle coming quickly to the boil, she made tea – very strong – poured out two large beakerfuls, added double the amount of sugar they usually took, and placed one before her husband, who nodded his thanks.

They sat for several minutes sipping their tea, both, they fully appreciated, in a state of shock. Eventually, the rector spoke, "We could have been killed, Celia – both of us. Could have been killed," he repeated then lapsed back into silence.

His wife nodded, continuing to sip her tea. Her husband's comments, she knew, did not exaggerate. Emptying her cup, her very positive nature gained control.

"We're still here, though, Luke – it'll take more than that to rid the world of us."

She got up from her chair, put the cup in the sink then, her sharp mind and active approach taking control, said, "I'm going to look around to see exactly what damage has been done to our room, and whether any other rooms are affected."

She left her Husband sitting, still somewhat in shock, certainly in very deep thought, and proceeded up the wide, scarred, wooden stairway, to inspect the carnage visited by the storm. It was almost a quarter of an hour before she returned – and found her Husband still sitting in the same spot, gripping the now empty cup in his hands.

"Over half of the ceiling in our room has come down," she reported, "And looking up I can see a very large hole in the roof – perhaps as much as ten feet across. So the water is pouring in as it's still raining heavily. All the other rooms seem to be all right though. Clearly we'll have to move into another bedroom – that's one thing with this house, we've got plenty. You'll have to ring the Church Office in Plymouth, though, Luke – this morning as soon as there's anybody about. Clearly they're going to have to do something about the roof urgently. Today, in fact, or else further winds could rip half the roof off. The ceiling as well, of course, but that's not quite as urgent. So they'll need to be told as soon as possible so they can get a builder in right away to make it safe and get some covering on it – don't you agree?" She asked the question in somewhat sharp fashion, her husband seemingly still in something of a daze. However, when he looked up at her, she could see that his eyes no longer displayed shock – rather there was something in them, plus the grim set of his mouth, that suggested there was gathering, within him, immense anger.

"Oh, I agree," he rasped. "I agree, all right – they will be told, Celia, never fear. The office opens at nine – and I shall 'phone that very minute. Oh yes, I will indeed – and I feel sympathy already for whoever picks up the phone because I will take no prisoners." He shook his head: "We could have been killed, Celia – so easily."

His wife nodded her agreement, then practical as always, said, "There's nothing we can do until full light, so I might as well make some more tea. It'll do us no harm, that's for sure."

Luke nodded his agreement – he was a big tea drinker at the best of times, at the worst, even bigger. Muttering his thanks to this wife for another beaker of the sweet beverage, the vicar relapsed into silence, clearly a prisoner of major thought processes.

Such silence reigned in the kitchen for half an hour or more, the rector transfixed by the major matters gripping his mind, his wife dozing gently in her chair. She was suddenly, though, fully awakened by her husband uttering – a little louder than normal – words which came from the heart:

"I owe you an apology, Celia – a very big one. I've been selfish and foolish; but no more. No longer."

His spouse looked at him in astonishment. It was several seconds before she spoke. "What do you mean, Luke; an apology? Why – what have you to apologise for? You've got your faults as have we all, but you've never been a difficult man to live with. I've not regretted our marriage for a single day."

"I owe you an apology because I've sentenced you to over thirty years of living in this wretched house. You've never liked it, I know that – and with good cause. But despite everything, all the dampness, problems, dilapidation over the years, you've just got on with things, taken it in your stride. I know it – and I appreciate it, but I should have done something about it years ago."

"You've lived here as well, Luke. You've had to put up with it as much as I have."

158

He shook his head – "It's been easier for me. It's generally easier for a man – a woman's the homemaker, after all. And you've made this a good home for me – for all of us, with the children so well cared for when they were growing up. But you shouldn't have had to spend over three decades in this dreadful barn of a place. We should have moved out long ago, as I knew you wanted to; rented, if we could not have afforded to buy."

Celia shook her head. "It's not been that easy, Luke, has it? The house goes with the job, it's as simple as that. And you were right when you said in effect that we would be spending money in a way we could ill afford if we'd rented when we had this place to live in, far from ideal though it was – and is. You've done your best over the years to get them to either really renovate it properly, or sell and buy a newer, smaller place in the parish – you've tried time and time again, but got nowhere – which has not been your fault."

"Clearly I've not tried hard enough, but I know one thing – it's about to change, with a vengeance. When I phone the office at nine, I will not ask for action, but demand it. And I don't just mean repairing the roof – I don't doubt that even they will see that as some sort of priority. And they'll probably get around to putting a new ceiling in. But that has to be the beginning, not the end. They have to put in place major renovations, refurbishment of this Rectory, and house us whilst they do so – 'cause you're talking months of work here, six, at least, I fear. Nothing's really been done for probably half a century or more. If they're not prepared to do this, then they must sell it – and very, very soon – and buy a smaller house or bungalow here in, or close to, the village, as the new Rectory, and do it before they sell this place, so that we can move in very soon. This is what I will demand – and I'll give no ground on it."

"And if they don't agree, Luke? If they dig their heels in or, as has been their way over the years, prevaricate – and I fear they will – what then? What happens then – what can we do we've not done over the years?"

"Simple – I can resign," came the blunt but straightforward answer. "Be, no longer, rector of this parish – although we could continue to live in it. It's too late for us to buy, of course – I'm aware of that, and to blame for it – but we could rent; perhaps a small bungalow or cottage. There are a great number of rented houses in the village."

"But how would be live, Luke? You're still four years short of your old age pension, and whilst you'd get a small pension from the church, you would have to carry on several years yet before you received your full entitlement – and even then it would not be very generous. The fact is, Luke, whilst I understand the way you feel, it's not practical – you've no option but to soldier on for the time being."

Her husband smiled – for the first time that morning. "But I have, Celia – believe it or not, I have. You thought I had been sitting here all this time beside the range in shock: Not so. Certainly I was to start with – we're getting a bit old to have ceilings fall on us in the middle of the night, and gaping holes in the roof. But anger soon superseded shock – perhaps bitterness also. Certainly this awful business has shaken me out of a kind of torpor – and made me think. I realise now something I should have acknowledged years ago – I have to make a stand. And I think God is on our side, because He has thrust into my mind a way forward – a way of making a living even if I resign from the living here and we leave this house. About three weeks ago I bumped into George Grant at Home Park. He's not a regular Argyle follower but he goes now and again. Although I know him reasonably well, it's the first time I'd seen or spoken to him in over twelve months. I really believe it was The Lord who caused us to meet that day, because as I sat here this morning it came to me, for the first time – though it really should have registered before – the possible importance to us of what he told me. I knew he had resigned as the rector of a big rural area up towards Okehampton, largely because his wife is in very poor health and, naturally, he wished to devote far more time to caring for her. He's a couple of years older than me but still short of drawing his old age pension and, again like me, whilst he gets a small pension from the church, he has officially retired too early to get the full one. How he makes up his income to a level which can keep them tolerably comfortable is that he does locum work. He has a friend doing such work in North Devon who put the idea into his head. What you do is to put your name on a central register in the office of the Bishop of Exeter – in charge of the entire county, of course, and the Bishop of Truro to cover south of the Tamar – then await the call to cover for a rector on holiday in one parish, or perhaps sick in another and so forth. When he first said about it, whilst I thought it was probably a good way to earn a bit of pocket money, I assumed there was no way in which anybody could earn a meaningful amount from it. I was wrong. Apparently he could do the job virtually full time if he wished, but because he doesn't, he has to turn work down. As he said, so many parishes now do not have curates or the like, if for any reason the rector is unavailable for even a week – perhaps even a day, if that day's a Sunday – then somebody has to cover. Also, in these parishes, often he will conduct weddings and bury the dead – extra earnings. Surprisingly there aren't that many on the list of locums so they are always in demand. This is probably due to the fact, most understandable, that the vast majority of ordained men prefer greatly to minister to a flock familiar to them, not a bunch of strangers. Clearly there could never be quite the same satisfaction in the work which one gets from deep involvement in your own parish, but assuredly it is an interesting, reasonably reliable way to make a tolerable living. So, Celia, with your agreement, if we can get no long term satisfaction and commitment from the Bishop's office in Plymouth regarding this rectory – or a new one – then that's the direction in which I feel we should go."

His wife's response was instant: "Luke, you have my agreement, and I think you know that without even asking – though I expect to be asked and consulted, of course. That's the way we've always been throughout our married life, and it's worked for us; mutual respect, something far too many people lack. Still, yes, that's the way forward. Whatever happens, we'll be able to stay on this lovely peninsula for the foreseeable future. If the Bishop's office do the honourable thing then we'll have a decent home to live in, either this one or something else in the parish (though, if I'm honest, I'd prefer the latter – somewhere a bit smaller). And you'll be able to continue your much loved ministry here. Should they not, then I know for you it will be a dreadful blow to no longer be directly involved in this community in the way you have for half your life; but you will still be able to continue in your calling and way of life, and make a living for us both."

Her husband nodded, smiled, and thanked his much loved wife. "So on the dot of nine o'clock, I'll phone the Bishop's office – and we'll see what transpires."

Thus did Luke Maxwell make the call, the tone of his voice courteous but totally uncompromising. "We might have been killed," were the words which came to his wife's ears on three occasions, likewise the demand that something be done immediately regarding the hole in the roof and the collapsed ceiling; This was followed by a demand that major works be put in hand to make the old rectory into a decent, habitable residence or that a newer, smaller dwelling be purchased in the parish as a new vicarage, with the old one sold – and that action in this direction be put into motion within the next month. These were the demands the rector put forward. Though he had couched them in civilised fashion, his tone and directness to the official at the other end of the phone left that somewhat harassed fellow fully aware that were not the clergyman's wishes followed, with some alacrity, then the clerical gentleman would be back in contact – and would not seek to take prisoners.

Initially, Luke's verbal confrontation appeared to work. For a surveyor appeared at the rectory before the day was out, and within three more, the hole in the roof was sealed. Then at the beginning of the following week, a carpenter and plasterer appeared on the scene tasked with replacing the bedroom ceiling, a job they had completed satisfactorily within a few more days.

So swift had been the response of the Bishop to their plight, so reassuring had been the words coming their way from officials and the surveyor regarding tackling the vital, so long over due renovations needed to the large dwelling, that Celia and Luke felt, at last, genuine optimism that the sprawling hovel in which they had lived for most of their married lives, would be brought up to a standard fit for human habitation. The ceiling having been done, further work to the house, they were told – major repairs, as well – would be put in hand probably within a month, certainly six weeks at the outside.

The month passed – but builders did not reappear. The Vicar, who could be terrier-like when the spirit moved him – and when upset – phoned the Bishop's office the very day after the calendar month had passed, pointed out courteously, but forcibly that the promise of work commencing in such a framework of time had not been kept, and demanded to know of an official, who sounded somewhat harassed, when it would start – the date. The fellow, sounding more than a little confused, was unable to state an exact day, but was sure – nay, certain – that a beginning would be made possibly within a fortnight, assuredly within the month.

The Maxwells bided their time. A fortnight came and went, then three weeks, then another month had passed on its way – June was but days away. Once again the vicar phoned the Bishop's office and spoke to the same official. This time, his patience worn threadbare, he wasted little time with a fellow who sounded young and certainly seemed perpetually to be stressed (or, at least, he was when he conversed with the irate clergyman), and clearly had no real idea as to what was going on, demanding to be put through to someone in a senior position. After waiting on the end of the line for almost five minutes, finally he was connected to a chap called Frank Bradley who held the grandiose title of 'Projects and Maintenance Manager'.

The rector, fed up with having his time wasted, angry at further prevarication on the part of the Bishop's office, despite all the promises – came brusquely and directly to the point, eschewing most of the basic pleasantries:

"When, Mr Bradley, can we expect a start to be made on the renovation of our rectory. It was promised to start weeks ago, yet nothing has been done. My wife and I need a starting date – and need it now."

For several seconds there was silence, then a hesitant voice came over the line: "Well, Reverend Maxwell, it's not, I'm afraid, not possible to give you an actual date at present. It is definitely on our priority list – and – and – and will be done in the very near – well, the near future, all being well. We do have a limited budget, of course, which as I'm sure you'll appreciate, we have to keep within, but we would hope to put the work in hand within the next – the next – the next twelve months, I would say. Certainly it's our intention to. . ."

"Twelve months? Priority – the near future? It's been priority, the near future for a quarter century and more – and I see no prospect of it changing." With that he slammed the receiver down and for a couple of minutes sat on the hard chair in the hallway by the phone, his head slumped forward into his hands. Then he straightened up and went off to see his wife. He knew what he had to do – and was confident she would back him totally. It was, after all, the fall back strategy they had planned that early morning after the ceiling had collapsed.

Celia backing him fully, that same day he phoned the relevant office – that of the Bishop of Exeter – to check firstly there were vacancies for locums (and was assured there were) and sought confirmation that he would be suitable to fill one of them. Again he was given assurance that in principle a minister of his experience, but well under seventy, would fulfil the criteria for the role, though, naturally, certain formalities would have to be gone through.

Replacing the receiver on this call, Luke Maxwell consulted his list of numbers, and phoned, directly, the Bishop of Plymouth. Speaking to his secretary – a lady, Miss Cornish, who had held the post for twenty years or more, whom he knew quite well to speak to, but whom he had never actually met – he asked to be put through to the Bishop, only to be told he was out and would not be available until later that evening. Wondering whether or not to phone back then, he decided, rather, to 'strike while the iron was hot', and asked Miss Cornish to inform the Bishop that he intended to resign his living in the parish and would formally put it in writing and send it off the following day.

The good lady was surprised to the point of shock at such news (she had been around a long while, thus was very conscious of the fact that any clergyman in situ before she came was long standing, indeed, and, by leaving his parish so suddenly and unexpectedly, would cause ripples – even waves). He also informed the lady of the reason, above all, for his resignation:

"The fact that my wife and I, for the duration of my entire ministry, have been promised by the Bishop's office that renovations would be carried out to our wreck of a vicarage. Following the two of us almost being killed by part of the roof being blown off and the ceiling falling on us in the middle of the night, we were promised that not only would this calamity be put right – which, to be fair, it was – but that also major works of renovation and improvement would be commenced within two months. Not only has this not happened but I've been told by the Maintenance Manager that there is not sufficient funding for it to be done in the near future. Also there appears to be, on the part of the church, no desire to pursue another option with which my wife and I would be most happy, and one which, I feel, would make financial sense for the church; the purchase of a much smaller dwelling in the parish to be used as the Rectory and, thus, the sale of the present Victorian edifice. Seeing as Celia and I have been so grievously let down on this crucial matter, then I have no option other than to resign my living, leave the vicarage and find other accommodation. If you would, verbally, inform the Bishop of this as soon as possible, Miss Cornish, I would be grateful. As I said just now, I will put this – and more – in writing, and post it off to you tomorrow."

The Secretary assured Luke Maxwell that the Bishop would certainly be informed of this before the day was out, leaving the vicar and his wife to contemplate their future, their momentous decision having been made.

They had little time to do so, for the next morning just a little after ten o'clock, Luke received a phone call from the Rural Dean. Mervyn Walton had held the office for a dozen or more years and whilst he and Luke Maxwell were not close friends, they had always had a good relationship based on meaningful mutual respect. The Dean's tone was reasonably casual, but there was nothing vague in his request. "Luke, I need to see you. I've had a phone call this morning from the Bishop and he wants me to see you and have a chat as soon as possible. Would you be about later this morning, if I drive over to see you?"

The rector smiled to himself. His message to Miss Cornish, clearly relayed to the Bishop, had elicited response and action far quicker than he had expected. Indeed, so shabbily had Celia and himself been treated over the years, he was far from certain that his sudden, and shock, announcement of resignation would cause the slightest concern to the Bishop. He felt that in the fullness of time there would be a polite, standard letter from the mitred minister, thanking him for his service and wishing him well for the future. It would appear, though, his message had caused the Bishop sufficient alarm for him to despatch the Rural Dean – if that, mind you, was the reason for his visit (he could think of no other).

"Yes, Mervyn, that'll be fine. We'll both be here. There'll be a cup of tea waiting for you."

The Rural Dean arrived on the stroke of noon. He was greeted by the Maxwells. Celia made a pot of tea, and soon they were seated in the large front room, the beverage and biscuits before them. The vicar had a feeling that the senior clergyman would like to have spoken to him on his own, but he insisted his wife remained – anything which affected him, affected her.

Mervyn Walton came, almost instantly, to the point – Luke Maxwell's resignation and the principal reasons for it. Clearly Miss Cornish had given a faithful and accurate summary of that stated to her by the rector.

"The Bishop's very upset, Luke, about you taking such a – well, drastic step. He would like you to re-consider. A man of your calibre is such an asset – he certainly doesn't want to lose you."

"We've been forced into it, Mervyn, for the reasons I've given. Look around you – if this place was owned by the council, tenants would refuse to live in it. We've been promised action to upgrade it for years – no, decades. Yet nothing's happened. We've had enough – I'm going to retire."

"And be a locum, I'm told."

"How do you know that?" There was astonishment in

166

Maxwell's tone – he'd only talked to an anonymous (to him) official in Exeter the previous day, so how could a Dean in West Devon, and apparently, the Bishop of Plymouth, know about it already?

"The Bishop was told that first thing this morning, Luke. Do you think the sudden resignation of a very long serving, most highly regarded rector, and his enquiry as to the immediate availability of places on the locum list would go unnoticed? Of course not. The official at Exeter who gave you the information immediately contacted the Bishop's office at Plymouth to inform them that it would appear you were contemplating a major change – shall we say, career-wise. Then you made your call to Miss Cornish asking her to inform the Bishop of your resignation, and reasons. It doesn't need Sherlock Holmes to work that one out, does it? The Bishop apparently was told all this in a phone call from Miss Cornish late yesterday evening after returning following a service at Truro Cathedral, and as I said, he phoned me early today – 7am."

The rector smiled, and shook his head. "No, I suppose not," said he. "Still, my resignation is seriously made Mervyn – made after long, heart searching discussions between Celia and myself. Also my intention to take up locum work. It'll not be the same, of course – not be the same as having my own parish. In fact, initially I've no doubt it'll break my heart to give up my ministry on this Peninsula, even though we'll rent a place and continue to live here. We've been given no choice though, I'm afraid – none at all."

The Rural Dean emptied his cup of tea, gratefully accepted another poured by his hostess, along with a Rich Tea biscuit, then looked directly at the rector: "There is a choice, Luke – you can both stay, continue the marvellous service you've given to this parish for over thirty years – and move into a new Rectory."

The final words were delivered with the effect of a torpedo – albeit, a friendly one. "A new Rectory, Mervyn? You mean, the church will buy a new place here in the parish – we would leave this one?"

The words stumbled from his mouth, his face registering a

combination of shock and hope. His wife looked even more bemused – unusual for her. "But why has nobody told us about this, Mervyn – why have we not been informed of the intention – or, at least the possibility of a new Rectory. After all, if that was to happen it would change everything – we would have no need to move and even less desire."

"Because it's only been decided this morning, Luke," came the Rural Dean's reply, following the swallowing of a large portion of biscuit. "In the past five hours more action and progress has been made regarding the rector's accommodation in this parish than has been made during the past quarter century. The fact is, the Bishop is incandescent – which is unusual, because generally, as you know, he is a quiet, courteous, very even-tempered man. He had not realised the Rectory was in such a state."

"Well he should have – he's visited quite often over the years. To be fair, I suppose, those visits have been brief and for business purposes, so he might well not notice much. But surely he must be aware of all the complaints we've made over the years – increasingly. He must be aware of those."

"Apparently not. He was not even told of the ceiling falling in on you back in March, when, it is generally accepted, you both could have been killed. Frank Bradley, the maintenance officer, is the one to blame for this. He was got from his bed at half past six this morning when the Bishop phoned him and, I fancy, gave him hell. Bradley, apparently, said he'd not wished to worry the Bishop about such matters, his department perfectly able to sort out problems of this nature. The Bishop pointed out, fiercely I imagine, that it was obvious, as a hugely valued rector was resigning his living because of the state of his Rectory, the Maintenance Manager could not be trusted to address such problems, was not doing his job properly and clearly had not been for some time. His job is under threat, Luke, you can be sure of that. The Bishop can be quite ruthless if he feels somebody is not up to the job – or doing his job. Anyway, Bradley's been like a dynamo this morning – trying to avoid the sack – and I've been busy as well, exceedingly so. The upshot of all this 'too-ing and fro-ing', and there's certainly been plenty of that with the surveyor involved, the builder who repaired the roof and ceiling here, the Diocese Accountant, a couple of land and house agents in Tavistock, in fact, just about everybody except the Queen – and I suppose she could be in theory. After all, we the Church of England are the established church and she is its head. We serve her as much as we serve God."

He ceased, briefly, to laugh at his own joke, then continued:

"Well, to get to the point – which I'm never that good at doing – the decision has been made by the Bishop this morning to sell this Rectory – as it is – and buy a smaller, much newer property, in the parish, as near to the church as possible, naturally. It was mooted to renovate this place, the Bishop as you know – like the Bishop of Exeter – always keen to retain large rectories, no matter what their age (and invariably they are Victorian, or older) as in his view (their view in fact, the both of them) it gives the church a boost in those numerous parishes in the South-west where the non-conformists hold the whip hand in terms of congregation numbers. At least the rectories will almost universally be larger and far more imposing than the manses, as, for that matter, will the churches be far grander than the chapels. In reality, it is of no real importance in my view as it adds not one soul to a congregation. Here it's the message that comes from the pulpit, the overall quality of the man giving it, that counts. Your church is full because of your huge presence in this community, and your erudition in voicing the word of God, not because you dwell in a big rectory. Whatever, in the final analysis, it's been down to the surveyor who, when he was here back along inspecting the roof and ceiling, noted the deplorable state of the rest of the building. He told the Bishop it would be so expensive to restore it to a decent standard that it could never be cost effective. He recommended selling it – possibly to a builder who would convert it to, perhaps, three or four dwellings – and buying a decent, but modest property nearby. So that is what is to happen – and in the very near future. The Diocese will not wait until this place has been sold first, but rather will raid its reserves to purchase somewhere for Celia and yourself, hopefully, within the next two months. One firm of agents in Tavistock have two

h

properties here on the Peninsula on their books at present – and one appears ideal in all directions. It's only a quarter of a mile from the church and is priced modestly because the owners want a quick sale. That, of course, is what they will get if our surveyor, who will inspect it this afternoon, is happy with it – and as it's less than twenty years old, one would feel he will be.

"So there it is Celia, Luke – that's the situation. The Bishop is shocked by the way you've been treated and mortified to contemplate you leaving the ministry in this parish – and I know he is in the process of writing to you to express this. So, may I go out and use your phone – in the hallway, I notice – call the Bishop, and give him news which will truly lift his spirits (mine as well) that you have withdrawn your resignation, as yet only verbal, and will carry on as rector of this parish?"

The joyful expression on Celia's face said everything as far as she was concerned, but her husband was the incumbent, not her. So she left it to him to make the decision, though she had no doubt what it would be.

For some seconds the Reverend Luke Maxwell said not a word. Then before he gave an answer, asked a question:

"Mervyn – I'm bemused. For years we've felt neglected – increasingly so. Now, having given notice of resigning, well, I don't know about Celia, but I almost get the feeling that the Bishop's world will come to an end if we give up the ministry in this parish; I mean – what difference can it make to him?"

The Rural Dean smiled, then shook his head: "Luke, I've always seen you as a modest man, but I did not realise just how modest – more, humble – you are until now. Luke – you are the Bishop's star turn, the very, very last man in the area he would want to lose. I'll go further and say the 'big boss', the Bishop of Exeter, who, of course is supreme throughout the county, would also be most upset if you turned your back on this parish. You know as well as I do, that whilst we are the established church and in probability, over most parts of the country, the dominant one, here in Devon and Cornwall we have for decades – in fact, a hundred years and more – played second fiddle to the non-conformists. As far as the eye can see, both sides of the Tamar,

Methodists, Weslyans, Baptists, Congregationalists and so on, dominate. We've got the fine old churches, some of them massive, but half the time we've nobody in them. Granted, the non-conformists don't get the congregations they did before the war, but they still get far more than we do – except in this parish. Here, even on a Sunday in January, with a force nine gale coming up the Tamar, when the chapels are three quarters empty, your church, a big one too, will be three quarters full – and a fair number of them will have been brought up to go to chapel, not church. You are unique, Luke – a legend in your way, and I do not use the world lightly. We all prize you – the Bishop probably most of all. You give up the ministry here and within a month – probably less – congregations will be halved, whilst those at the chapels will be boosted. We all know it – the Bishop probably more than most, which is why he spent a sleepless night when he was given the news of your intended resignation by Miss Cornish yesterday evening; and he definitely had spent a bad night because he told me when he rang me at a ridiculously early hour this morning."

The Rural Dean spoke the final words with a touch of ire. He looked at the vicar and his spouse, then said, "So I ask again – can I use your phone and inform the Bishop, who is awaiting my call – very nervously – that you have withdrawn your resignation and will continue your inspirational ministry in this parish for, hopefully, very many years to come."

The rector looked at his loyal spouse – herself a major contributor to the wellbeing of the local community – saw her smile, then nod her head. He turned towards the Rural Dean. "Make your call, Mervyn – and tell the Bishop of my change of heart; there will be no vacancy in this parish for a while yet. And apologise to him for me – I did not mean to give him a sleepless night. Also, thank him for his remarkably prompt actions – it is appreciated by us both." He stopped, then shook his head. "I wish I'd gone to him direct – and done it years ago."

The Rural Dean rose from his chair and began to move towards the hall – and the telephone. He stopped briefly and looked back at the minister: "There's a lesson there, Luke – one which a mature man like yourself, with a wideish experience of life should have known. Always go to the top if you want to get anything done. Well, by that, I mean the top locally. The very top, the Boss we all serve, is probably a touch too busy trying to save the world to worry about the state of this Rectory."

VII

High Noon

Ronald Penrose was 'long headed'. His father had been 'long headed', also. He had been headmaster at the village school for decades, and a member of the Parish Council likewise, being chairman many times. A sharp, wise man he had been much trusted and respected, but having, at times, a sharp tongue and uncertain temper, not universally liked. A strict disciplinarian, it had been a rare girl or boy in the village who would ever disobey him – and virtually all for a very long period of time would have attended his school, probably until they left to enter the working world at the age of fourteen (although many at the outbreak of the Great War had left at as young an age as twelve, their labour needed on the farms of the parish and suchlike). A few, though, won scholarships to Tavistock Grammar School, Roland being amongst them.

Very intelligent like his father – although somewhat more amiable – he had done well, and upon leaving, being very good at science, especially chemistry, went to Plymouth to work in a large pharmacy, learning the complex craft of becoming a dispensing chemist. As in most things he did, he flourished in the job and having completed his many years of training, gained a position as a dispenser in a chemists in Tavistock; within five years he had become the head of the small team at the chemists, and only four years later became owner of the chemist shop in the village – his father helping his only son buy the business.

By this time, Roland had married Cynthia Burns, daughter of a local farmer. The future looked good for him, and so it was. The business thrived. This was down to many things, Cynthia certainly playing her part. Often serving in the shop, she was efficient, courteous and kindly, always making customers feel welcome. Her husband, though, was the real source of the business's success. For beyond being knowledgeable and very obliging, he was innovative – very much so.

He was, in fact, a master of concoctions, seemingly able to mix up a 'dollop of jollop' which would relieve many an ailment. Headaches, upset stomachs, flu symptoms, boils and myriad more daily complaints would so often be alleviated – sometimes cured – using his potions. When asked advice regarding cures, he developed the habit – which became almost a catch phrase – of saying, "I often get this, and this nearly always cures it," before mixing up some, often, foul smelling, unpleasant tasting liquid. If the problem was voiced by a woman, and clearly could only be suffered by one of that gender, he would revert to the back stop of, "My Cynthia often gets this, and this will usually put things right."

Folk often sought his advice with other matters, also, well beyond the remit of his profession. Marital problems were brought to him, many sought financial advice, others would ask his opinion in terms of changing their jobs or regarding personal disputes; and even, at times, on legal issues. Rarely did he fail to give advice, but always pointed out that basically it was only his opinion and he could well be wrong – though, in reality, he rarely was. A 'long headed' man, indeed. And after being elected, like his father, to the Parish Council, he was inevitably often approached on council matters, many well beyond his jurisdiction.

Roland also had a keen interest in photography and after a few years, extended his shop by taking in a small room that was part of their dwelling house, filling this extra space with cameras, films and various accessories. Like with most of that which he did, he became very knowledgeable on the subject. This expertise, plus his ever helpful, approachable manner, meant this side of his business took off beyond anything he could have

174

hoped for, with people coming, at times, from Tavistock, even beyond, to avail themselves of his advice and his stock. Still photos, though, were a minor passion of Penrose – a greater one was moving pictures.

Roland loved the cinema. He had enjoyed the silent era, often going to screenings when the opportunity arose, but it was the coming of the 'talkies' which really seized his imagination.

When Roland Penrose was enthused, he usually took action, and so it proved here. Talking motion pictures were very much the future – so he would bring that future to the Peninsula. Great numbers took the train to Tavistock – at times to Plymouth, to go to 'the pictures', some twice, or even three times a week. It occurred to Roland that if there was a facility in the village for the viewing of films, then there would certainly be a market. So, it became his project – he would provide a community asset and, being ever-shrewd in business terms, he would 'make a few bob' as well.

There were, though, three essentials which needed to be sourced – projectors and other necessary gear, which would not be cheap, even if it was second hand (and it would be), a source for obtaining films (they would need to be reasonably current) and, clearly vital, somewhere to show them. One of his many contacts was a fellow, Henry Wallace, whom he had worked with when learning his business in the Plymouth pharmacy those many years earlier.

Even more interested than Roland in moving pictures, Henry had gone into the cinema industry not long after the Great War, when, using his natural technical skills, he had joined the projection unit in a large Plymouth cinema, soon taking charge of it. After just five years he became a manager and within a further three years, being a man who was excellent at making contacts and possessing the surest of touches in terms of business acumen, had branched out on his own, mainly as a distributor of films to smaller local cinemas. Also, he had sources when it came to the acquisition, at a very fair price, of second hand projection equipment.

Roland had never lost contact, even though it had been many

years since they had worked together – and had been good friends. Thus, the promise of the necessary projection gear and a regular supply of up-to-date films – all at reasonable price and hire rate – was rapidly forthcoming.

The third side of the triangle, though, was a little more difficult to put into place – location. The chemist knew that the most desirable – of the very limited number there were to choose from – was undoubtedly the village hall. Built to commemorate Queen Victoria's Golden Jubilee it was an impressive, granite built construction, by far the biggest possessed by any village in the Tamar Valley – probably beyond that. Locally, certainly, only Tavistock Town Hall was superior.

Thus it was that the chemist brought the matter to a meeting of the Parish Council. As a member he had the right to speak of the matter and explain what his plans were, to give the sound view that it would be a popular addition to the village facilities, providing an entertainment avenue which was escalating, at a galloping pace, in popularity.

"It'll give us something which no other village in this area possesses – that's as far as I'm aware, anyway. I've asked folk as they've come into the shop and a big, big, majority would be delighted if it went ahead. As this hall is the centre of activity in the parish – and right in the middle of the village – it's clearly the place to put on the films. I'd probably put on shows at least once a week – twice if it became very popular – and, obviously, I'd be paying the proper hire charge for the hall, so good regular income for the council and a help for the rate-payers. We're always saying the hall is underused – and so it is. Well, this would put up the usage a great deal, and in regular fashion. And I wouldn't expect it at weekends when it's so much easier to hire out the hall – especially Saturdays. I'd probably put on a weekly show on Fridays – possibly Wednesdays. But whatever, I do feel it would be a success, happily received by most people in the parish." He rested his case, confident that it was a good one and would be supported by a large majority of councillors, with little debate.

He was wrong on both counts. Not able to take part in the discussion, or vote, as he had to declare a personal interest, he was forced to sit and listen to a debate which assuredly did not go as smoothly as he would have wished. Very occasionally he answered questions and enquiries regarding the proposed film shows, put to him by the many councillors dubious about the scheme. Old Andrew Merton, past eighty now and the longest serving member of the council, was opposed, as Roland expected. A pillar of the Congregational Chapel, he saw the cinema in largely the same light as he saw alcohol – instruments of the Devil. Others though were, at best, unsure of the project, at worst against it.

"The trouble with the pictures is that as far as I can tell – or from what I hear, anyway – it's always American stuff and nonsense; Gangsters, cowboys and suchlike, none of which should be encouraged in this parish, especially by us as a council," opined Councillor Stuart Harper, who market gardened some ten acres running down to the river. "Folk look to us to set an example."

"Well, some films are British – or so I'm told," said Councillor Ida Crossley, who ran a small wool shop in the village – "I've never been to see any," added she, hastily. She wasn't sure they were necessarily an instrument of Satan, but felt it wise to hedge her bets. "I'm not sure that Councillor Penrose's idea is a good one."

"Could it lead to bad behaviour?" enquired Rollo Barnes, who helped to look after the local roads for the County Council. "All those people together – it could be a film might stir them up. Who knows what it might lead to. Could be fights, all sorts."

Roland Penrose caught the eye of the chairman, received a nod, and interjected hastily – "I think I can assure Mr Barnes that such an occurrence is very unlikely. People go to the pictures to sit and watch and enjoy themselves. I've never heard of a fight in a cinema. I would also point out to Mr Barnes that dances and the like often take place in this hall and often there are those a little the worse for drink – yet even then it is very rare there is any trouble. There'll be no trouble, I can guarantee that."

Councillor Margery Anthony caught the chairman's attention. "The problem I have, Mr Chairman, is that I can only class these cinema shows as being a commercial exercise. Mr Penrose will make a profit from it. Now there's nothing wrong with such in the correct place, but this is a public hall – a community hall – there for the benefit of the people of the parish. And I would point out, partially subsidised out of the rates. I do not feel that it is right for any individual, or business, to gain from the hire of the hall." A lady of the strictest moral code, the chemist might well have expected such a reaction from her.

The chairman, Dick Conway, the village newsagent, looked in the direction of the parish clerk. "I'm not aware that there is anything in the rules concerning the letting of the hall that prevents us making it available to commercial or business organisations," said he (knowing full well that there was nothing in the rules to prevent Roland hiring the hall).

The clerk, the very able Reg Perkins, confirmed this. "Nothing at all, Mr Chairman. And we already do hire it out at times for this. We had a furniture sale in the hall last month. A firm from Plymouth that had bought up bankrupt stock – though a lot of it looked more like war damaged stock, or so my wife said. Frankly, I wish there were more commercial bookings. As we all know, the hall is underused overall – and greatly underused by local groups and societies. Frankly there are just not enough of them. Speaking in purely financial terms, a regular income from Mr Penrose's cinema enterprise would help finances to a fair extent, appreciably reducing what we have to take from the rates to upkeep the place. And, as everybody knows, it's no bad plan to keep down the rates as much as possible. It is, though, of course, a matter for the council."

A classic Reg Perkins' manoeuvre, was this, giving his opinion succinctly, but strongly, as to what a decision should be, but making it clear it was totally a matter for the elected members. As was so often the case, it had an effect. Money always spoke, the clerk knew that; to be able to reduce the rate – even to hold it steady – had to be desirable. So although the debate meandered on just a touch longer, the chemist felt that he was likely to get the nod for his cinema plans. Eventually the chairman put the matter to the vote – and it was approved, though by no means overwhelmingly: Five voted for, three against, whilst four, strangely, abstained. Still, the vote was positive – thanks, Roland was aware, to the parish clerk's timely intervention, his sage opinion always being respected, and noted, by several councillors. Anyway, the Village Hall could be used and a large white screen was painted high up at one end of the hall. Roland then constructed a smallish, portable wooden booth, which would be put upon the stage, and which would hold the projector and operator.

Thus it was to a packed village hall on a raw Friday evening in October, that the first ever motion picture to be seen in the parish was shown. It was loved. Also keen on the enterprise was 'Curly' Frank Redman, who ran a small corner shop opposite the hall; for before the show started his premises were thronged with children having penny glasses of lemonade, and buying sweets and gob stoppers, whilst their parents stocked up with cigarettes for the evening. Curly would normally have closed well before the show took place, but had foreseen the possibility of a boost to business if he remained open until seven o'clock when proceedings began. Thus he would always stay open the extra two hours of a Friday night from then on. The fish and chip shop, just up the hill from the hall, also had cause to be grateful as, following the end of the pictures – usually between half past nine and ten – they would do more business, by far, than during any other evening of the week. The only loser, really, was the Tamar View Inn as many of the regulars there would absent themselves on a Friday, and by the time they would have left the hall, it was usually too late for them to slake their thirst, the law demanding the landlord call time at ten.

The chemist's close association with Henry Wallace paid immense dividends. Always seeking more outlets for his films, the shrewd Plymothian sold the chemist the projection equipment – usually very pricey – for virtually cost price. Granted it was second hand, but it was in good order, having been little used. More vital, though, was the supply of weekly films – and here Wallace was remarkably helpful. For not only did he supply the best, most iconic films of the day, with the 'big name' stars, he ensured that Roland received them when still very much in the public awareness. Plymouth would get them first, naturally, Tavistock probably a fortnight later – especially the brand new, state of the art Carlton – and within another fortnight, sometimes even sooner, they would be upon the village hall wall.

Some younger folk would take themselves off to Plymouth on a Saturday night, there being a late night train back – although they would have to pay a lot more, plus the rail fare. Many went to Tavistock which was less pricey, but knowing the film would soon be up on the Parish Hall wall, most aficionados waited the extra couple of weeks to avail themselves of Roland's excellent service at a far lower cost, where the only transport they needed was provided by 'shank's pony'. Granted, the hall, with its hard chairs and unforgiving floors, lacked the comfort of custom built cinemas – and the acoustics – but some sacrifices had to be made.

So over the years, the people of the parish came in their droves to the Friday night shows – only failing to take place if Christmas Day fell on a Friday and, of course, during the 'Good' ones of that description, but even then, regulars were not deprived of their weekly 'fix' as the showing would take place on a different night, usually a Wednesday. There were those who never missed, enjoying everything from The Three Stooges to the main feature, others who came but rarely, if some special film such as *Gone With The Wind* or *The Wizard of Oz* took their fancy. A majority, though, went two or three times a month, which meant there were rarely many empty chairs. When a film was exceptionally popular, he would put it out on two separate evenings on the same week.

Once established, 'Roland's Cinema' became a very rewarding part of his business, in terms of both finance and satisfaction. The first was obvious, the second came from the sight of people enjoying themselves. A good natured, positive man, the chemist derived much pleasure from this. And it was pleasure at a cheap price, children under fourteen admitted for just a few pence, everyone for under a shilling. The youngsters always sat in the front (Roland, paying scant attention to film categorisation in terms of age, rarely banning them from anything), courting couples were at the back, and most others sat in between.

The number of couples at the rear decreased considerably during the war years when so many of the young men of the parish went off to fight for King and Country. Amongst them was Edgar Bright who, during virtually every showing for years, had been right at the back – up on the stage, in the projection booth. He had come to work for Roland and Cynthia in the chemist's shop straight from school, and proved himself very much in keeping with his name. Able, keen, hardworking and always pleasant and courteous to customers, he was an asset; also, Roland and Cynthia who had no children, took to him in a personal way, treating him almost like a member of the family – something he appreciated and did not forget.

Edgar's had not been an easy life. His Mother had been widowed, with three children, in her thirties and life for all of them had been hard. He left school as soon as he could to be able to go out to earn to help the family live – hence his employment with the Penroses. Aware, as were everybody else in the village, of the family's difficult situation, Roland and Cynthia were not only good employers to him, but also good friends to his mother and siblings. Any medication they needed was sent home via Edgar – minus a bill – along with the odd bar or, even, box of chocolates. Also crystallised fruit which Mrs Bright enjoyed, all of which was stocked in a small section of the shop dedicated to the desirable rather than the medical. Cynthia would often deliberately order more meat than she required from Ron Benton, the butcher, and give a goodly portion of it – often more than half – to Edgar to take home for the family's Sunday dinner.

In a quite brief period of time, Edgar Bright became to the Penroses, if not quite a son, then certainly a much valued nephew. To Roland, though, his value went far beyond a personal affection – it lay very much in his work abilities, especially in the fields of photography and film. For the young man possessed not only a quick, logical enquiring mind with a strong scientific bent, but also an acute ability to innovate – intelligence, reason and practicality all rolled into one. The chemist often felt that Edgar, in a sense, had been cheated by his circumstances in life. Had he been given the chance of higher education, even of going to a Grammar School as had been his employer, then he would be pursuing a career at a very high level. It had been to the chemist's advantage that the young man had never been able, as yet, to follow the path upwards, to greater things.

Edgar and Roland's interests were as one – photography and films. The young man loved both, especially the latter. In his dreams, he saw himself at the heart of the film industry – but not as a star of the silver screen, rather as a director, or even in charge of the technical side of filming.

Rapidly appreciating the youngster's natural acumen for such matters, Roland soon involved him in his Friday night screenings. It was not long before he became the projectionist, taking over from the combined, though often none too brilliant, skills of Roland and Alan Carter, an electrician by trade (but with an interest in film) who tended to alternate with Penrose in the projection booth. Both were tolerably able if things went to plan, but were generally stumped on those not infrequent occasions when the projector misbehaved, the film broke, the sound system failed or some other calamity befell the show. If this happened there would be, invariably, a break in proceedings – sometimes a long one – and the paying customers would become, at best, impatient, at worst hostile. If the system couldn't be got back up and running again, then the show would have to be abandoned, money refunded, his reputation dented and his bank balance reduced.

Alan Carter had no objections to losing his role as projectionist as, being a man quite easily stressed, he had found people's impatience, at times even abuse, unnecessary and upsetting especially, as was often the case, when he was not at all sure how to put matters right. He saw in Edgar abilities and knowledge well beyond any he possessed and was happy to see him take over. He still remained in the 'team' however, standing in for the young man on the rare occasions he was not available. More often though, he was there to keep an eye on the audience, assist anyone unwell, quieten the youngster (usually) who was being a bit too noisy and, possibly, disruptive.

182

As to Edgar – he was first class. If the projector broke down he, seemingly instinctively, knew what was wrong, and unless something major, would usually fix it in a few minutes. The film very rarely broke for him, largely because he was adept at placing the film in a fractionally different way when loading the projector. The amplifier, which often crackled and could be, at times, a little indistinct, became much clearer after receiving his attention, he 'fine tuning' it in a way which would possibly have been beyond the talents of all but an expert.

Nobody in any employment in the parish was more valued by their employers than was Edgar Bright. There could, of course, be only one reasonably certain development in such a situation – he would change his employment. Someone would offer him a better job, or Edgar, modest young man though he was, would become aware his abilities were superior to his present opportunities – and salary – and would seek one. This circumstance came some twelve months before the outbreak of the war when, one morning, clearly ill at ease – almost embarrassed – he approached his employer, Roland being in the storeroom. "Could I possibly, Mr Penrose – please, could I have a word with you for a minute?"

" 'Course, boy." The chemist spoke the words in friendly fashion, but he felt a touch apprehensive – largely because Edgar was clearly uneasy, which was not like him at all. "Come in the office, Edgar – and we'll have a chat. The shop's quiet at present, and Mrs Penrose is there if anybody comes in."

They went into the office, the proprietor closing the door behind them.

"Well, what can I do for you, boy?"

The young fellow looked ever more ill at ease – even more so when he took the chair indicated by his employer. The chemist said nothing, but fixed his employee with an enquiring look. Edgar cleared his throat – and stated his case. So nervous was he, the words almost tumbled from his lips.

"Well, Mr Penrose – it's like this. I've worked here now for almost five years, for you and Mrs Penrose – and I could never, will never, work for anybody better, kinder or fairer. You've always been so good to me – and my mother and sisters; I'll never forget it, nor will they. I enjoy working here – and I certainly love working on the photography side of things and, of course, being the projectionist on Friday nights. I love that, Mr Penrose, as you know, and – well, I think I'm quite good at it. More than this, though, film work is what I want to do – full time." He paused, seemingly not sure how to proceed.

The chemist helped him on his way: "And there is, perhaps, a way you can do this?" he asked helpfully and perceptively.

Edgar hurtled through the opening he had been given: "Well, yes, there is, Mr Penrose. I heard a few days ago that the Odeon Cinema in Plymouth is looking for an Assistant Projectionist; I went round to the newsagents on the way home last night and bought the *Evening Herald* – it's in there, an advertisement for the job. I've got to apply by this time next week if I want the job, in writing. I've got to say what I've been doing, and am doing. As well as this, I've got to send two full references, one for character – I'll ask my old teacher at school, Miss Blake, if she'll do that for me (and I think she will as we always got on). But more vital, I need a reference from either a former or present employer. Well, obviously I've got no former employer, only a present one – you and Mrs Penrose, of course. So, well, I feel a bit silly about this – well, definitely a bit cheeky, even perhaps, rude, but I'm asking you if perhaps you would give me that reference. I'd understand, mind you, understand completely, if you said no. It's so, so, well, as I said, so cheeky of me to ask."

For a few seconds the chemist gazed at his employee, his expression dead pan. Then his lips eased into a gentle smile. "No, Edgar," said he after what to the shop assistant, seemed an eternity, "it's not cheeky of you at all. You see a chance to pursue a good career – certainly one with a good future to it. Films, motion pictures – call it what you will – they will become bigger, more important, ever more popular. And they'll be better, the technology will improve as it always does, in everything. When you're an old man, Edgar, I reckon they will be very different from what they are now. Mind you, the world will be very different to what it is now. It's not only your ambition to go along this line, Edgar – it's your dream; I know that. Though by giving you a good reference I'll stand far too great a chance of losing a good employee and an outstanding projectionist, if I did not so do then I would be telling lies. So I will just tell the truth; and for sure if I don't, my wife will give me hell. There's no guarantee you'll get the job, obviously, but if there's anybody better than you, they will most certainly be good, exceptionally so."

Thus did he sit down and write a reference so glowing one could almost see it in the dark. He showed it to his wife, and she nodded her agreement – "Yes, Roland, that's fine. It does him justice. You've praised him highly in all directions but not once have you exaggerated."

Edgar Bright was shortlisted, then interviewed. There were five others, but he got the job. The manager who interviewed told him that he and one other stood out from the rest – but Roland Penrose's reference was, he said, the most noteworthy and praising of any he had ever received in over fifteen years in his role.

So Edgar left the employ of the Penroses – with their blessing, but also sorrow. He continued to live in the village, though, so they saw him quite often. He worked successfully at the Odeon for three years before being called up into the navy. Here he was lucky, as after his initial training he was posted to a shore base to join a team showing instructional films – in Plymouth. He was to remain there for the duration, which meant he was able to put in many a shift, when off duty, to keep his hand in as a projectionist in the Odeon, which fortunately escaped the wide-scale bombing of the city, and was packed out every night, the pictures providing much needed distraction from the fraught reality of life.

Likewise did Roland Penrose's village cinema prosper during those dark years. The people of the parish, like those of Plymouth, needed a diversion from all that was happening in the world – including the local one – and he provided it. Often with popular films, he would put on two showings a week – even occasionally three. The cartoons were also popular, along with such regulars as The Three Stooges and, of course, Pathé News – followed avidly with its widespread footage of world happenings and of the Home Front, news eternally given in an upbeat way no matter how grave was the situation in reality. And he continued to get, in good time, all the popular films of the day – along with the dross and B movies.

After the conflict finished, village life – like that everywhere – began to get back to something resembling normality, though the pre-war world they had known would probably never return, the war having naturally changed people, their perspective on life, plus, crucially, their expectations. Large numbers, though, continued to gaze for a few hours every week, at the wall of the Parish Hall, taking in the Ealing Comedies, the villains of gangster-ridden Chicago, the constant conflict between cowboys and Indians in the Wild West – plus laughing at the antics of Laurel and Hardy or Abbott and Costello.

The forties passed, but people's passion for cinema did not – the Parish Hall shows still, generally, sell outs, with a fresh generation now having come along to enjoy the wonders of the silver screen. With the coming of the fifties, folk began to feel better times lay ahead as rationing was, at last, being eased, more items coming into shops and, most importantly of all, more – and a wider range – of food becoming available. Not that there had ever been a desperate shortage of many food items in the parish. Being a farming, growing area, potatoes, root and green veg, apples, pears and the like had always been available in sufficient quantity, whilst strict meat rationing had been augmented by the catching of rabbits – prolific in their burrows – and the occasional illegal slaughter of pigs. But now sweets, even chocolate, came into shops, along with such exotic fruit as pineapples, bananas, even peaches (which many of the younger generation had never seen), albeit still in very short supply. And some excellent films came to the screen, out of both British studios and Hollywood. Henry Wallace continued to supply Roland with these pictures, and, as always, within a fortnight of them having been shown in Tavistock. And it was the same supplier from Plymouth who contacted the chemist one morning with news, and a proposal, which excited him.

"Roland," said Wallace, after the brief courtesies had sped by, "I would imagine you'd want to have *High Noon* as soon as

186

possible, wouldn't you?" To the chemist this was akin to asking, "Would you like to win the Football Pools?"

"*High Noon*? Henry, I'd take *High Noon* this very minute. It's said by many to be the best western ever made – nominated for several Academy Awards, including one for Gary Cooper. Great favourite of mine he is, and Cynthia – very popular with many of the ladies, come to that. Probably the highest rated film for years. I could fill the Parish Hall for that one even if we showed it in the middle of the night. They love westerns around here – love them. So I'll take *High Noon* as soon as I can get it." He paused briefly, then enquired, a touch of concern in his voice – "Why do you ask, Henry? Is there a problem? I can see it might be perhaps difficult for you to get one to me to show a couple of weeks after Tavistock, as you usually do, but I'll have it even if it comes a couple of months after. Folks will turn out for that one, whenever."

His old friend laughed; "No, nothing like that, Roland. The opposite. I've had a stroke of luck which I want to pass on to you – we've done business now for so many years, I think to the advantage of us both. In fact, I've been dealing with you far longer than anybody else; the established cinemas in the towns all change hands or managers from time to time and, strangely, there have been few running shows in villages the way you do, which has always surprised me. And anyway, we go back a very long time in terms of both friendship and association. The fact is, I've just received some copies of *High Noon* for the various town cinemas that I supply, including the Carltons at both Tavistock and Okehampton. For the first time I've ever known, though, I've been sent one copy more than normal – clearly a mistake. The problem normally with a film as popular as this would be to get enough. It's a wonderful piece of luck though. I can send out a copy to each of my regulars to whom I have to give priority, as you know, by the terms of the agreement I've got with them – only fair, as they have so many different titles over a month with, in many cases, three changes of film every week; and once they've got it, they'll schedule showings in two or three weeks – including the Carltons. As to the spare one, though, I thought I'd send it to you. Now, when you show it is a matter for yourself, of course, but it strikes me you would be in a position, for the first time ever, to screen it before either of the Tavistock cinemas. You could even put it on for two, three even four nights if you could hire the hall. People would come from Tavistock if you've got it before it's shown there. You could pack out – make a few bob. You could probably put prices up a bit for a film such as this, especially if you were the first in the area – outside of Plymouth, of course – to screen it."

"I'd never raise the prices in that way," replied Roland instantly. "Most of these folk have been very loyal to me over the years. Two decades in many instances. But I would certainly put on extra screenings if, as you say, I can get the hall. And, as you say, I'd draw a fair number from Tavistock if I put an advert in the *Times and Gazette*. Henry, this really is good, well, exciting news. To be able to put on a film before the Carlton – and one of the quality of *High Noon*. Brilliant, boy! Thank you – thank you for giving me the opportunity." He paused, then in more measured, serious tones, enquired, "But won't it upset your regulars in the cinemas, Henry, you giving me a chance to put a film on – and a big one – before them? I might be a regular customer of yours, and a long term one, but I'm only a part timer – they're professionals, and crucial to your business. I mean, I can't imagine old Cecil Bryant at The Carlton in Tavistock being impressed – he can be a funny devil a the best of times. Men like him are your bread and butter – not me, I'm just the odd dollop of jam. I wouldn't want you to lose anybody's business over this, boy, even though, as I say, I'd be delighted to have it, and be given the chance of showing it before anybody else locally."

A laugh came over the line. "They'll have no way of knowing how you got hold of it so early. Yes, they'll know you've got it – or Cecil Bryant will, at least – but they'll not know you've had it from me. After all, you've been getting films from me for donkey's years and you've never had any early before. Why should you now? And being small, independently run picture houses, they wouldn't find it easy to get a supplier. The Odeons and Gaumonts of his world, the Ranks – that's who dominate. Ninety per cent of all films go to them first, sometimes up to a month before the others. Anyway, Roland, you putting out a few early showings in your village hall is not going to affect their business – not when it involves a film of the stature of *High Noon*. Folk'll be queueing round the block everywhere to see it. So don't worry about it; just get on and advertise it. The Carlton will probably screen it starting a fortnight on Saturday – that's their usual timescale. So if you could get it up on your village wall the week after next, then you'll have people queueing."

"Henry – you've talked me in to it. Not that it's been a hard task for you. I'm grateful, boy – oh yes, so much. This'll be the high point of my cinematic career;" said he chuckling.

"You'll be a cinema proprietor, yet, Roland, I can see it. Anyway, you should get the film within the next few days; certainly by early next week. And good luck with it. Though with a film like that, you'll not need luck."

The chemist wasted no time, and could not afford to, for it was crucial that he booked the extra evenings for the shows. Bookings for the hall were always taken by Sally Courtney, wife of the Post Master. Thus after telling Cynthia of their excellent fortune in getting the film so early, and receiving her agreement that they go for as many showings as possible – certainly at least four – he left the shop at a brisk pace and made for the Post Office. Fortunately it was quiet there, so Sally was not occupied behind the counter as was so often the case. She was thus, almost immediately, able to consult her hall bookings register.

"So what extra nights were you looking for, Roland? The week after next I think it is, you said?"

"Yes, that's right, maid. Well, Tuesday, Wednesday and Thursday would be ideal, as well as the usual Friday, of course."

"Four – four nights? Whatever for, Roland – what are you showing?"

"*High Noon* – and, for the first time ever, we'll have it here before they show it in Tavistock. Usually, it's a fortnight or so after – but this time we'll be first, and with a truly top class film." Enthusiasm oozed out of every pore of his body.

"*High Noon*," she exclaimed. "Well, that really is a prize. They say it's a wonderful film – and it's starring Gary Cooper. He's probably my favourite actor. Arthur and I will be along for that one – he loves westerns."

Sally perused the open hardback book laid out on the counter. "You've got Friday night automatically, so there's no problem there, and you're in luck for the Tuesday; the WI had it booked for a couple of hours for a special meeting they were having – several different village groups in the area all getting together to be addressed by the President or Chairman, or such like, of all the Devon WIs but it's been switched to Tavistock Town Hall for some reason. They only cancelled a few days ago. Thursday is fine, too – no bookings that night. Wednesday, though, poses a problem; the scouts have got it. They've been meeting there for the past month and have got it booked Wednesday nights for just over another month. Their hut was badly burnt back in August when some stupid boy, because it was wet outside, lit a camp fire to fry sausages inside. So they've booked it for scout nights – always Wednesdays from 6.30–8.30 – until they are able to return to their hut, which will be in about five weeks' time. Funny place in some ways for the scouts to meet, in a big hall like that, but there was nowhere else they could go – and it is a community hall, of course. Anyway, the council took pity on them and let them have the hall at a much reduced rent. My only worry is that the stupid boy who started the fire in the hut might try to arrange a fry up in the hall." She laughed as she spoke the words, but Roland could see she was not entirely jesting. "So I'm sorry, Roland – Wednesday is out. I can't see any way around it. The only way would be for you to get Albie Dunster, the scoutmaster, to cancel the scouts that evening."

Sally ceased talking for a few seconds, a positive expression dominating her face.

"Knowing Albie, Roland, there could be a way of doing it. He is, after all, an easy going sort of man and he'll be aware that many of his scouts gaze up at your screen most weeks, and would be quite happy to miss a couple of hours of knot tying and field-craft to watch *High Noon* – especially – especially if you were to

190

let them in free of charge on that Wednesday evening; Albie as well, of course – assuming he is a picture goer."

Roland fixed this most helpful lady with a serious look. "Come to think of it, Sally – he is. Not quite a regular, but I reckon he comes along once a month or so. Do you know, maid, that's one first class idea. And another way to get on the right side of Albie is to buy him a few drinks – Guinness and whisky. A regular in the Tamar View Inn, or so I hear. Certainly he's nearly always in there when Cynthia and myself drop in for a drink on occasions, usually on a Saturday. Mind you, he can hold it – never seen him the worse for wear; was a Merchant Seaman back in the war, was Albie; was on the Russian Convoys – torpedoed once as well. Hellish business that – brave men all of them. I reckon he's earned his whisky, maid." He ceased for a few seconds, then opined:

"Do you know, Sally, I reckon he's earned a few more whiskies. I might go round to the pub tonight and see if he's there. It's quite possible he will be. If he is I could well stand him a round or two then make the offer you so kindly suggested – free tickets all round for him and his troop. So book me in for the Tuesday and Thursday evenings if you would, and if I'm successful tonight with the scoutmaster, then I'll be back to book the Wednesday night as well."

He returned home and told his wife of the booking situation and what he proposed to do. She agreed it was probably worth a go, but doubted it would be successful. "If he's serious about his role as scoutmaster, Roland – and I imagine he is as he's been doing it for many a year now – then I don't think he'll be bought off by a few drinks and some free tickets to *High Noon*."

Cynthia was generally right about most things, but this time she was to be proved wrong. That evening Roland went round to the bar of the Tamar View and there found Albie Dunster leaning against it. He was soon in conversation with a man whom, whilst he did not know him particularly well in a social capacity, knew him reasonably well professionally. For the scoutmaster – who earned his living as a self-employed carpenter – often suffered gastric problems, assuredly not helped by his, occasional, over indulgence in alcohol. The prescriptions the doctor gave him were ineffective, but the jollop he got from the chemist – mixed on the premises by the proprietor himself – often worked well.

Thus Albie had a high regard for Roland Penrose, and the chemist used such regard – plus a Guinness and two double Scotches – very much to his own advantage. After little more than an hour the scoutmaster had agreed to cancel the weekly scout session on that Wednesday night, electing to spend the evening in the Parish Hall – along, no doubt, with most of his troop – watching *High Noon* for free rather than indulging in the normal run of scouting activities.

The following morning saw the chemist around at the Post Office to book that Wednesday night, and to thank Sally Courtney for her inspired suggestion regarding the free tickets for the scouts plus the free liquor for the scoutmaster, before returning to his shop to phone through adverts to both the *Tavistock Times* and *Tavistock Gazette* to go in the papers when they came out the following Thursday, regarding the early, pre-Tavistock showing, on four separate evenings, of *High Noon* at the Village Hall the following week. Things were going so very, very well.

The film arrived from Henry Wallace the following Monday and Penrose put it in his secure drug store for safe keeping. Also that week he put a few posters about the village advertising the film and the extra screenings. There was nothing more he could do in terms of promoting the film. He now just had to sit back and take what came. Hopefully it would prove a highly successful enterprise but nothing in life, he well knew, was certain. He noted with satisfaction the sizeable advertisements which had gone into the two Tavistock newspapers – which covered not only the town but a sizeable area around it and had not been cheap – then sat back, looking forward, more than a little nervously, to the following week which would, he so greatly hoped, be the high point of his long career locally in bringing 'the pictures' to the people.

On the Friday, though, he thought of something he had not done which normally would have been amongst the first actions he would take upon receiving the new film – check there was no damage to the celluloid. All the manifold preparations, though, all the bustle and planning had caused him to forget this basic safeguard.

Thus is was that at the end of that morning, when he closed the shop and dispensary for lunch, he went into the drug store, collected the film, a vivid label, *High Noon*, stuck to its metal exterior, and carried it out to the kitchen at the rear to where Cynthia was producing, from the oven, a sizeable pasty. Taking, with thanks, the large portion given him by his spouse he proceeded to eat and enjoy the same. Having finished, he drank half the cup of tea before him, then proceeded to open the can of film. He reached in, pulled it out – and gazed at it. The gaze became fixed, his expression changed rapidly from benign contentment to concern, then to mild horror. For the words on the film said nothing about *High Noon* – rather, there printed quite boldly, was, *Sands of Iwo Jima*. The Wild West on the outside had given way to the Far East within. He continued to gaze at it in shock, then looked up at Cynthia, now aware that something was very wrong.

"What is it, Roland – what's happened? You look in a terrible state."

Her husband looked across at her shaking his head in bemusement: "It's the wrong film, maid. This isn't *High Noon* – it says that on the outside, but inside it says, *Sands of Iwo Jima*."

"Well – well – perhaps the outside's right and it's the inside that's wrong. In fact, that's probably it – somewhere they've made a mistake and it is *High Noon*, but they've stuck the wrong label on. That sort of thing could happen easily."

Ever the optimist was Cynthia. Her husband sprung suddenly to his feet – "I'll soon find out." He lifted the reel from the can, detached the end of the spool, and held it up to the light, revealing a few stills of the picture. His expression of horror did not abate: "This definitely does not look like the Wild West, maid – and it certainly isn't the Wild West. It's the wrong film, Henry's sent us. He wasn't to know, I suppose but, dear me, this is a calamity. Four screenings we've got next week, of what's said to be the best ever western – and we've not got it. What are we going to do, maid?"

j

Roland rarely panicked, but he was in danger of doing so now. His wife, though, never did:

"You phone Henry Wallace and you do it right away. It could be he's just sent the wrong film by mistake. If he has, there's still time to put it right. If the worse came to the worse, you could always go into Plymouth and collect it from him."

"Yes, you're right – I'll do it now, this minute."

With that he was out of the kitchen and into the back office. Within three rings, Wallace had answered the call. So alarmed was the chemist, he wasted no time on the usual courtesies, although in essence he was a very courteous man. "Henry – the film, Henry; it's not *High Noon*, it's *Sands of Iwo Jima*." Not only had the chemist failed to give out a "Good afternoon," or such-like – he had failed to give his name. The film supplier, though, recognised the voice with its good, soft, but distinctive Devon accent.

"What do you mean, boy? – Of course it's *High Noon*. I checked every single can. Anyway, my suppliers don't make mistakes like that. It has to be *High Noon*, Roland." The last few words did betray a little uncertainty on the part of Wallace.

"Oh yes, it says *High Noon* on the outside, but the *Iwo Jima* film on the inside. I've looked at a bit of the celluloid and it is a war film, not a western – it's the wrong one, Henry, which means I've got problems. I've booked the Parish Hall for four evenings next week, even advertised in both of the Tavistock papers – and at the moment I've no film to show them. Can you get a copy of *High Noon* up to me over the weekend – even Monday would be all right, as the first showing's not until Tuesday evening. If need be, I could drive into Plymouth and collect it – that would be no problem. I could even come down this afternoon; I've got to have the film, though, Henry – I've advertised it, and the showings, for miles around. There'll be folk coming from all over to see it – I'll be in real trouble if there's no film for them to see – no *High Noon*, that is. They'd not come far to see *Sands of Iwo Jima* – not even from the village. So when can you let me have it, Henry – or when can I collect it?"

There was, for several seconds, a silence from the other end of the phone which was both eloquent – and ominous. Eventually there was a response.

"Well – well, Roland," replied Henry Wallace, his voice hesitant and somewhat concerned. "Well, there could be a problem to tell you the truth. I'm not sure I've got another copy of *High Noon*. No, let's be honest, boy – I owe you that; I've not got another – and there's no real chance of me getting another, either. Gold dust, they'll be – gold dust they are. Clearly they made a mistake at the distribution depot, and sent me a *Sands of Iwo Jima* with *High Noon* marked on the outside. I should have checked, clearly, and for the fact I did not, and consequently have put you in a – a – well, a difficult position, I can only apologise, Roland. Not that my apologies can help much, I appreciate that."

A few seconds passed before the chemist replied. When he did, his tone was milder and far less frantic:

"Well, Henry, to be fair, it's not your fault. It said *High Noon* on the can, so you had every right to assume it was *High Noon* on the inside – it's just one of those things. All the years you've been supplying me, boy – and we're talking some twenty now – this is the first time it's ever happened, so I've no real cause for complaint. It's just that – well, sod's law really. The first time it's happened is the very worst time in all these years that it could have. How I'm going to get around it, I really do not know – if I can't show *High Noon* next week, then I really am in trouble. And it would seem there is no realistic way in which I can expect to show it. All those potential customers – many very regular – and I'll be letting them down."

"Perhaps if you explain to folk before the showings it will be all right. I find people, on the whole, are quite reasonable if they know something is a genuine error – and that in no way there can be any blame laid at your door. And it could be that *Sands of Iwo Jima* will go down well – it's a war film and, even better, it stars John Wayne. They don't come much more popular than John Wayne, Roland."

The chemist's retort was instant. "Quite so, boy – Wayne is very popular, but only in westerns. I remember showing him in *Stagecoach* back before the war, and several since – all have been popular. But this is different – this is John Wayne winning the war. Worse, it's the Yanks winning the war. People won't have it, Henry. They won't have it in this parish, in Plymouth or, probably, in any other part of Britain – and you know it. And why should they, when you think of all the sacrifice made by the people of these islands to get rid of the Germans and Japs."

"Well, yes – I see what you mean to an extent, Roland," came the voice over the phone, "but a majority of films folk see are American – a majority of all films made are shot there. Yet generally people flock to see them – most of the big stars are Yanks, most of the storylines likewise. So what's the problem with a war film?"

"The problem, boy, is that it offends, and does so because in a sense it is just that – offensive. Folk are happy enough to see Wild West shoot-outs between sheriffs and desperados – as long as the goodies win, mind you. The cavalry pitched against Red Indians always goes down well; gangsters in Chicago obliterating each other, the legendary screen comic actors playing things for laughs, musicals and lighthearted, escapist stuff of that nature – all of it is enjoyed, and brings people in to watch. But war films – that's different. That's too recent and too raw; also many people feel – and I wouldn't disagree with them – that Hollywood churn out films that give the impression the war was fought and won by American Forces, nobody else having played any part. Both the Jerries and Japs were beaten by forces under the Stars and Stripes – the Union Jack never features. It's outrageous, Henry – and folk resent it. There are numerous men in this village who fought in the war – and there's an awful lot of names on the War Memorial pointing out those that did not come back; and many of them fought in the Far East – Burma. Some, poor devils, were prisoners of the Japs. I'll not insult them by showing John Wayne – who to my knowledge never fought anybody, anywhere, in reality – beating the 'Nips' single handedly. No way, Henry."

For a few seconds there was no response from the film distributor. He had known Roland Penrose for many a long year, had always had an excellent relationship with him as friend, colleague and customer – and had never before known him to be upset, even remotely. The chemist, now though, was close to it, however – and Wallace was aware of it. He immediately made efforts to placate:

"Fair enough, boy – I see what you mean, totally. *Sands of Iwo Jima* would not be suitable – I can see that. So – so – it's finding something that is. I'm thinking, Roland, as I'm talking here – thinking as to what films I've got about. Most of them come to me, I distribute them, take them back when they've been shown, then send them back to the main distributors. I do have a few about the office which I've held on to over the years – some going back over twenty years. I'm wondering if I've got something decent amongst these – perhaps an old classic." He paused momentarily, but before the chemist could speak, continued: "Tell you what I do have, Roland – had it for years. Ever since it came out back in the war. Not sure how I managed to keep it, but I'm glad I did 'cause it's a classic. It's a war film, again, but it's British – *The Way Ahead* with David Niven; and he did fight in the war, in the British Army. Terrific film, Roland – I could sent that up to you. I reckon that would go down all right – people would enjoy it, I'm sure."

The chemist's rebuttal of the offer was instant. "No, Henry, thank you. I know the film, of course, and it is a good one – as good a war film as has ever been made. And I showed it back in the war not long after it came out. It was popular – good, patriotic, defiant stuff that was needed then. But that was the best part of ten years ago, boy. Folk have moved on from then – inevitably and rightly. The war is past, and most of us don't want to be reminded of it any more than we have to be. People want a bit of frivolity now, a bit of escapism, some good entertainment – and *High Noon* fits that role admirably. But it would seem there's no way I can show it at the moment – so that's that. I'll just have to cancel it all – put up notices and so forth. It's too late to get it into the local papers now, so that's not an option. I'll just have to hope that word of mouth will tell most people who were going to come that there's nothing to come to see." His voice tailed off, the tone dominated by despondency.

Henry Wallace made an attempt – not with measurable success

– to raise his old friend's spirits: "I'll phone around, Roland, and do so right away – there could possibly be a copy of *High Noon* somewhere that I can get hold of before Tuesday. It's not likely, I would have to say, but I'll not know if I don't try; I'll get right on with it. And Roland – I'm sorry boy, I really am. I've never had such a thing happen before – but once is too often, especially when it causes the massive problems for you which it has at present."

"It's not your fault, Henry – as I said earlier. You thought you had an extra copy and went out of your way to do me a huge favour – which is appreciated, very much, even though clearly things have not gone to plan. It's not the end of the world, of course – it's just so very, very disappointing."

It was more than that, though, a fact of which Henry Wallace was well aware (which increased his feelings of guilt over the entire sorry episode, it being in no way lessened by Roland's patient understanding, and the fact he knew there was, in reality, nothing he could do about it).

The chemist, also, was desperately conscious of just what a disaster loomed. The following week, which should have given him the very best moments of his long career as a cinema proprietor, would now, assuredly, provide him with the worst. He told his wife the grim news, and she, like him, spent a stressful afternoon and evening trying to think of the solution to the problem, both knowing there was only one – they needed to get their hands on a copy of *High Noon* within the next three days. They knew also, realistically, chances of that appeared to be nil. As they went to bed, Roland told Cynthia that he would arise very early the following morning, write out some posters giving the bleak news of the cancellation of the following week's showing of *High Noon*, and get them, at first light, pinned up around the village. He would then await the fallout – which, he had not the slightest doubt, would be substantial.

Roland, who was not the greatest sleeper at the best of times, lay – as he had expected – fully awake, searching, pointlessly, he well knew, for a solution. Cynthia, on the other hand, who scarcely suffered with a sleepless night ever, quickly went off.

The chemist heard the wall clock chiming the quarters, and, at three o'clock in the morning decided to get up, make a pot of tea, and put the rest of the night to some positive use by drawing up the posters which had to be put about the following day. Putting on an ancient dressing gown, he went slowly and despondently down to the kitchen and put the heavy iron kettle on to one of the range's three hotplates. Awaiting its coming to the boil, he searched out some large sheets of plain white paper and a black marker pen in preparation for, firstly, composing his dismal message, then committing it in large letters onto the sheets – a laborious task, one which could occupy a large part of the remaining hours of darkness, and one which would be so depressing for him. It had, though, to be done.

The kettle having boiled, he made a sizeable pot – a great tea lover was Roland – poured some of the dark contents into a large mug and added a little milk, plus three spoonfuls of sugar. He usually took only two, but his mother's maxim (which he had followed always) was that an extra spoonful – at least – should be added at times of worry or stress. He stirred the turgid liquid, then slumped down onto a hard kitchen chair, and sipped it. He needed this tea, and assuredly he was going to empty the beaker down his gullet before he contemplated the message of failure he had to write upon the bleak sheets of paper which lay before him.

As he sipped the beverage, he cast his eyes about the kitchen, his mind wrestling with the best form of words to use to convey the bleak tidings of the demise of *High Noon* as the promised major feature to be illuminated on the village hall for an unparalleled four nights the following week.

His gaze fixed upon a wedding photograph standing on a nearby shelf. It stood beside one of himself and Cynthia, and was of the marriage of Edgar Bright to a local girl, Maudie Baxter, daughter of Jim Baxter who ran a small plumbing business in the parish. Because of the closeness of the Penroses to Edgar – he looking upon his former employee almost as family – the chemist and his wife had not only been invited to the wedding, held in the Parish Church some three years earlier, but Roland had acted as an usher, and been honoured to do so. The couple still lived in the village and now had a daughter just over twelve months old. Cynthia, as well as Roland, had been honoured this time, both becoming godparents to the child just a few months earlier; and they saw quite a bit of the Brights, they often dropping into the shop – usually for a prescription, to buy something or, in Edgar's case, just for a chat.

Career-wise, Edgar had done well. After being demobbed late in 1945 he had returned to his job as a projectionist at the Odeon, Plymouth (not that he had ever fully left, of course, thanks to his being able to fulfil the odd shift in his off-duty hours from the navy). Just before he got married, he had received a decent boost to his salary, having been promoted to the highly responsible position of Assistant Manager, whilst just three months before he had, due to the serious, and potentially life-threatening illness which had struck down the long-serving Manager of the cinema, taken on that role, albeit in an 'acting' capacity. Thus was he, at present, in charge of the largest cinema west of London with a strong possibility existing that he would remain in command in a permanent, and long term, capacity.

Edgar's successful career and the fact that he and Maudie appeared to have a very good marriage were a source of much satisfaction to Roland and his wife, the still young man ever being, in a sense, the son they never had.

Draining the remainder of his tea, Roland returned the mug to the table, musing as he did so that Edgar had had no problems getting hold of *High Noon*, as the Odeon in Plymouth had been showing it for the best part of a fortnight, it being due to finish that very day, Saturday. He turned his attention to his bleak task of creating the sorry announcement which would disappoint so many – and could well anger some. He picked up the marker pen, looked down at the blank paper on the table – but then froze. After a few seconds, he turned his head and looked again at Edgar Bright's wedding photo. It occurred to him – no, hit him, suddenly; Edgar could be the one to put right the problem – he could be salvation. He had mused that his former employee would be in possession of a copy – indeed, probably copies – of the priceless film. Now, granted he didn't own them and when the

200

cinema stopped showing the classic western the following day, no doubt all reels of it would have to be returned to the head office, wherever that was. But the reality remained that at the moment, and for at least a day more, Edgar Bright could lay hands on the precious motion picture and, if a copy of it could end up, for a few days, in the hands of the chemist (and local 'movie mogul') then assuredly all would be well – and no bleak notices of cancellation would need to be printed and posted about the parish.

He poured himself another cup of tea, fresh hope coursing through his veins. It could be, mind you, that Edgar might not be able to help, but Roland knew that his good, loyal, kind and ever affable former employee assuredly would if he was able. He would postpone the writing and distribution of cancellation notices until he had seen Edgar – and that he would do as soon as it was decently possible. Having a young child, he and his wife would not linger late in bed of a morning, so Roland reckoned that if he arrived at the couple's semi-detached home (built and bought just a couple of years earlier) at about half past eight, he would find them up and about. The nature of Edgar's work and position meant that he would be at the cinema on most Saturdays, but as showings of the films did not start until after lunch, almost certainly he would catch the 12.30 train from the village station to Plymouth (his regular custom), to be in his office at roughly one o'clock – so he no doubt would be at home for a large part of the morning.

Roland knew there was little point in returning to his bed as his chances of sleep were virtually nil, so spent the next couple of hours catching up with some office work. At half past seven he took up a cup of tea to Cynthia as was his custom, and told her of what was in his mind – how, if good fortune smiled upon them, they could yet obtain a precious copy of *High Noon*.

His wife was as enthused with the idea as was he and wished him joy in his mission – one which would be fraught, but if successful, so rewarding.

Just before twenty-five past eight, Roland went out the kitchen door and made the short journey to the home of his former employee, leaving Cynthia to open up the shop and dispensary at

8.30. He promised he would not be long as Saturday mornings were always busy. His wife, though, was not too worried if he took a while as long as he was successful in his quest for the reel of film, its acquisition being almost as important to her as it was to him. The chemist knocked on Edgar's front door on the dot of half past eight and within seconds it was opened, a fully dressed Edgar Bright standing before him.

"Mr Penrose," said he, surprise in his voice, "I didn't expect it would be you – though, to be honest, I had no idea who it would be this time of the morning. Come on in, Mr Penrose – it's nippy out there."

Even though Edgar had left the chemist's employ so very many years previously, he still addressed his former employer by the formal 'Mr', likewise Cynthia, as 'Mrs'; a very respectful traditional fellow was Edgar. The chemist entered, voicing instantly his apologies:

"Sorry to disturb you so early, Edgar – I really am. Hope I don't catch you and Maudie at too difficult a time. If it is, then please do say and I'll come back later. Nothing worse than being disturbed early in the morning just after you've got up."

The younger man laughed. "Just got up? I wish that was true. The fact is, we've been up for ages – the nipper's had a funny old night, hardly slept. That means we've hardly slept either. Still, that's the way it goes – wouldn't be without her, that's for sure. So you've definitely not disturbed us, Mr Penrose – and it must be important for you to come around early like this, when normally you'd be opening up the shop. Anyway, I've just made a pot of tea – you'll have one, won't you? Strong, a touch of milk and two sugars as I recall." Edgar knew the habits and tastes of his former boss very well – and was aware that it was exceedingly unlikely he would refuse the offer of a freshly made brew.

"Thank you, Edgar – that'll go down nicely." His host led him to the kitchen, ushered him in the direction of an upright wooden chair by the table, then proceeded to pour out a couple of cups of tea from the capacious pot.

Putting the beverage upon the table before his guest, Edgar fortuitously brought up the subject which had brought about the chemist's early and urgent visit. "I'm delighted to see, Mr Penrose, that you've got hold of *High Noon* a week before they've got it in Tavistock. Brilliant. You're showing it for four nights too; I doubt you've ever done that before – I certainly don't remember you doing such a thing, not that you've anything to worry about when it comes to attendances – you'll sell out every night, I reckon. A terrific film, had massive publicity, and you've got it before Tavistock – you can't fail. They've been queueing around the block at the Odeon for the fortnight we've been showing it. Last day today, of course."

The chemist gulped down a decent measure of tea, then looked at his host: "Unfortunately, Edgar, at the moment failure is inevitable – I've not got a film to show or, at least, I've not got *High Noon*."

He proceeded to tell of the calamity which had befallen him and how, if he was not able to locate a copy within the next couple of days, then the four showings would all have to be cancelled. Having completed his dire tale, the chemist gazed at the acting manager of the Odeon, an expression mingling despair and desperation upon his face: "So there it is, boy – I'm in a bit of a spot as you can see, and frankly I don't really see a way out of it – except if there is any way you can help me. Clearly you've a copy or two of the film – a film you'll stop showing after today. Edgar, if there's any way you could let me have a copy for the coming week, well – well, I'd be forever in your debt. It probably can't be done, I accept that. You don't own the film – as soon as its run's finished, you have to return it, that I don't doubt. But I feel I've got to ask you – you're my only hope."

Edgar Bright smiled. "Mr Penrose, the only man who owes a debt here is me to you – and Mrs Penrose, of course. In the personal sense, you were always – and are still – so very kind and generous to myself and my family (my mother and sisters will never forget your goodness to them years ago); and the fact I've a good job doing work I love is down to you – totally. You gave me the chance, the encouragement and constant support regarding pursuing a career in the cinema and a marvellous reference; that is something I'll never forget. No, sir, the debt here is mine – and I think, probably, I can make something of a start in terms of repaying it. You want a copy of *High Noon* for next week – and I see no reason why I can't supply it."

Roland Penrose gazed at this fellow with an expression little short of joy on his face: "Really, Edgar – you can let me have a copy? Really? And for the week?"

"I see no reason why not. I've got three copies of the film – there's always spares in case anything goes wrong with the one in the projector. After tonight, clearly, we'll not be needing them any more. The normal routine is for all the films – including cartoons, newsreels and so forth – that have been shown, to be put in a metal canister either on the Sunday or a Monday morning, then sent back to the organisation's distribution centre in London. In accordance with procedure, that will be done in the next couple of days, by myself – but an error will be made in that I will fail to return one of the copies of *High Noon*; an easy mistake to make, of course. Naturally it will be discovered at head office that there is a copy missing, and I'll be informed of the fact. I'll search my office at the cinema and find the missing copy; I shall apologise for the mistake, and as this situation will, I shall ensure, take several days to materialise, I'll suggest that I return the missing copy with the other films on the following Monday. I've no reason to feel that such a solution will not be totally acceptable to those at head office. So, I see no reason why I cannot deliver a copy of the film to you in the morning – and if you return it to me next Saturday, after your fourth and final showing of it, then nobody will be the wiser – that all right by you?"

For a few seconds, words escaped the chemist – but he found his voice at last: "All right, Edgar? All right, boy? It's fantastic – a life saver. Thank you, boy – so much. It means I'll not let people down – it's worried me so much that I would."

And knowing his former employer's character, Edgar Bright knew that such concerns regarding giving folk the opportunity and pleasure of seeing, early, a top film would rate far higher with him than the loss of income which, inevitably, cancellation would cause.

Edgar was as good as his word, as the following morning he

delivered into the Roland's so grateful hands a priceless copy of
High Noon. The marker pen and sheaf of large white sheets of
paper would not be needed. The chemist, now, began to look
forward to the week to come – and the pinnacle of his 'movie
mogul' career.

The saga, though, took a further twist in the early afternoon of
the Monday. Just as Cynthia and he finished their lunch, the
phone rang. Lifting the receiver to his ear, Roland was almost
deafened by a loud, excited voice coming down the line – a man
who got directly to the point – a most urgent one, without even a
nod towards the traditional courtesies and formalities: "Roland –
it's Harry Wallace. Have you cancelled this week's showings of
High Noon?"

"Well – well, no, Harry," he stuttered, taken aback by this
verbal assault.

"Thank heavens for that – don't, boy, don't 'cause I've got you
a copy of *High Noon*." The voice at the end was bursting with
excitement and pleasure.

Roland Penrose was far too amiable a chap to burst such a
balloon by saying he already had a copy. "That's great news,
Harry," he responded enthusiastically. "How did that come
about?"

"Well, boy – in a simple way really, and probably I'm to blame
for not thinking of the explanation why you had *Sands of Iwo
Jima* in a container marked *High Noon*. Why I didn't think of it,
I really don't know, but it's simple and, basically, logical. The fact
is that since the terrible mix up with *High Noon* and the problem
it caused you, I've been opening up every can of film and
checking it says on the reel the same film that it says on the can.
I ordered a copy of *Sands of Iwo Jima* for a small cinema down
in Cornwall – it's been out more than two years but they wanted
a copy for a special showing for some obscure reason; some
goodwill visit from some Yanks next week or some such thing.
Anyway, literally five minutes ago I opened up the can marked
Iwo Jima to check all was in order and what did it say on the reel
– *High Noon*. Obviously, at the distribution centre they put the
films in the wrong containers. When you think of it, there's a

logic to how such a mistake can be made – and I really should have thought of it. Still, it looks like there's still time to put it all right. What I intend to do, if it's all right with you, is to get in my car as soon as I've finished talking to you, and drive up to you bringing *High Noon* with me; You'll have it in good time for tomorrow night, and I can collect the Iwo Jima film and get it sent down to Cornwall. How does that sound, Roland?"

"First class, boy – an absolute life saver," enthused the chemist in highly exaggerated fashion. He and Henry had been good friends for very many years, and also Roland had generally been very well treated and looked after by the independent film distributor from Plymouth. Thus, he was not about to deflate this good man who, clearly, was feeling ecstatic relief that he was able, at the eleventh hour, to supply such vital cargo. He would accept it with grateful thanks and use it rather than Edgar's – which had been temporarily 'lost' by the Odeon Cinema, Plymouth. He would, though, hang on to Edgar's just in case anything went wrong with the one which Henry was about to deliver to him.

It was as well that he did, for on the first night of the showing – to a packed village hall – with little over half an hour of the running time having passed, the film broke. It was something which was fixable, but it would have taken at least half an hour to do so; as it was, the broken reel was taken out, Edgar's Odeon copy put in, and in fewer than five minutes, normal service was resumed to a satisfied audience.

Problems, though, were not confined to the first night. On the second, the Wednesday, there was a violent thunderstorm – and electricity throughout the village ceased. It had come virtually dead on seven o'clock just as the show was about to commence – again to a packed hall. Roland stood before the assembly, apologised for the calamity – though he, and fortunately, the gathered masses, were well aware it was in no way his fault – and suggested that they waited for three quarters of an hour to see if power was restored. If it was not, then naturally entrance fees would be refunded. Virtually everybody agreed to this, their desire to see the film exceeding their impatience or desire to be elsewhere. And fortunately for one and all, the power returned after thirty-five minutes and the screening proceeded.

On the third night, an ambulance had to be called when a fellow, not local, collapsed with a heart attack (fortunately not fatal) and on the Friday – the normal 'picture' evening – proceedings were again delayed, this time for half an hour, when a large rat was seen in the front of the hall on the floor beneath the screen. This, naturally, caused some consternation and it was apparent to Roland that nobody would settle to watch Gary Cooper eliminate the evil Frank Miller and his henchmen of the Wild West until this undesirable rodent was eliminated from the building. Des Dymond – possessor of a ferocious but valiant Jack Russell that could dispose of rats probably better than any other dog in the parish – was, fortuitously, in the audience and suggested, immediately, that he 'nip home', collect his bitch, bring her back and let her loose to hunt the vermin. This was done as quickly and efficiently as it was possible to do, the sturdy little canine, once released into the hall, taking but five minutes to locate, and dispose of the pest. However, it was past seven-thirty before the show could begin, Roland having to allow farm worker Dymond time to return his magnificent beast home and get back to take his seat. So, despite all the calamities, the four showings of *High Noon* were completed – to, overwhelmingly, very satisfied audiences.

The phone call came on Saturday just after lunch, as Roland and Cynthia sat at the kitchen table sipping tea, with the chemist about to drain his cup prior to opening up the shop for afternoon business. Roland took it and recognised the Plymothian tones of Henry Wallace.

"Just to check that all went well for you this week, Roland – that you had a good turn out and that there were no problems. I've been thinking about you all week."

"Well, that's good of you, Henry – it really is. We had one or two problems of – well, varying nature, but we got over them; and we had packed houses. Truly a great film – everybody enjoyed it, I think, including Cynthia and myself. So thanks, Henry – not just for this call, but for all you've done. It is appreciated."

"Welcome, Roland – good to be of service. And I'm sorry about the original problems about supplying the film – a lot of it down to the fact I didn't check as I should. I've learned a lot there. Everything will be checked – and double checked – from now on, I can assure you of that. And if in the future I can get hold of any other big, box office films early as I did with *High Noon*, then I'll call you right away so again you can screen it early – and perhaps have extra showings."

Roland Penrose was unusually rapid in his reply: "Henry, again thanks. Kind and thoughtful of you – but no thank you. Cynthia and me have aged ten years over *High Noon* – even though we've made a few extra bob out of it. We're both getting too old now to go through all that again, or even anything like it, even though it all came right in the end. No boy, from now on we'll just take the films in the normal way and show them once a week on a Friday night as we have over the years – that's enough excitement, and profit, for us."

And that is the way it was from then on – with no exceptions.